Roni and Beverly talked for a while longer, until they saw Hallie posting the election results in the foyer, and then they walked over to check out the list of new officers.

They both looked, and squealed at the same time, hugging each other.

"Omigod! You're the new ZZT President!" Roni cried as Beverly shrieked with excitement. "That's incredible!"

"I can't believe it!" Beverly beamed as other ZZTs crowded around her offering hugs and congratulations.

"You're going to do an amazing job," Roni said, squeezing her hand.

"And so are you, Miss Newly Elected Formal Planner Assistant," Beverly said.

"Thanks." Roni blushed, feeling a thrill race through her at being elected to the position. "I can't wait to get started."

She checked the list again, and just as she was finishing, the ZZT doorbell rang. Through the decorative glass oval in the door, she could see Lance standing outside, smiling at her.

"*Hello*, hotness," Beverly said in a low voice, scooting to Roni's side. "Um, you failed to mention how completely gorge your date is."

"Glad you approve," Roni said, grabbing her purse and taking a deep breath.

"Have fun," Beverly said as Roni headed for the door. "You know tonight's a full moon, so watch out. It can make you do crazy things."

Roni laughed as she opened the door. Crazy had never been her MO, but tonight with Lance and the moonlight and the lakefront dining, who knew what might happen?

the Formal

KATE HARMON

speak
An Imprint of Penguin Group (USA) Inc.

SPEAK
Published by the Penguin Group
Penguin Group (USA) Inc., 345 Hudson Street, New York, New York 10014, U.S.A.
Penguin Group (Canada), 90 Eglinton Avenue East, Suite 700, Toronto, Ontario, Canada M4P 2Y3
(a division of Pearson Penguin Canada Inc.)
Penguin Books Ltd, 80 Strand, London WC2R 0RL, England
Penguin Ireland, 25 St Stephen's Green, Dublin 2, Ireland (a division of Penguin Books Ltd)
Penguin Group (Australia), 250 Camberwell Road, Camberwell, Victoria 3124, Australia
(a division of Pearson Australia Group Pty Ltd)
Penguin Books India Pvt Ltd, 11 Community Centre,
Panchsheel Park, New Delhi - 110 017, India
Penguin Group (NZ), 67 Apollo Drive, Rosedale, North Shore 0632, New Zealand
(a division of Pearson New Zealand Ltd)
Penguin Books (South Africa) (Pty) Ltd, 24 Sturdee Avenue,
Rosebank, Johannesburg 2196, South Africa

Registered Offices: Penguin Books Ltd, 80 Strand, London WC2R 0RL, England

Published by Speak, an imprint of Penguin Group (USA) Inc., 2008

1 3 5 7 9 10 8 6 4 2

Library of Congress Cataloging-in-Publication Data
Harmon, Kate.
Sorority 101 : the formal / Kate Harmon.
p. cm.
Summary: The sorority sisters of Zeta Zeta Tau are planning their
annual formal, but not without a few trials and tribulations along the way.
ISBN 978-0-14-241055-4
[1. Friendship—Fiction. 2. Greek letter societies—Fiction. 3. Universities and colleges—Fiction.
4. Balls (Parties)—Fiction. 5. Florida—Fiction.] I. Title. II. Title: Formal.
PZ7.H22719Soi 2008 [Fic]—dc22 2008029725

Speak ISBN 978-0-14-241055-4

Printed in the United States of America

ACKNOWLEDGMENTS

The publishers would like to extend their thanks to Marley Gibson for her contributions to the Sorority 101 series.

CHAPTER 1

Roni Van Gelderen stopped the overflowing luggage cart just short of room 714 and hesitantly knocked on the door.

It swung open and her best friend, Jenna Driscoll, stood there, by turns laughing and rolling her eyes. "Okay, Miss Manners," Jenna said, tossing her long blonde hair and putting a hand on her hip in the same fashion Roni'd seen her use with her three younger sisters. "This is *our* room now, remember? You don't have to knock."

"I know, I know," Roni said with a giggle. "I'm still trying to break the habit." It always made her laugh to see five-foot-two Jenna, with her nymphlike frame, shifting into her Little Napoleon mode. The truth was, sweet-natured Jenna wasn't capable of intimidating a flea.

Roni and Jenna shimmied the cart through the door and lugged the boxes onto the floor. "*Our* room," Roni said, smiling happily. "I love the way that sounds."

"Me, too. I couldn't have asked for a better roommate."

"Thanks," Roni said. "But after your hellish experience with Amber last semester, you're not a very tough critic. You'd think *anyone* was better than her." Poor Jenna had had to live with Amber Ferris for the entire fall semester, and Amber's biatchitude had almost been too much for her to take. Luckily, Jenna'd finally gone to Tricia, their resident adviser, about the problem, and that's when the idea had hit Roni that she could be Jenna's new roommie for the spring semester. It had all worked out perfectly, especially since Roni was footing the bill for her room and board now. This way, she could save herself a little money and get a wonderful roommate in the process.

"Poor Amber," Jenna said with a sigh. "I know she was awful, but when I heard from Tricia that she'd dropped out of Latimer, I just felt sorry for her. She had such a hard time making friends here."

"I wonder why," Roni mumbled. "Could it have been her alter ego, 'The Grudge,' that did it?"

Jenna gave her a scolding glance. "I just hope she'll be happier now that she's living at home with her family again and going to community college." Then she smiled. "And I know we're going to have a fab time together this semester. But there might be one problem. . . ."

"What's that?" Roni asked, twisting her long black hair worriedly.

"Where we're going to put everything." Jenna laughed.

Roni blanked for a second, then glanced around at the mountains of clothes, shoes, and boxes taking up nearly every inch of free space in the small dorm room. "Omigod." She gasped. "I never realized how much stuff I had."

"Come on, Boston," a husky voice rang out from the doorway. "Your wardrobe is big enough to clothe an entire third-world country."

"Lora-Leigh!" Roni and Jenna both yelled, and turned around to see Lora-Leigh Sorenstein, her wild curls and menagerie of earrings (an array of vintage-style amber dangles today) flying hysterically in every direction as she bounded into the room. Roni smiled. Last semester, she, Jenna, and Lora-Leigh had all joined the Zeta Zeta Tau sorority and had grown into best friends as they went through recruitment, new member education, and initiation together. But Roni hadn't realized until this moment how very much she'd missed both Jenna and Lora-Leigh over the last six weeks, and how glad she was to be back at Latimer with them.

"I missed you so much!" Jenna squealed, grabbing Lora-Leigh in a fierce hug.

"I figured as much from the e-mails I got from you at least three times a day," Lora-Leigh said, smiling.

"I'd be willing to part with some of my wardrobe for a pair of those," Roni said, taking her turn at hugging Lora-Leigh, then pointing to her camel-colored cords. They went perfectly with her rust-orange, peasant-sleeved top, no doubt handmade by Lora-Leigh herself, their resident fashionista. "Looks like you stayed busy with your sewing machine over winter break."

"It's true," Lora-Leigh said. "I was one with my bobbin. It was the only way I could stay sane during the whole month and a half at home. If my dad wasn't the dean of students here, I would've tried to tell them that school started two weeks ago just to move back to Tuthill Hall early."

"It couldn't have been that bad," Jenna said. "You and your mom didn't get into a fight again, did you?"

Lora-Leigh and her mom had had a face-off last semester when Lora-Leigh'd decided to pledge Zeta Zeta Tau instead of Tri-Omega (her mom's sorority); but they'd finally made peace with each other, and as far as Roni knew, there hadn't been any family drama since then.

"Nah, Mom and I are good," Lora-Leigh said, grabbing a soda out of the minifridge and flopping down on Jenna's bed. "She helped me put together the first part of my ZZT scrapbook, and I helped her make knishes. I tried not to nag her about her June Cleaver clothes, and she tried not to nag me about my latest piercing. For us, that's some serious bonding."

"You got another piercing?" Roni asked, slightly horrified, still counting the same six holes in each of Lora-Leigh's ears that had been there in December.

"Check it out." Lora-Leigh grinned, then lifted the bottom of her sweater to reveal a silver navel ring with her ZZT initiation pearl dangling from the end.

"That is so cool," Jenna said admiringly. "I'm jealous. You get to wear glam jewelry in your belly button, and I have to wear my stupid pump."

"Your pump's not stupid," Roni said, squeezing Jenna's hand. Roni knew Jenna hated the insulin pump she wore to regulate the medication for her diabetes, and she and Lora-Leigh tried their best to support her by downplaying it.

Jenna just shrugged and changed the subject. "So, what else did you do over the break, Lora-Leigh?"

"Not much. When you've lived in the same town your whole

life and you go to college there, too, it's the 'been there, done that' prob. I hung out with my best friend from high school, Elizabeth, and we went out a few times. We mostly laid low and watched really awful dramality shows." She absently skimmed through the issue of *Lucky* she'd brought in with her. "So, what about your breaks? I want all the sordid details—parties, guys, mug sessions, et cetera."

"Mug sessions?" Roni asked blankly. "Why would you want somebody to get mugged?"

"Not the 'steal your purse' sort of mugging, Boston," Lora-Leigh said. "*Mugging,* as in making out with a choice guy."

"That must be a southern term," Roni said with a laugh. "I'm sad to report that there was no *mugging* on my end."

"Holding out for a certain guy on the LU swim team?" Lora-Leigh smiled knowingly.

"We'll see," Roni said, thinking of Lance McManus, the dark-haired hottie she'd met last September and had a casual on-again, off-again flirtation with. "We talked a couple of times over break, and he mentioned hanging out together once classes started again, but nothing official."

"And what about being home with the Royal Van Gelderens?" Lora-Leigh asked. "Any cathartic, memoir-worthy breakthroughs with the 'rents?"

Roni laughed. "They're still emotionally thwarted, but they did stop calling LU 'that hick school,' which I guess is progress." After her big blowup with her dad over her Amex bill last fall, she'd decided to write off her parents once and for all. But when Roni hadn't come home for Thanksgiving, her mom had written her a letter cordially inviting her home for Christmas and promising to try to be more supportive of her choices. Since Roni was a bridesmaid in her friend Kiersten's wedding anyway, she decided to go back to Boston to try to make the best of things. Her parents would never change, but at least they'd made an attempt to reach out to her. It was a start.

"And I see by your new Burberry coat that they didn't disown you yet, either," Lora-Leigh said, holding up the sleek black raincoat that had been lying on top of one of Roni's clothing piles. "They have impeccable taste, I'll give them that."

"That was my Christmas present," Roni said. "But that'll be the last addition to my designer labels for who knows how long. My dad agreed to keep paying for my tuition and books. But I'm on my own for room and board, ZZT dues, and spending money. Which is why I didn't have to spend much time over break tête-à-tête-ing at Beacon Hill holiday soirees. I was so busy helping Kiersten with her wedding plans and working at How Sweet It Is, I escaped the *snob*-nobbing functions." She rummaged through one of her boxes and pulled out two cheerfully wrapped bags of truffles and handed the sugar-free one to Jenna and the other to Lora-Leigh.

"*Pour vous,* courtesy of Madame and Monsieur Beauchamp," she said proudly. She'd loved every minute she'd worked for the elderly French couple in their gourmet chocolate boutique on Newbury Street. They'd treated her like more of a granddaughter than an employee, inviting her upstairs to their tiny apartment above the store for home-cooked meals and even having her over for a Christmas Eve lunch with their grown children and grandchildren. "I never knew how good it felt to get a paycheck until this Christmas."

"Yeah." Lora-Leigh snorted as she bit into one of the truffles. "I wouldn't have a problem getting paid to spend all day in a chocolate store, either. Especially with chocolate like this. Heaven."

"Tell me about it," Roni said. "I think I gained five pounds just from smelling the chocolate every day. It's a good thing I start life guarding at the natatorium on Monday so I can burn it all off again."

"I don't know how you're going to have time for everything," Jenna said as she dove into her own bag of chocolate. "I had a hard enough time balancing band and class and ZZT last semester, and I didn't even have a job."

"But I don't have band to worry about," Roni said as she started hanging up some of her clothes in her half of the closet, "so I think I'll be okay."

"And what about you, Jen-girl?" Lora-Leigh asked. "Was it all warm fuzzies and familial bliss in Marietta, Georgia?"

Jenna smiled. "Sort of. My mom let me sleep in every day and even came home early from work most nights to cook dinner. So I finally got back on track with my diet, and I didn't have to worry about my 'betes hardly at all. The Little Js fought the whole time, but that's the norm. And I missed them so much that I didn't even mind driving Jayne and Jordan around to their Christmas pageant practices and Jessica to her sleepovers and ballet."

"You are one truly warped individual if you enjoyed that," Lora-Leigh said with a laugh. "But forget about the fam; how's coupledom treating you?"

"You mean Tiger?" Jenna said, blushing. "He's great. We

talked on the phone every day over break, and e-mailed each other, too. He even sent me a little Christmas present." She held out her arm to reveal a delicate, silver bracelet with a ZZT pendant dangling from it.

"Jewelry already?" Lora-Leigh asked, and exchanged a knowing glance with Roni. "That is *such* a boyfriend gift."

"I know," Roni said, elbowing Jenna playfully. "Sounds pretty serious."

"I'm not sure, but we're getting closer," Jenna said, giggling giddily as she fingered her bracelet. "He just got back into town this morning, and I think I'm going to see him later tonight." Her smile grew even wider. "I've never felt this way about anyone before . . . ever."

"'Love is in the air,'" Lora-Leigh singsonged.

"And what about you and DeShawn, Lora-Leigh?" Jenna countered.

Lora-Leigh smiled mischievously. "Now that football season's over, it's sayonara to the platonic game. We texted a few times over break, and he wants to hang out as soon as he gets back in town."

"As in, *date* hang out?" Roni asked.

"That's what I'm thinking," Lora-Leigh said. "Of course I don't want anything serious, and I'm sure he doesn't, either. But I know he's still into me, so I'm ready to make my move."

"The question is, is DeShawn ready for you?" Jenna teased, giggling.

"Ready or not, here I come." Lora-Leigh winked.

Roni giggled, wondering if DeShawn had any idea what he was in for. He and Lora-Leigh had chemistry that gave off heat for miles, but as the star running back for the Latimer Red Raiders, DeShawn's focus had been all about football last semester. He'd made it clear to Lora-Leigh that nothing could happen between them while the season was under way. But now Roni knew it would be a whole different game, and the ball was undeniably in Lora-Leigh's court.

"He's going to call me sometime this week," Lora-Leigh said now. "And when he does . . ."

"Watch out," Roni interjected, and all three of them burst out laughing. Then Roni surveyed the mess around them. "Guys, as former ZZT New Member President," she said, "I'm about to make an executive decision."

"Uh-oh," Lora-Leigh said. "If this involves enlisting your former minions to alphabetize your closet by designer, forget about it. We're all on equal ground now."

"No alphabetizing," Roni promised. "I just don't think I can deal with any more unpacking right now. What do you think about heading to Heavenly BBQ for dinner? I've missed pulled pork po'boys like you wouldn't believe."

Lora-Leigh stood up. "I could kill for one of their corn muffins."

"Mmm," Jenna said, grabbing her purse. "And their black-eyed peas."

"Good," Roni said. "Eat now, clean later."

As they headed out the door, Roni smiled at her friends. After being apart for more than a month, their threesome was complete again. Tomorrow night would be their first ZZT house meeting as official actives, and Roni couldn't wait to catch up with her Big Sister Beverly as well.

Now, as they stepped out into the mild Florida evening and talked about what fun ZZT events might be happening this spring, Roni had the surreal feeling that something inside her had shifted. Boston wasn't home for her anymore; it had become a place to visit. Latimer, this small town that she'd known for only a few short months, was home. And she couldn't wait to see what her new hometown and her new ZZT family had in store for her.

Lora-Leigh stumbled out of the Supe Store, struggling under the weight of the semester's worth of textbooks she'd just bought. She was already dreading meeting her profs when classes started tomorrow. After all, what kind of sadistic instructor would have a ten-pound Political Science text as required reading? Add to that her Calculus, English Comp 102, Anthropology, and Art 210 texts, and she had to be carrying at least fifty pounds. She couldn't wait to dump the books in the back of her Jetta and meet up with her Big Sister Camille at the ZZT house for dinner and the Sunday-night house meeting.

She hurried to her car and jumped in just as it began to pour, and soon the rain was battering her windshield with such force that she barely heard her cell phone ring. When she saw her mom's number pop up on her caller ID, her heart stampeded across her chest just like it always did these days when her mom called. Logic told her that it was way too soon for any news, of course. But it didn't matter; a small part of her was always under the delusion that she might get an answer this early.

"Hi, Mom," she said breathlessly. "What's up?"

"Hello, dear. I just wanted to check your schedule this week. I was hoping you might come home for Shabbat dinner on Friday night."

"Oh," Lora-Leigh said, trying not to let any sign of disappointment creep into her voice. But of course her mom's superhuman powers of perception picked up on her tone right away.

"What's wrong?" she asked, but before Lora-Leigh could even answer, she added, "Oh, you didn't think I was calling about FIT, did you?"

"No no," Lora-Leigh said quickly, but then decided there was no use pretending. She sighed. "Well, actually, I sort of thought something might have come in the mail."

"Not yet," her mom said softly, "but you only sent in your application two months ago. These things take time."

"I know." Lora-Leigh nodded into the phone as she stared out at the streaks of rain racing down her windshield. She'd spent hours prepping her portfolio and rereading her essay for her application to the Fashion Institute of Technology in New York City before sending it out last Thanksgiving. And within a week of mailing it, she began checking the mailbox every single day without fail. Waiting for an answer from FIT was like waiting for the sales at Macy's on Black Friday—excruciating. All she could think about was getting accepted so that she could finally say good-bye to the hometown that she'd been trying to escape for, oh, the last nineteen years or so.

"I know it's hard to be patient," her mom added, "but I'm sure you'll hear something soon. And I'll call the second anything comes in the mail. I know how much it means to you."

"Thanks, Mom," Lora-Leigh said. "And about Shabbat . . . Since it's my first week to hang out with my friends, I'll take a rain check, if that's okay."

"Of course that's all right," her mom said. "Your dad is just suffering from Lora-Leigh blues. He misses you. I have to admit the house feels a little empty without you."

Lora-Leigh snorted. "I thought you'd be relieved I'm gone. No more dealing with my train wreck of a room."

Her mom laughed. "Oh, it wasn't that bad. Besides, you know we love to have you home."

"I know," she said. "Well, I'm about to be late meeting my Big Sis for dinner, so I better go. Tell Dad I miss him, too."

"I will."

As she hung up with her mom, Lora-Leigh felt an inkling of disappointment gnaw at her stomach, but then shook it off. She knew FIT was a total long shot. In fact, she'd intentionally downplayed the whole thing with Jenna and Roni since she'd applied because of that. But still, part of her was dying to know if she'd made the cut, if she had what it took to take her fashion talent all the way. She pulled out of the parking lot, willing herself to forget FIT. She had just enough time to drive back to Tuthill to leave her car in the far reaches of the student lot before hurrying over to Sorority Row to meet up with Camille.

When Lora-Leigh arrived at the ZZT house twenty minutes later, Sandy and Danika were on the front porch catching up with Jenna and Roni. After sharing hugs and hellos with them, Lora-Leigh bounded straight up the stairs, heading for Camille's room on the second floor. She got halfway up and froze in front of the row of conglomerate photos hanging on the wall, a triumphant smile creeping across her face. This was the first time she'd been upstairs in the ZZT house. No new members had been allowed there until initiation. She could see now that the upstairs wasn't anything extraordinary. It was basically two long hallways stretching out in either direction housing three dozen bedrooms and two massive shared bathrooms. But it was the fact that Lora-Leigh was free to roam where she wanted that gave her a small thrill. She took the last few steps two at a time, then knocked on Camille's door.

"Hey, stranger!" Camille said, hugging Lora-Leigh.

"Hey, Big Sis." Lora-Leigh smiled. "I've come to steal your makeup, try on your clothes, read your diary, and perform other annoying little sis duties."

"I don't buy it for a sec," Camille said, laughing. "My clothes are way too cliché for you, Miss *Hot* Couture. And I don't have a diary, but you won't find anything in my blog that I haven't already told you."

"I don't know," Lora-Leigh said. "I'm sure there are some juicy details about Mike that even your blog doesn't spill." She had set up Camille and Mike Muti on a blind date last fall, and they'd been dating steadily since then.

Camille grinned slyly. "Maybe so. But there are some details you'll never get out of me, no matter how much you nag, Little Sis."

"Such a killjoy." Lora-Leigh sighed theatrically. "Well, if I can't harass you about your love life, at least let me drag you to dinner. And if you don't eat every single last one of Miss Merry's pickled Brussels sprouts, I'm telling."

"You're enjoying this way too much," Camille said, elbowing

Lora-Leigh as they headed down to the dining room.

"Hey, I've been starved for sisterly attention for six weeks," Lora-Leigh said, sitting down with Camille across from Roni, Beverly, Jenna, and Darcy. "My big brother Scott just doesn't cut it, and he was home from Germany for only a week anyway. So you and I have some catching up to do."

"You're so right," Camille said. "I want to hear everything. You first."

Lora-Leigh grinned. Camille's "tell it like it is" demeanor and sense of humor complemented Lora-Leigh's blunt sarcasm perfectly. As they talked a mile a minute, filling in each other on their respective breaks, laughing as they traded stories, Lora-Leigh decided she had the best Big Sis in ZZT (not that she was biased or anything). In fact, Camille already knew her so well that when Lora-Leigh's cell beeped with a text message, Camille called it before Lora-Leigh even had a chance to check the screen.

"DeShawn," Camille said confidently, sharing a knowing smile with Jenna and Roni across the table.

"Show-off," Lora-Leigh teased Camille, downplaying the whole thing even as her heart performed an involuntary skitter across her chest.

Pritchard#33: Hey, Curly! Guess which hot commodity got back in town last nite? Did u miss me?

DesignsOnU: Wouldn't u like 2 know?

Pritchard#33: That's my grl. =) Wanna hang 2morrow nite at Mario's Pizzeria?

DesignsOnU: What's in it for me?

Pritchard#33: My constant adoration and a beer, my treat.

DesignsOnU: Worship me at ur own risk. The beer, I'll take.

Pritchard#33: U *so* missed me. =) L8tr.

Lora-Leigh snapped her phone shut and smiled.

"And?" Camille asked expectantly.

Lora-Leigh shrugged. "And, we're meeting tomorrow night to catch up."

"To catch up, huh? I don't think so. Not from the conniving look on your face. My guess is after tomorrow, you're going to have some juicy details of your own to spill." Camille giggled until Lora-Leigh threatened to launch one of the putrid-smelling Brussels sprouts at her. "Okay, okay, truce," Camille cried. "God, we really are like sisters, aren't we?"

"Yes," came the resounding vote from the other side of the table.

"Now behave yourselves before Mrs. Walsh sends you to your room," Beverly teased. "And eat something. The house meeting starts in ten minutes."

Lora-Leigh shared an eye roll with Camille and stifled a laugh, and they both quickly finished eating. But Lora-Leigh smiled over her plate as she thought of DeShawn. So he'd texted her almost the second he got back into town. That said something. And now that he was back, their flirt fest could finally turn legit, assuming that was what he wanted, too. She couldn't wait to see him and find out.

Jenna pulled out her planner as soon as she sat down in the ZZT living room with Roni, Lora-Leigh, Darcy, and Camille for the house meeting. Over the break, Jenna'd vowed that she was going to start this semester on the right foot—no more all-nighters (except maybe one or two for parties!), no more junk-food binges that messed with her 'betes, no more letting course work pile up until the last possible minute, and no more missing out on ZZT functions.

While everyone around her was hugging and happily chatting about what they'd done over break, Jenna flipped to the calendar section of her planner and lined up her pen and a rainbow of highlighters next to her on the floor of the ZZT living room.

"What's with the art supplies?" Lora-Leigh whispered. "Are we having a Martha Stewart night or something?"

Jenna giggled and shook her head. "I'm writing down all the dates for ZZT functions so I make sure I don't have any scheduling conflicts. I'm going to color-code everything according to activity. Band is orange; ZZT blue; and classes pink."

Lora-Leigh's jaw dropped. "Warning: Certain people in this room may be more anal than they appear," she said, laughing and elbowing Jenna. "Let me guess; Tiger's color is the color of true *lurve* . . . red."

Jenna blushed. "I know it seems stupid, but I'm just trying to keep my schedule under control."

"I think it's great," Darcy, her ZZT Big Sis, said, smiling

proudly at Jenna. "And marching band is over now, right? So that should make this easier for you, too."

Jenna nodded. "We have two out-of-town parades this month and next month, but then I'm done with marching band until next fall. Of course I joined the Raiders Concert Band this semester, but the practices for that are a lot less intense. The concert band's smaller and way more laid-back. And—major stress reliever—Papa Skank isn't my section leader. He's in the concert band, but he lost the section-leader spot to Heidi Clifton. So I don't have to worry about him raking me across the coals. He has been nicer to me since he found out about the 'betes, but he's still a total tyrant."

"I'll bet he's nicer to you now. I mean, you almost gave him a coronary when you collapsed on the field," Darcy said.

"And me, too!" Lora-Leigh added.

"I bet he really felt guilty about yelling at me for being late to practice *that* day," Jenna said, finally able to joke a little at the vague memory of the diabetic seizure she'd had at band practice a few months ago. That was another thing she didn't want a repeat of, which was why she was going to take better care of herself this spring. "I normally hate when people go easy on me because of my 'betes, but in Papa Skank's case, I think I'll milk it for all its worth."

Jenna laughed with the girls, then quieted down as Marissa, the ZZT President, started the meeting. Jenna grabbed her pen, armed and ready to start scheduling.

"It's so good to have y'all back," Marissa said with a warm smile, "and to have our new actives joining us for a brand-new semester."

Jenna clapped and whooped along with the rest of her former new-member class, loving the fact that she was called an "active" now. It sounded so much more permanent than "new member," like she was here in ZZT to stay.

"I'm proud to say that ZZT had the highest GPA of all the sororities last semester," Marissa said to the cheers of the roomful of girls, "and I have no doubt we'll have the same success this semester, too. We're going to have an amazing spring with some great activities, including Greek Week and our annual spring formal. We'll go over more details about both events as the semester progresses, but for now, I'll give you a brief overview of what's in store." Her eyes lit up with enthusiasm as she looked around the room. "Greek Week will kick off on Wednesday, March fourth, and end Saturday, March seventh. It's a huge event that brings all of the fraternities and sororities at Latimer together for five days of fun competitions that celebrate the spirit and camaraderie of Greek life. It's also a chance for the LU Greek student body to unite in a massive community-service endeavor, since the proceeds earned from Greek Week will be donated to the Latimer Special Olympics. Some of the events this year will include a talent show, softball tournament, Twister contest, three-legged relay race, slip-'n'-slide obstacle course, tug-of-war, cheer competition, and chariot race."

"So does that mean we get to drag the Tri-Omegas through the mud in a tug-o'-war?" Lora-Leigh asked. "If it does, just tell me where to sign up."

"Not quite." Marissa smiled and shook her head as the room bubbled with giggles. "Here's how it works. All of the twenty-two houses will be combined into eight Greek teams. There will be seven teams made up of three houses and one team made up of four houses. ZZT will be matched with another sorority and frat to make a team. For some events, like the talent show and cheer competition, ZZT will compete against other houses, earning points for our team. For other events, we'll be paired with members of other frats and sororities from our team to compete and win points. The Greek Week champion is the team with the most points earned for winning competitions and for the highest level of participation in the competitions and in the overall community-service effort."

"Guys and girls together?" Bonni, another new active, said gleefully. "It doesn't get much better than that."

"I hope we're on the same team as the Foxes," Jenna said, thinking of Tiger's frat, Phi Omicron Chi.

"I think it'd be more fun if you and Tiger competed *against* each other," Lora-Leigh said. "I bet he'd love a little wrestle with you on the Twister mat. I heard there's even whipped cream involved in that contest."

"Lora-Leigh, hush!" Jenna covered her mouth to stifle a giggle, feeling the blood rush to her face.

"Last year, we were on the same team as Zeta Theta Mu," Darcy whispered to Jenna, "and Holly Kendall, one of our seniors, met Matt Hughes, the ZΘM President. The two of them fell for each other and ended up getting engaged this year." She winked. "You never know what might happen."

"Greek Week is a great time for you to get to know other Greeks, and it will be tons of fun," Marissa continued. "But there will be even more fun to come later on, too, with Romance and Roses, our Spring Formal."

"Beverly showed me pictures of Formal from last year," Roni whispered to Jenna and Lora-Leigh. "It looked amazing!"

"The formal banquet and dance will be held at the end of April," Marissa said. "It's a time for us to celebrate the completion of our school year and our year at ZZT—a night for us to enjoy being with our friends, boyfriends, and sisters."

Jenna grinned, already imagining herself with Tiger at Formal. Just the idea of what he'd look like in a tux was enough to make her wish it was this weekend instead of three months away. Of course she didn't know for certain that they'd still be together in three months' time, but she had a good feeling about it. When she'd stopped by the Fox house last night to see him after dinner with Roni and Lora-Leigh, they had picked up right where they'd left off before break. They sat on the front porch talking (well, not *just* talking) for two hours before Jenna'd finally pulled herself away. Somehow over the last four months, Tiger hadn't just grown into her boyfriend but into one of her closest friends, too, and she'd never had that with a guy before. And there was no question she'd ask him to be her date to Formal, and of course he'd say yes.

"We haven't decided on a venue for Formal yet," Marissa was saying, interrupting Jenna's thoughts, "but we'll let you know when we do. There will be plenty of opportunities for y'all to get involved in the planning process for Greek Week and Formal as well, starting tonight. Which leads me to my next announcement . . ."

Marissa motioned for Heather Bourke, Stacy Fagen, Betsy Bickford, and the other ZZT officers to join her at the front of the room. "We'll be organizing a number of committees for the spring, including one for Greek Week and Formal," Marissa said. "But in addition, it's also time for our annual chapter elections. The elections will be held next Sunday during our first official chapter meeting. At that time, all initiated members of ZZT, including our newest actives, will be able to vote for their officers. Assistant positions are also available for any new actives who want to learn more about certain offices and help the officers with their responsibilities over the next year. We'll be passing out a list and description of the offices now, along with a list of the spring committees. Remember that you can nominate yourself or others for an office or assistant position. We'll accept nominations at the end of this meeting. Also, sign-up sheets for the committees will be on the table in the back of the room, so please sign up for any you'd like to join."

Marissa made some brief final announcements and then the meeting came to an end. She and the other officers passed out the information sheets, and as Jenna browsed through the list, at least half a dozen of the assistant positions and committees piqued her interest. She'd love to assist the new Philanthropy Chair with some community-service functions, or even the House Manager in improving some things around the ZZT house (like the dinner menus, for starters).

"What are y'all going to sign up for?" she asked her friends.

"Greek Week Committee," Lora-Leigh said. "Where there's a talent show, there're costumes. And when costumes call to Lora-Leigh Sorenstein, great guru of fashion, she must obey."

"First, I'm going to nominate Beverly for President," Roni said. "I know she'd make a great one, and she mentioned to me last semester that she'd been thinking about running."

"I'd vote for her," Lora-Leigh said. "She did a great job as New Member Chair."

"And I'm definitely going to nominate myself to be the Formal Planner's assistant," Roni continued. "I mean, I just went through Kiersten's wedding planning with her, so I have some great ideas already. And I'm going to sign up for the House Beautification Committee, too. I saw the bathroom upstairs today." She shuddered. "The ZZT sister who picked out the green vinyl curtains and the lemon linoleum flooring must have been colorblind. If there's one thing I learned from my mom, it's how to decorate a room with class. So I think I'll give it a shot."

"You won't be getting marble floors and silk window treatments with the ZZT budget, Boston," Lora-Leigh teased. "But maybe I can help you pick out some nice fabric at the Sewing Bee to work with. It won't be Dupioni silk, but it'll be workable."

"Thanks," Roni said, grinning.

"I think I'm going to sign up for the Greek Week and Formal Committees," Jenna said. "And I'd love to nominate myself as assistant to the Philanthropy Chair, too. That sounds so great."

"That seems like a lot for you, doesn't it?" Roni asked.

Jenna almost protested, but then she caught herself, remembering her promise to herself to keep things balanced this semester. She didn't want to get in over her head like she had before.

"You might be right," Jenna said reluctantly, then turned to her Big Sis. "Darcy, how much of a time commitment do you think two committees and an assistant position would take?"

Darcy thought for a second and then said, "Well, assistant

positions can be pretty time-consuming. Sort of like the commitment Roni had when she was New Member President. And each committee will take about as much time as your new member activities and classes did."

Jenna flipped through her planner, mentally running through her schedule. She already had a lot going on, just like last semester, except this semester she hoped she'd be able to spend even more time with Tiger. "I better only sign up for the Greek Week Committee, then," she said. "Just to be on the safe side."

"I think that'll be perfect," Darcy said, nodding in approval.

Jenna smiled as she jotted down her name on the sign-up sheet underneath Lora-Leigh's. Even though she would've liked to get more involved and be the overachiever she'd been in high school, she knew she was doing the right thing in limiting herself this time. Besides, now she could make sure that her activities, classes, friends, and *boyfriend* (she loved that word!) would all get the attention they deserved.

CHAPTER 2

Roni looked down from her perch in the lifeguard chair, scrutinizing the Olympic-size swimming pool for any sign of danger or distress. There was a "Mommy and Me" baby swim class going on and a few Latimer students doing laps, but other than that, everything was relatively quiet.

She'd come to the natatorium right after she'd finished up her Monday classes this afternoon, and so far, her first day of life guarding had been pretty cushy. In fact, she probably couldn't have picked a better way to earn money for room and board. She got to hang out by the pool (which she loved) and swim (which she *really* loved). Of course she couldn't study, or even read a magazine, while she worked, because her eyes had to be focused on the water at all times. But as long as there weren't any real emergencies to deal with, lifeguarding would be fun.

As she scanned the pool for the hundredth time, a movement over by the guys' locker room caught her attention. A dozen guys were headed for the pool, all wearing matching red LU

Speedos. Roni's heart sped up as she watched the Latimer swim team warming up and stretching, looking for the one familiar face she knew had to be there. She finally spotted him chatting with one of his teammates. With his dark, unruly hair and tan, lean frame (not to mention his disarmingly gorge hazel eyes), Lance McManus was a tough guy to miss.

She scooted forward in her chair, hoping he'd glance up. When he did, his eyes lit up and a smile of recognition spread across his face. Roni smiled, too, thankful that he was far enough away not to see her cheeks catching fire. She raised her hand, and even though it was oh-so-tempting to motion him over to say hello, a half wave was all she allowed herself. She couldn't leave her lifeguard post, and she knew she needed to keep her mind on the water. Maybe, if she was lucky, he'd stick around after he finished his practice and she'd see him when she got off work in two hours.

After flashing her one more smile, Lance dove into the pool and caught up with his teammates in a flawless butterfly stroke. Roni leaned back in her chair, watching Lance's arms swing up over his head in powerful strokes, lifting him out of the water gracefully. Oh yeah, she could keep her eyes glued to the water now. There was no doubt about it. She was going to *love* this job, especially on swim-team practice days.

Two hours later, after she'd showered and changed, Roni made a point of walking back through the pool area on her way toward the exit. She sighed. No sign of Lance. His practice had ended an hour ago, so she'd figured it was a long shot that he'd still be here. But as she opened the door to the late-afternoon sunshine, there he was, sitting on a park bench by the rec-center fountain, an open Anatomy textbook on his lap. He immediately lifted his head and waved her over, and Roni wondered if he'd been waiting for her this whole time.

"So you did decide to take Anatomy 101 this semester," she said, motioning to his textbook as she sat down. He'd told her last fall that he was thinking of going premed. "And is it improving your odds with girls like you thought it would?"

"Well, I'm going to be intimately acquainted with one Claire Jenkins in a few weeks," he said. "But I don't think she's the right one for me. She's a little too old. Five decades too old, actually, and she's pretty antisocial."

"Really?"

Lance nodded. "She's not the best conversationalist, being a cadaver and all. And if *you* hang around me enough, who knows? Claire might be in for some tough competition." He smiled.

Roni made sure to smile back, tilting her head to twirl her hair around her finger in a flirty way she hoped would look irresistible.

"So, how was your first day of classes?" he asked.

"Not bad," Roni said. "First days are always great. You get the syllabus and then get let out early. I had Business Math and English Comp today. Tomorrow it's Archaeology and Poli Sci. The usual core classes."

"I have Poli Sci tomorrow, too," Lance said. "Which class are you in?"

"Dr. Fillburn's nine-fifteen," Roni said.

"Me, too!"

"Oh no." Roni shook her head. "I'm not falling for that again.

Last semester, we were supposed to be in the same Geography lab, but you disappeared halfway through the class and left me alone with that god-awful TA."

Lance laughed. "I promise, no more switching classes. I heard Dr. Fillburn's a complete geriatric who mumbles so badly that no one can understand a thing he says. But we can suffer through it together."

"I'll save you a seat in the back so we can snooze unnoticed," Roni joked. It would be fun to share a class with him, especially a boring one like Poli Sci. "Well, I better go. I'm having dinner with my Big Sis Beverly at ZZT in a little while. And then I have to finish unpacking my dorm room." Roni'd given up on the last of her boxes late last night. She and Jenna had crammed as much of her stuff as they could into the dorm room, but there were still three boxes of clothes left and nowhere to put them. So tonight, Roni would go through the boxes, pull out one or two of her fave outfits, then ship the rest back to her parents in Boston. She hated to do it, but it was a small price to pay for having Jenna as a roommate, so she'd deal.

"So I guess I'll see you in Poli Sci?" she said to Lance now.

"Tomorrow morning, it's a date," Lance said. He hesitated, looking uncertain for a second, then added, "And, um . . . speaking of dates, maybe we can have a real one sometime?"

Roni blushed, a surge of heat flashing through her. "I was hoping you'd remember." She smiled. If he hadn't finally gotten around to asking her, she would've been so disappointed.

"There's no way I'd forget," Lance said, shaking his head. "I've been waiting for this since last semester."

She grinned. So that made two of them.

"How about Sunday night?" Lance suggested.

"Oh." Roni's face fell. "That's the night of our first ZZT chapter meeting. I can't miss it."

Lance grinned. "Why not? Isn't it just a bunch of gossip about cute boys, such as yours truly?"

Roni laughed. "Oh sure, and then we sit around giving each other manis, pedis, and facials," she joked back, then shook her head. "No . . . believe it or not, we actually have intelligent conversations about community-service projects, budgets, and lots of other things."

"Of course you do," Lance kidded. "But the boy talk, I mean, the meeting ends pretty early, right? So I could pick you up at the ZZT house afterward. There's this cool restaurant I've been to that's right on Latimer Lake. We can go there."

"That sounds great," Roni said.

They talked for a few more minutes, and then Roni said good-bye, leaving Lance standing by the bench. She chanced one glance back at him as she walked away and saw that he'd packed up his stuff and was leaving, too. So he *had* been waiting for her. She smiled as she headed toward Sorority Row on a hottie high. Between rooming with Jenna, the fun activities planned for ZZT, and her date with Lance on Sunday, this was shaping up to be a great semester. And it was just the beginning. . . .

Lora-Leigh reached for a slice of Mario's famous Gut-Buster pizza and snuck another glance at DeShawn across the table. In a navy crewneck that stretched tightly across his broad shoulders and J.Crew jeans, he was looking fine, and she realized how good it was to see him again. Of course she'd never admit that to him, but she could allow herself a few seconds of subtle DeShawn-scoping every now and then. He'd never notice.

"I'm a tough guy to resist, I know," DeShawn said suddenly with a mischievous smile. "But if you don't quit staring at me, Curly, you're gonna give me a complex."

Lora-Leigh blanched. Okay, so he'd noticed. "Don't flatter yourself," she said coolly, making a quick recovery. "You've got pizza sauce on your chin, that's all."

DeShawn laughed. "It's good to be back, Curly. Nobody at home keeps me on my toes like you do." He leaned across the table. "But don't kid yourself. There's not a drop of sauce on my chin. You know it, and I know it."

Her heart accelerated as she tried to read the glimmer in his eyes. What was he saying, that he knew she was ready to be done with the whole "just friends" facade? Well, now was her chance to lay it out on the table. "All right, so you caught me staring." She shrugged. "I dare you to do something about it."

His eyebrows lifted in mock surprise, and he laughed. "Don't tempt me."

"Funny," she said, giving him a harmless kick under the table, "that's exactly what I'm trying to do. Is it working?"

DeShawn grabbed another slice of pizza and shrugged. "Maybe try a more hands-on approach, and I'll let you know."

"Ach." She slugged him on the arm, laughing as she realized her chances of having a serious conversation with him over pizza and beer were about as slim as one of Nicole Ritchie's skirts. "You are such a mood killer, Pritchard, you know that? But you better watch yourself. You don't have me in any of your classes to save your butt by keeping you awake this semester. Why aren't you taking Art 210, anyway?" She'd been hoping she'd see him in her art class earlier today, but no such luck.

"I wish I could," he said, "but I'm taking Advanced Architectural Engineering this semester, thanks to my Architect prof from last fall. When I told him I didn't think I could swing a summer internship with an architecture firm, he recommended me for the senior-level course, and my adviser approved it."

"That's amazing!"

"Thanks," DeShawn said, grabbing two more slices of pizza, layering them like a sandwich, and digging in. "It'll get me a lot further along in my degree, which will be great, considering I don't know where I'll be with school next year."

"What do you mean?" Lora-Leigh asked, her stomach dipping suddenly. She didn't like the sound of this.

"Coach Bradshaw called me into his office this morning," DeShawn said. "He hinted that a couple of scouts were checking me out last season, especially from the Green Bay Packers. He thinks I might have a shot at being picked up by a pro team this year."

"With the season you had last fall," Lora-Leigh said, "I'm not surprised. You set the field on fire at every game. You probably have a dozen scouts drooling over you right now."

"I'll try not to let that go to my head," DeShawn said with a laugh. "Anyway, I'm thinking about declaring myself eligible for the NFL draft. I'm putting in a request with the NFL College Advisory Committee to give me an idea of my potential draft status."

"I didn't even know they could give out info like that," Lora-Leigh said.

"They're the only ones who can," DeShawn said. "I can't work with an agent or any pro teams before the draft. But the Advisory Committee can give me an unbiased estimate of the highest round I could be selected in during the draft. If they tell me my chances are good enough, I'll write up my official declaration and give it to the LU director of athletics. Then all I have to do is give a signed petition of eligibility to the NFL, and I'm good to go."

Lora-Leigh whistled. "Sounds like *somebody's* been doing some serious research," she teased.

"Gotta prep for my big break, baby," he joked. "I'm just not sure whether I should go for it now, or wait until next year so I can get my degree. If I go to summer school this year, I'll have enough credits to graduate early next fall, and then go pro. But that's if I decide to wait that long."

Lora-Leigh smiled as she watched DeShawn's eyes light up at the mention of going pro. God, he wanted it badly. It was written all over his face. "Whether you do the draft this year or next, you'll go all the way," Lora-Leigh said with certainty. "I know it."

DeShawn smiled. "We'll see. I'd love to be able to call my mom and dad and tell them I got drafted, and to go buy some oceanfront property in Palm Beach and hire a housekeeper."

"I hate to think of you giving up Architecture, though," Lora-Leigh said. "It's your gift."

"Who said anything about giving it up?" DeShawn said. "I can still finish my classes correspondence, if I have to. Don't get me wrong; I love Latimer. But I've got to go for the prize, too, you know?"

"I know," Lora-Leigh said. And she did know, all too well. That's how she felt about applying to FIT, so who was she to expect DeShawn to do anything different? They both had dreams, and they both had to decide what was right for them. The problem was, that meant big changes for both of them, and that was something Lora-Leigh didn't even want to think about just yet.

They finished their meal while they talked about the rest of their plans for the semester. Then, all too soon, Lora-Leigh found herself reluctantly walking toward Sorority Row with DeShawn. She didn't want the evening to be over, especially since she was sure that there was even more electricity ricocheting between them now than there had been last semester. She was trying to decide whether she should stage an all-out ambush on him, when DeShawn suddenly caught her hand and pulled her onto a bench outside Billado Hall.

"What the—" she started, but his lips on hers froze the rest of the words. It was a playful kiss, short enough to be teasing but long enough to make her head spin. It was a kiss she'd been wanting for months, and finally . . . *finally* here it was.

"That," DeShawn said when he pulled away, "should answer your earlier question. I've been tempted since day one with you, Curly."

Lora-Leigh let out the breath she'd been holding and grinned. "I'll try not to let that go to *my* head," she said as they kept walking.

"There is one thing," DeShawn said, looking at her more

seriously. "You've still got to know I'm in limbo here this semester with the draft question and everything. I'm all for us dating when we can, but there're no guarantees. . . ."

Lora-Leigh held up her hand to silence him. "I can live with that. Just answer one question for me."

"What's that?"

"Are there more where that kiss came from?" she asked.

DeShawn grinned, then wrapped his arms around her, pulling her close. "What do you think?"

And before she could say another word, her breath was gone again, flying away with his kiss.

"Come on, Boston," Lora-Leigh said, throwing herself back on Roni's bed in frustration on Friday night. "I'd like to get to Brad Johnson's party *before* Armageddon, if at all possible." Jenna was hanging with Tiger tonight at a Fox party, but she and Roni were supposed to meet up with Camille, Beverly, Sandy, Bonni, and Betsy over half an hour ago for the party at Betsy's boyfriend Brad's house off campus. But Lora-Leigh'd had to call Camille five minutes ago and tell her they'd meet them there. It was only a short walk from Tuthill down University Drive, anyway, so it wouldn't take them long to get there. *If* they ever left Tuthill, that is.

"I know, I know," Roni said. "I'm sorry. It's just that . . ." She sighed, throwing up her hands in frustration. "This has never happened to me before."

"What, you've never had a wardrobe crisis?" Lora-Leigh asked. She laughed. "Well, with your runway-worthy clothes, I guess I can buy that."

"I really wanted to wear my suede skirt, but then I remembered I wore that once already this week," Roni said. "And the same with these pants, and this top." She plopped down on the bed beside Lora-Leigh. "I should never have mailed the rest of my clothes back to Boston." She sighed. "I miss them."

Lora-Leigh snickered. "It is possible to live with a limited number of clothes, Boston. Most people do. But I'm willing to accept that this is a somewhat trying time for you and your closet, so let's work through it together. First, let's get one thing straight. There is no cardinal rule of fashion against wearing the same outfit twice in one week. It's all about accessorizing. You glam up your clothes with some choice hardware, and no one will notice it's the same thing you wore three days ago."

"You pick for me, then," Roni said. "I've hit a stalemate."

Lora-Leigh reached into the closet with her eyes closed and pulled a pair of jeans and a top from the rack, then opened her eyes. "Perfect," she said, proudly holding up a cranberry silk BCBG sleeveless wraparound and some Sevens hip-hugging flares. The dark top would really set off Roni's black hair, and the jeans would make her slender legs look fab. "Wear your Miu Miu boots and"—she pulled a chiffon beaded scarf belt from the depths of the closet—"tie this into your hair."

Roni grinned. "You're a miracle worker."

"Don't I know it." Lora-Leigh laughed. "But let's save the deification for after we're out the door."

"Right," Roni said.

Ten minutes later they were walking across campus toward University Drive.

"So," Roni said, "how did everything go with DeShawn on

Monday night? We've all been so busy with classes this week, I never got to hear the details."

"Oh, there's not much to tell. A little Heineken, a little hanging out . . ." Lora-Leigh grinned. ". . . a little hooking up."

Roni froze midstep, staring wide-eyed at Lora-Leigh. "Omigod, that's great!" she squealed, grabbing Lora-Leigh's hand. "And it definitely took you two long enough."

"Tell me about it," Lora-Leigh said. "But the whole thing's still low-key, you know? We're going to have some fun, no doubt, but DeShawn's got a lot on his mind right now, so this isn't going to turn into the romance of the century." She filled Roni in on what DeShawn had told her about the NFL draft. "He's not sure what he's going to do," she finished. "But I feel like he's just killing time until he figures it out. Like he's half here, half gone already. I can't believe the school year's only half over and everyone's already obsessing over next year."

"Who's everyone?" Roni asked. "I'm not obsessing." She giggled. "Although my parents are, mostly about me not having declared prelaw as my major yet."

"And I am, too," Lora-Leigh blurted. Then she froze, feeling Roni's eyes on her, waiting.

"Lora-Leigh?" Roni asked, looking her in the eyes. "What's up?"

"Well, you know I applied to FIT over Thanksgiving. . . ." Lora-Leigh started.

"I remember." Roni nodded, her face suddenly very serious. "I've just been blocking it out, hoping it might disappear completely." A small smile crossed her face. "It's selfish, I know, but I hate the thought of you leaving us." Then her eyes widened. "Why, did you hear from them already?"

"No," Lora-Leigh said. "But I probably will within the next month or so, and then I have to decide what to do. I've been thinking about it a lot lately."

"But you never talk about it with me or Jenna," Roni said.

Lora-Leigh shrugged. "Because it feels weird to talk about leaving y'all when we're having so much fun with ZZT and everything."

"But, Lora-Leigh, we're your best friends. You *should* be talking to us about it." Roni seemed lost in thought for a minute, and then she slipped an arm around Lora-Leigh. "Of course I don't want you to leave Latimer, and neither does Jenna. But we also know that it wasn't your first choice to come here. You did what your parents wanted, but now you have a chance to do what's right for you." She smiled. "I know how important that is. That's why I came to Latimer instead of going to Harvard or Wellesley, like my parents wanted."

Lora-Leigh shrugged. "I'm not going to get accepted anyway, so I should just forget about the whole thing."

"You'll get accepted," Roni said matter-of-factly as they crossed over University to the row of duplexes on the other side. "You have such a passion for designing, and FIT will see that. And then the choice will be yours to make, and it won't matter what any of the rest of us think."

"Maybe you and Jenna can come with me," Lora-Leigh said. "Ever thought of transferring to Columbia or NYU?"

"I think I'm here to stay," Roni said. "We'll miss you horribly and harass you with e-mails and IMs nonstop. And if you go to

FIT, I have the perfect excuse to visit Manhattan! Of course I won't be able to afford to shop at Bergdorf's anymore, but I'll live."

Lora-Leigh smiled. "Oh, celebs love to unload the designer clothes they're tired of at little thrift boutiques in the Village. So we can get fab names at prices even us common plebes can afford. If you've never shopped south of Saks, you don't know what you're missing out on."

"Then you'll just have to show me," Roni said.

"Sure thing. But that's if I get accepted," Lora-Leigh said, "*and* if I decide to go. This semester, I just want to live in the here and now. No more talk about FIT until I say so. Got it?"

"Got it," Roni said.

They walked up the steps to Brad's house and rang the doorbell. Lora-Leigh could hear muted laughter and shouting and the bass from the sound system, even with the door closed.

"Y'all made it!" Betsy said when she threw open the door. Camille was right behind her, holding two cups of Trashcan Punch out to them.

"Come on," Camille said, leading Lora-Leigh and Roni into the room of wall-to-wall people. "We were waiting until you got here to get the real party going."

"There is no party without Lora-Leigh Sorenstein," Lora-Leigh said, lifting her cup to toast Camille and Roni, "but there will be one now!"

Jenna had no idea how long she'd been dancing with Tiger, but that was just fine by her. The feel of his hands on the small of her back as they moved to the music made her want to stay just like this all night long. And she probably could've, too, if it hadn't been for her sore feet and the stifling crush of bodies surrounding them. The Fox party had been in full swing since eight o'clock, and it had to be close to midnight now, but there was still no sign of the party letting up. It seemed like every inch of the downstairs living room and den of the Fox house was crammed with people talking, laughing, and dancing. Some of the people Jenna recognized from other Greek houses. There were a few guys from Pi Theta Ep manning the ice-block shots (no surprise there), and some Kappa Omegas in their telltale cowboy boots hanging out with a group of girls from Beta Xi. But a lot of the partygoers were non-Greeks who were friends or girlfriends of the Foxes, too. It was insanely loud and a total blast, and Jenna had been having a great time until about ten minutes ago, when she'd started to hit the wall. But she didn't want to be a downer, so she was doing her best to stifle her yawns and keep a smile on her face.

"Hey," Tiger said, pulling her close so she could hear him over the blaring music. "Are you all right?"

"Sure," Jenna shouted back. "Why?"

Tiger pointed to her feet. "You haven't moved your feet for the last ten minutes."

"I'm fine," Jenna lied, but even as she said it, her feet screamed out in protest. And on top of that, she was starting to feel twinges of dizziness now. She sighed. There was no point in trying to pretend. "Okay, I'm not fine." She lifted one foot gingerly and grimaced. "My feet are killing me. We marched a practice parade route today in band to prep for the Mardi Gras parade we have in two weeks, and even my blisters have blisters now. I'm completely wiped."

Tiger slipped his arm around her waist, leaning over her in concern. "Why didn't you say something before?"

Jenna shrugged, hesitating. "I didn't want to stop dancing, and I didn't want to ruin the night for you," she said quietly. "But I think I might need a break now. It's been a long week, and I think my 'betes might be sending off some warning signals. Maybe I should just get home." She remembered she'd left her backpack, the one stocked with juice boxes, back at Tuthill. Not a smart move.

"Listen," Tiger said, guiding her off the dance floor, "the only way you'd ruin my night is if you left." He squeezed her hand. "Come on, let's get you somewhere quiet to relax for a minute."

He led her upstairs to his room and shut the door, muting the party sounds from below.

"You sit there and put your feet up," Tiger said, motioning to his futon. "I'll get you something cold to drink."

Jenna was too tired and too unsteady to argue, so she gratefully slipped off her shoes and sat back. The ache in her feet lessened a bit, but she still felt like her head was in some sort of strange vacuum.

Tiger opened the minifridge, and Jenna's jaw dropped when she saw half a dozen juice boxes lining the top shelf, all with her name on them. He handed her one with a smile, then sat down on the edge of the futon to gently rub her feet.

"You got those juice boxes for me?" she asked in disbelief.

"Sure," Tiger said with a shrug. "I figured they'd be handy for when we hang out here." He smiled shyly. "And I thought they might help convince you to come over more often."

"Thank you. That's so sweet." She loved that he was considerate without hovering over her like she was a sick person. She smiled and reached for his hand as she sipped her juice. "And for the record, I don't need any convincing. I'll come over as much as you want me to. All you need to do is ask."

"Watch out," Tiger teased. "You might get sick of me."

She laughed. "I doubt that."

As Jenna finished her juice box, Tiger asked, "How are you feeling now?"

"Much better," Jenna said, feeling her body stabilizing again. She checked her insulin-pump readout just to be sure and then nodded. "But I think I'm retiring my dancing shoes for the night. Don't worry about me, though. You should go down and enjoy the rest of the party with your friends."

"Nah," Tiger said. "Right here in this room is something I care about a lot more than the party."

Jenna's heart pounded furiously. Omigod. He'd never said anything like that before, and the great thing was that she felt the same way about him. The L-word flitted across her mind, but she wasn't sure she was ready for that just yet. Still, she knew her relationship with Tiger was turning into more than just mutual like-like, something more serious, and more meaningful. And now it seemed like he felt that way, too.

Her breath caught as he brushed his lips against hers, and as the kiss deepened she felt a new dizziness that had nothing to do with her 'betes. Tiger slipped his hands around her waist, and she fell gently back onto the futon in his arms as he moved to kiss her ears, her neck, her collarbone. She tucked her hands up under his henley, loving the warmth of his skin.

Getting deliciously light-headed from his kisses, Jenna lost all sense of time and place. Before she realized it, the two of them were a tangle of arms and legs and rumpled clothes. They were moving in a direction they'd never gone before and it felt incredible. All she wanted was more, except for a nagging voice inside her that said maybe more was a little too much.

"Tiger," she mumbled through his kisses. "Tiger, wait . . ." She forced herself to draw back, putting some space in between them.

"What's wrong?" Tiger asked. "Are you okay? Is this too fast?" His cheeks were flushed and his sandy hair tousled, making him look absolutely, positively . . . irresistible.

Jenna could've kissed him again, giving in to herself, but instead she flopped back on the futon with a sigh. "I'm fine," she said. "And you didn't screw up. It's me . . ." She took a deep breath, feeling her already heated cheeks blazing even hotter. "It's just . . . I'm not sure I'm ready for, well, you know . . ."

"Oh, right," Tiger said quietly, nodding in understanding as he sat up. He brushed her hair away from her face and said gently, "Okay, so, talk to me."

Jenna swallowed, nervousness roiling in her stomach. She hoped she wasn't about to ruin the best thing that'd ever happened to her, but she had to be completely honest with him. Her experience with guys before Tiger was virtually no experience at all, aside from a few harmless porch-light kisses. She'd held back on the big "V," wanting her first time to be with someone special, someone she could see herself with for more than just a few dates. Not fessing up to that truth now would only end up frustrating both of them down the road, and he deserved to know. "See, I've never, um, been with anyone before," she said slowly. *God, could this get any more embarrassing?* "I've been waiting for the right guy."

"Wow," Tiger said, and Jenna wasn't sure if it was an impressed "wow" or a freaked-out "wow." But then he took her hand in his and added, "That's amazing."

"Thanks." Jenna smiled at him, wondering how many guys might've rolled their eyes instead. She was so lucky she had such a great, understanding boyfriend. "I've just always wanted my first time to be special, *with* someone special."

"Of course you do," Tiger said. "Everyone's first time should be."

There was something about the way Tiger said it that brought a new question stampeding into Jenna's mind. She wasn't sure she wanted to know the answer to it, but at the same time she *had* to know the answer. "So, um, have you ever . . . been with anyone before?"

Tiger met her eyes, and Jenna could see the concern and hesitation in them. "Well, yes," he said finally. "I have. There was a girl that I went to camp with in high school, but it was a long time ago. . . ." He blushed, clearly uncomfortable with the idea of sharing any more details.

"Oh," Jenna said quietly, staring at the carpet, disappointment sweeping over her. She should have expected this. Really, she should have. But part of her had hoped that he would be just as inexperienced as she was. Lately, she'd been starting to feel like she could share anything with Tiger, maybe even *everything* with him. And she'd thought that if they did go down that road, they'd be heading down it for the first time together, making it even more unforgettable. But—she argued with herself now—it was completely naive to think that. Tiger was older, and she knew he'd had girlfriends in the past, so she shouldn't have been surprised by this. But, still, the whole idea of him *with* someone else made her uneasy.

"Jenna?" Tiger said softly. "You're not upset, are you? Because I had to be honest about this . . ."

Jenna shook her head, clearing the fog in her mind. "No, no, of course I want you to be honest." She tried to give him a reassuring smile to let him know she was okay, but he still looked doubtful. "I'm fine . . . really."

Tiger lifted her chin until she had to meet his eyes. "Hey," he said quietly, "just so you know, it's not something I took casually. It meant something to me."

Jenna nodded, wanting to feel relief, but instead all she felt was uncertainty. If Tiger was way more experienced than she was, could he even really understand what a big deal this was to her? Or what if she decided to be with him, and then, afterward, they broke up? Would she regret the choice she'd made? Or, what if she decided not to take the leap with Tiger, and then he got frustrated with waiting and broke up with her? A whirlwind of questions spun in her head, and none of the answers seemed simple or easy.

"I'm glad you don't take it lightly," she finally said, "because I don't either. It would be a big step for me, and I guess I just need some more time to think everything through."

"I understand," Tiger said. "Listen, I'm so glad you told me. That took a lot of guts. And I want you to know that I'm fine with whatever you decide." He smiled sweetly. "But am I allowed to say that whoever your first ends up being, he's one lucky guy."

Jenna giggled. "Thanks."

Tiger kissed her lightly and softly on the lips one more time, but as he pulled away, Jenna suddenly found herself stifling a heavy yawn. She didn't know whether it was her band practice and the partying earlier, or if it was the seriousness of the discussion she'd just had with Tiger. But it had been a long, long day, and all at once she could barely keep her eyes open.

"I'm sorry," she whispered through another yawn. "Maybe I should get back to the dorm to get some sleep."

"Sure," Tiger said, helping her up. "I'll take you."

As they walked through campus, Jenna tried not to rehash their discussion in her mind. She knew that it was way too late, and she was way too tired, to make sense of her feelings right now. But despite her best intentions, the same nagging thoughts thrummed in her head. *She would never be Tiger's first. He'd already been with someone else, or maybe even more than one someone.* She tried to tell herself that she couldn't be upset about this. It wouldn't be fair to Tiger. After all, the past was past, and whatever had happened before didn't matter. But hours after she'd kissed Tiger good night, she lay in bed with her mind reeling and her stomach churning relentlessly. And she knew that it did matter to her, more than she'd ever imagined. Now she was more confused than ever about what she wanted—or didn't want—to happen with Tiger.

CHAPTER 3

Roni felt a rush of excitement as she stood in between Amy Tubbs and Sue-Marie Weiss outside the closed living-room doors. Along with all the other actives lined up in alphabetical order, she was waiting to be let into her first formal ZZT chapter meeting. Not only was her first chapter meeting tonight, but so was her first date with Lance. He was picking her up at the ZZT house after the meeting, and just the thought of finally getting to spend some time with him made her heart flip-flop.

As she waited to be let into the meeting, she could see Lora-Leigh farther up the line, twisting one of her six garnet earrings in boredom, and Jenna toward the front, biting her lip nervously. This wasn't as big a deal as initiation had been—not even close. But still, attending a chapter meeting made Roni feel that much more an official active in ZZT. And if she was elected the Formal Planner's assistant tonight, then she'd be even more involved, which was exactly what she wanted. Now that ZZT was her family, she wanted to devote herself to it as much as she could.

The living-room door opened a few inches, and Stacy Fagen, the current VP of Finance, stepped out. She nodded somberly to the girls. "Once you give the ZZT knock and secret password," she said, "you will be permitted to enter." With that, she shut the door again.

Roni watched as Heidi Anderson hesitantly stepped up to the door and tapped a sequence of long and short knocks, spelling out the letters *Z, Z, T* in Morse code. When Stacy opened the door an inch, Heidi whispered the secret password, then smiled with relief as the door opened wider and she disappeared behind it. Each girl performed the same motions to be let into the meeting, and when it was finally Roni's turn, a thrill shot through her as she tapped out the special knock and whispered "Rosebud" into Stacy's ear. The door opened, and Roni hurried in to grab her seat at the table. She saw Lora-Leigh, Jenna, and Beverly already in their chairs, and for a second wished she could sit with them instead of in alphabetical order. But Beverly had already told her that the protocol for chapter meetings had to be kept, and it made sense to Roni that this setup was the most efficient way to run the meeting.

Once the last of the girls was admitted, Marissa stood up at the front of the room. "On this, the twenty-fifth day of January, I hereby call the meeting of the Delta Chapter of Zeta Zeta Tau to order. We will now proceed with the roll call and reading of the minutes from our last chapter meeting at the end of the fall semester." She read off the roll, and each active had to stand and say "present" before the minutes could be read.

Roni listened intently as Hallie Stoops, the Secretary, read the minutes, and then each officer and current committee head gave her report. Beverly was the only one who didn't have a report to give, since her duties as New Member Chair had ended in the fall semester. After that, there were several votes by voice, including one on whether or not to spend money from the house budget on a new plasma TV for the living room (a unanimous yes). Then, finally, after all the unfinished business had been taken care of, the moment came that Roni'd been waiting for all night.

"Now, as current ZZT President, I move that we vote on our new officers for next year," Marissa said.

"I second the motion, Madame President," Heather Bourke said, standing up.

Hallie quickly and silently passed around ballots, with each of the offices and the nominees listed. Roni smiled when she saw Beverly's name as a nominee for ZZT President and her own name for Formal Planner Assistant. Only one other sister was nominated for the Formal Assistant role, Emma Cox. Roni knew that Emma was the über-organized type, but she was also a little too dictatorial about it, and where was the fun in that? Roni knew Emma'd get the job done and done well if she was elected. But so would she. Ultimately, it was all up to their sisters.

Roni meticulously filled out her ballot, double-checked it, then slipped it into the ballot box at the back of the room. When everyone was finished voting, Marissa made a few final announcements, then led everyone in the closing ritual. All of the girls linked hands and soberly recited the oath of loyalty, swearing to uphold the laws and integrity of ZZT through their words and deeds. Then Marissa officially adjourned the meeting.

"Y'all can hang out in the living room now that the meeting's over, if you want. For those of you who'd like to know the results of the election," she added, "they'll be posted in the foyer in about half an hour."

"Thank God that's over with," Lora-Leigh mumbled after Roni'd reconnected with her and Jenna. "What was with Marissa's pallbearer face? And all the motions and 'herebys' and 'wherefores' and 'the ayes have it'? I thought I'd never live to see the end."

"Marissa was using Robert's Rules of Order," Roni explained. "It's standard procedure for formal meetings like this." She smiled. "I think it's great. This way, no one talks over each other and everyone gets a chance to take the floor and be heard without interruption."

"Of course you think it's great, Boston," Lora-Leigh said, rolling her eyes. "You probably had to memorize the whole rule book in cotillion, right?" She turned to Jenna. "Let's just hope our Greek Week Committee meeting isn't that torturous. I can only sit through so many motions in one night."

Jenna laughed, then waved to Roni. "We'll see you later."

As Lora-Leigh and Jenna left for their next meeting, Roni caught Beverly's eye from across the room. They both smiled in secret understanding and made for the couch.

"I was hoping you'd stick around for a few minutes," Beverly said, plopping down next to Roni.

"I want to see the results," Roni said. "And besides, Lance isn't supposed to be here for another forty-five minutes."

Beverly grinned. "So . . . are you ready for the big date? He sure took his sweet ol' time asking you out."

"Tell me about it," Roni joked. "But it was worth the wait." She glanced down at her outfit, an Armani black skirt and satin cami. It was one of her power outfits—the kind that made her feel flirty and feminine and, well, just plain fabulous.

"Where's he taking you?" Beverly asked.

"He mentioned something about a lakefront restaurant," Roni said.

Beverly smiled dreamily. "Moonlight glistening on the water, soft waves lapping the shore in the background. Very romantic."

Roni laughed. "Sounds like you and Kyle had some romantic moments of your own over break." Kyle was Beverly's longtime boyfriend from her hometown, but since he went to Baylor, they did the long-distance thing for most of the year.

Beverly giggled. "Is it that obvious?"

"Moonlight and glistening water and soft surf?" Roni said. "You sound like an ad for eharmony.com."

Beverly shrugged. "What can I say? Love has turned me into one blubbering mass of poetry and cheesy eighties ballads."

"That's not such a bad way to be," Roni said. She'd never felt that way about any guy. She'd watched Kiersten fall hard for Phillip, and now Beverly. . . . She could only hope that it would happen for her someday, too.

They talked for a while longer, until they saw Hallie posting the election results in the foyer, and then they walked over to check out the list of new officers.

They both looked, and squealed at the same time, hugging each other.

"Omigod! You're the new ZZT President!" Roni cried as Beverly shrieked with excitement. "That's incredible!"

"I can't believe it!" Beverly beamed as other ZZTs crowded around her offering hugs and congratulations.

"You're going to do an amazing job," Roni said, squeezing her hand.

"And so are you, Miss Newly Elected Formal Planner Assistant," Beverly said.

"Thanks." Roni blushed, feeling a thrill race through her at being elected to the position. "I can't wait to get started."

She checked the list again and saw that Melody Montgomery was the Formal Planner, so she walked over to the smiling Melody to give her a hug and congratulations, too.

"Roni!" Melody exclaimed enthusiastically. "I'm so glad you're the assistant. We're going to have a great time planning Formal."

"I can't wait," Roni said. "I'd love to help out as much as possible, so just let me know where I should start."

"That's great to hear," Melody said. "What's your schedule like this week? I was thinking maybe we could meet up at the Funky Bean Café on Tuesday or Wednesday to start working out the details."

"I don't have class until eleven on Wednesdays," Roni said, "so that sounds perfect."

She typed it into her BlackBerry calendar right then and there, and just as she was finishing, the ZZT doorbell rang. Through the decorative glass oval in the door, she could see Lance standing outside, smiling at her.

"*Hello,* hotness," Beverly said in a low voice, scooting to Roni's side. "Um, you failed to mention how completely gorge your date is."

"Glad you approve," Roni said, grabbing her purse and taking a deep breath.

"Have fun," Beverly said as Roni headed for the door. "You know tonight's a full moon, so watch out. It can make you do crazy things."

Roni laughed as she opened the door. Crazy had never been her MO, but tonight with Lance and the moonlight and the lakefront dining, who knew what might happen?

"Is there something wrong with your dinner?" Lance asked Roni, motioning to her plate.

"No, no, it's delish," Roni said. "Why?" Then she glanced down at her plate of shrimp linguini with clam sauce, and suddenly realized why. She'd barely made a dent in her food.

Roni looked up at Lance, halfway between blushing and laughing. "I guess I've just been too busy talking to eat," she said.

Lance smiled. "I'm hoping that means you're having a good time?"

"Definitely," Roni said. She was having a completely amazing time, in fact. The Water's Edge Restaurant jutted out over the lake, and one entire wall of the building was nothing but windows, giving an amazing view of the sparkling water. The two hours she and Lance had been at their table overlooking the moonlit lake had flown by effortlessly, and she hoped that Lance felt the same way. On the other hand, it suddenly occurred to her that maybe she'd been boring him to death with all her chatter about ZZT and her Big Sis being President and her own new position as Formal Planner Assistant. The excitement from the elections was still so fresh, she couldn't keep herself from sharing the news.

"I just hope I haven't been blabbering nonstop," she said to him now, apologetically.

"You have," Lance said, but then obviously seeing Roni's look of mortification, he added quickly, "but that's okay. I'm enjoying it. I had no idea how involved you were in ZZT. I guess I always thought of sororities and fraternities as being all about the parties. At least, that's what I saw when I rushed. And up until I met you, the other sorority girls I knew seemed very 'Delta Delta Delta Can I Help Ya Help Ya Help Ya.' "

Roni laughed. "Like, totally," she said, doing her best imitation of the classic *Saturday Night Live*–skit sorority stereotype. "You know, we just use our houseboys as eye candy and spend all of our time fantasizing about frat boys and planning parties."

"No offense, but sometimes that's what it seems like from the outside," Lance said.

"Oh, it's so much more than that," Roni said. "I feel like ZZT is my family now. I never thought it would be like that." She was about to launch into another ZZT story but stopped herself. "Sorry," she said, making a concerted effort to focus on actually eating her food. "Rambling again. I don't understand what's wrong with me tonight. It's not like me at all."

"You mean you don't normally talk on dates?" Lance teased.

"Actually, not much," Roni said truthfully, thinking about her awkward encounters with Ivy League poster boys from New England. "The guys I dated in Boston were more my mom's type than mine."

"That's a disturbing thought," Lance said with a laugh.

"It is." Roni giggled. "But my parents were big on me associating with the right type of people." She grimaced. "*Their* type." She gave Lance a rundown of her parents' hopes for her and their disappointments and her recent confrontation with them. But she treaded lightly on the issue of her parents' wealth. She always felt extremely awkward even alluding to her family's social status, but she figured if she had any chance of starting off on the right foot with Lance, she'd have to lay it all out there for him to take or leave.

"Wow," he said afterward, "and I thought my family had issues. I guess I was lucky I only had to deal with one control-freak parent, not two."

"Your dad?" Roni guessed, remembering that Lance had told her he was an army brat when they first met.

Lance nodded. "That's Colonel McManus to you," Lance said, saluting with mock seriousness. "Don't get me wrong, I love the man, but he was tough to grow up around. My bedroom had to be spotless, and so did my behavior. The other kids on base used to pay me to make their beds for them, because I could pull the sheets so tight a quarter would bounce a foot high off of them. And, I was the only kid on base who had a pantry alphabetized by food group. My dad called that 'kitchen discipline.' "

"That's harsh," Roni said.

"Eh, I should probably thank him for it now. I have the neatest dorm room on campus."

"And he's the one who got you into swimming, right? So at least you have that in common."

"Yeah," Lance said. "But even though I love it, I can't ever quite get up to his standards." He shrugged. "His frustration with me is something I've just learned to live with and let go of."

"Me, too," Roni said, thinking of her own parents. "It's really the only way you can deal and make your own choices."

"Exactly," Lance agreed. "So what about your swimming? You think you'll go out for the swim team next year? You'd make the team without even trying."

"Thanks," Roni said, blushing. "I'll have to see how my schedule works out. It's something I'd definitely love to do, but I think I'd enjoy getting more involved with ZZT next year, too. It all depends on what I have time for."

"I hear that," Lance said. "My premed courses are going to be grueling, and I have to stay at the top of my classes to up my chances of getting into a good med school later. Between studying and swimming, I'll be lucky if I get any sleep at all."

"There won't be room for much else, it sounds like," Roni said, suddenly wondering if Lance was one of those guys who was so completely focused and driven that he wouldn't even have time for dating.

Lance smiled, and leaned toward her, his hand almost brushing against hers across the table. "Oh, I have to make sure to leave room for *some* other things," he said, seeming to read her thoughts. "I'd go nuts if I was studying diseases and body parts all day long and couldn't at least have a little fun. Speaking of fun, are you up for something involving chocolate and fiddles?"

Roni smiled. "I have no idea what you're talking about, but I'm always up for anything involving chocolate."

"I was hoping you'd say that," Lance said with a smile.

As they finished dinner and left the restaurant, Roni wondered what Lance had planned. But he wouldn't give her any more hints until twenty minutes later when they pulled up to an adorable little coffeehouse called Celia's on the outskirts of the LU campus. It had a sprawling outdoor patio strung with brightly colored paper lanterns and draped in a trellis of bougainvillea, where a dozen or so people sat in comfortable clusters, sipping coffee and eating dessert. The whole scene was wonderfully inviting, but what really caught Roni's attention was the music she heard coming from the far end of the patio.

"I love Irish music," she said with a smile.

"I was hoping you might," Lance said. "That's why I brought you here. They always have live music, but tonight it's the Celtic Pirates, a band from Boston."

"I know them!" Roni cried with delight. "I heard them play once at the Black Rose with my friend Kiersten. They're great."

Lance grinned. "So I guess I picked the right place to come for dessert, huh?"

"Absolutely," Roni said.

"In that case, are you ready for some Boston cream pie?" he asked. "It's homemade here, and it's supposed to be the best in Latimer."

"Sounds delish," she said. She was touched that Lance had tried so hard to get everything about tonight just right, down to the tiniest detail. She took it as a good sign that maybe there'd be more dates with him down the road. At least, she hoped there would be.

They found a cozy table in the corner that was far enough

from the band that they could talk but close enough that they could enjoy the music. The next few hours flew by easily, and before she knew it, Roni was standing outside Tuthill with Lance, reluctant to let the evening end.

"Thank you for tonight," she said. "Everything was perfect."

"*Almost* perfect." Lance reached for her hand, sending an electric thrill through her. "There's one thing that would make it better."

"What?" Roni asked as her heart tap-danced excitedly.

"This," Lance said, just before his lips met hers in a light, refreshing kiss. "Not a bad way to spend a Sunday night, huh?" he whispered as he pulled away.

"Not bad at all," Roni said with a smile.

On Wednesday morning, Roni stepped through the doorway of the Funky Bean Café and scanned the room, looking for a familiar face. She immediately spotted Melody in the far corner, tucked away in a booth by the window, her nose buried in a massive textbook. She could see Melody already had an extra-large cup of coffee in front of her, so she quickly ordered herself a chai latte and made her way over to the booth. She was still on cloud nine from her date with Lance on Sunday, and now she couldn't wait to hear all about the formal planning. The week could only keep getting better.

"Hi, Melody!" she said cheerfully, sliding into the seat across from her.

Melody started, nearly spilling her coffee, and it was then that Roni saw the dark circles under her eyes and the harried look on her face. "Oh, Roni!" she gasped. "Hi! Sorry, I was completely zoning on these LSAT practice questions." She motioned to the book in front of her. "They're killers. I didn't even see you come in."

"No prob," Roni said. She took a peek at the pages of Melody's book. "Wow, I'm already lost and I only read half of the first question." She smiled. "I guess this is why I'm not on the prelaw track."

Melody groaned. "You don't know how lucky you are. I'm taking this LSAT prep course, and it's a complete nightmare. I have a huge practice test the week before Formal, which is supposed to help prepare me for the horror that is the *real* test. But I'm so stressed about the practice exam I don't even think I'll survive to take the legit one. I have to present an entire defense for a practice case in my Trial and Litigation class in less than a month, which makes up seventy percent of my grade. And right now I'm drowning in applications for summer internships, too. I already have one ulcer, and I'm probably on my way to another one. I'm starting to think prelaw is for the clinically insane."

Roni giggled, but Melody just sighed. "But that's why I'm so glad you're my Formal Assistant. You did a fantastic job as New Member President, and I know I can count on you for lots of help with Formal. With my schedule this semester, I need all the help I can get."

"Of course," Roni said. "I'll do whatever you need me to."

Melody smiled gratefully. "That's exactly what I was hoping to hear." She checked her watch. "I only have a few minutes before my next class, so let's go through this as fast as we can, okay?"

"Okay," Roni said with a little uncertainty. She'd thought

they would be meeting for at least an hour. From what Beverly had told her, Formal involved quite a bit of planning. But then again, maybe Melody had already gotten a head start on some things.

Melody rummaged through her messenger bag, mumbling to herself as she dug. "Now where did I put the to-do list? I know I had it in here somewhere. . . ." Finally, she pulled out a crumpled, coffee-stained piece of paper and flattened it out on the table, then handed it to Roni.

Roni studied it, trying to make sense of what looked more like chicken scratches than writing.

"We can go over the rest of the list later," Melody said, waving her hand dismissively at the paper. "You'll be organizing chartered buses to take us to and from Formal, and decorations, floral centerpieces, T-shirts, favors, the menu, and a DJ."

"Wow," Roni said, "I had no idea there'd be so much to do."

Melody nodded. "It seems pretty overwhelming, I know. But you seem like such an organized person, I'm sure you can handle it all, no problem." She smiled. "I really appreciate you helping me out with this. Otherwise, there's no way I could survive this semester without a complete mental meltdown."

Roni nodded. Melody seemed like she was already stressed to the max, and wasn't it in times like these that sisters needed to help each other out?

"So," Melody hurried on, "first and foremost, before we deal with the smaller details, we need to find a venue."

"Great!" Roni said, a pen poised in her hand for note taking. "Do you have any suggestions about places we should look into?"

"Not off the top of my head," Melody said, "but I'm sure you can come up with some great ideas. Besides, aren't you best friends with Lora-Leigh Sorenstein? She's one of the Latimer locals, so she'll know lots of cool places. Why don't you ask her?"

"Um, sure," Roni said, wondering if this was how it usually worked with the planners and their assistants.

"And we can touch base in a few weeks to see how you're progressing," Melody said. "We'll need a banquet facility that can hold at least two hundred people, maybe even more. And of course, somewhere that can host a DJ and provide food."

"Right." Roni furiously jotted down notes as Melody rambled for a few more minutes about liabilities and banquet contracts. She could barely make sense of anything Melody was saying, but she tried to keep up as best as she could.

"Okay, so that's a good start," Melody said after what couldn't have been more than ten minutes of haphazard instructions. She closed her book and dumped it into her bag. She chugged the last of her coffee, then stood up. "I've got to run, but you let me know if you have any questions about anything, okay?"

"Um, sure," Roni said in a haze of confusion. But before she could add anything else, Melody was rushing out the door. She stared after her. This was it? This was all the info she was going to get? That didn't seem right at all. Roni's first thought was to catch Melody at dinner tonight and ask her for some clarification. But poor Melody seemed so stressed. No, Roni was perfectly capable of taking this on. She would prove to Melody just how on top of things she was by finding the perfect venue in record time. Melody would be impressed with her efforts, and once they found a venue, Roni was sure Melody would feel a lot less pressure about the whole thing. Roni took a sip of her latte, slid her laptop out of her bag, and booted up. She had another hour before her first class, which was plenty of time to get started doing some research on venues. She'd get this done in no time, efficiently and effectively, Van Gelderen style.

Jenna opened the door to her room on Thursday afternoon and immediately smiled. Roni and Lora-Leigh were spread out on the floor with Roni's laptop between them. Roni had her iPod playing in the background, and the sunshine was shining in through the window above their beds. Jenna still needed a reality check every once in a while to accept that this was, in fact, *her* cheerful bedroom and *her* wonderful roommate. Compared to the dark cloud that had loomed over her room when she'd lived with sullen, brooding Amber, this was sheer bliss.

"What are you grinning at, Miss Sunshine?" Lora-Leigh asked her.

"Just thinking how lucky I am that I'm not living with someone who curses my very existence anymore," Jenna said.

"No joke," Lora-Leigh said. "And *we're* lucky to know someone who knows how to cook and shares her food with us on a regular basis so that we don't waste away on Miss Merry's mystery meats." She stood up and peered into the Tupperware container Jenna was holding in her hands. "What tasty delicacy did you create for us in Culinary Arts 101 today?"

"Who says I'm going to share?" Jenna teased.

"I'm afraid of what Lora-Leigh will do to you if you don't share," Roni said with a laugh, keeping her eyes intently focused on her laptop screen. "It's not just coincidence that she's magically appeared in our room every Thursday afternoon since you started your cooking class. She's a Chez Jen addict. Deny her at your own risk."

"All right, Lora-Leigh," Jenna said, popping the top on the Tupperware lid. "Cherry cream scones, just for you. Dig in."

"Sweet ambrosia," Lora-Leigh said, reveling in her first bite. Then she dramatically went weak in the knees. "Please overthrow Miss Merry, please, please, please."

Jenna laughed, secretly loving the fact that her friends couldn't get enough of the edible "assignments" she had in her Intro to Cooking and Baking class. And neither could Tiger. She always made sure to bring him a taste of whatever creation she'd made in class, and now he joked that he'd gained five pounds in the two weeks the semester'd been under way. Of course he was the one who'd encouraged her to take a cooking course this semester, and she was so glad he had. She was loving every minute of it, and she was starting to think more seriously about a degree in Culinary Arts farther down the road.

"Can I have one, too, Jenna?" Roni asked. "I'm completely stressed and in need of some comfort food."

"Sure," Jenna said, handing her one and then joining the girls on the floor. "What's the prob?"

Roni sighed. "I'm still trying to find the venue for Formal, and I've been surfing the Net for local places all afternoon. I thought it would be so much easier than this."

"I still can't believe Melody put you in charge of the venue," Jenna said, frowning. "It's such a huge job. I mean, I've been on the Greek Week Committee for two weeks already and the only thing I've had to do is make sign-up sheets for the sporting events."

"My job is a cakewalk, too," Lora-Leigh said. "I'm doing the talent-show costumes, but we're only making three costumes, and I could practically do that in my sleep."

"Well, Melody's got a lot on her plate right now," Roni said with a shrug. "I told you she's studying for the LSATs, so I'm taking on a few extra responsibilities." She gave Jenna and Lora-Leigh a quick rundown of the rest of her formal to-do list.

"That sounds like more than a few extra things to me," Lora-Leigh said.

"I don't mind, really," Roni said. "I want to help Melody out. And I'm sure she's doing her own work on Formal, too."

Lora-Leigh snorted. "It sounds to me like all she's doing is delegating."

Roni shot Lora-Leigh a scolding look as Jenna added worriedly, "You're doing way more than Lora-Leigh and me. But maybe I'm not doing enough for the Greek Week Committee. Or, maybe I should have gone for an assistant position."

Roni gave a halfhearted laugh. "I don't think so, Jenna. Even I'm a little overwhelmed with this, and I don't have band to worry about, too, like you do. I just want to make sure I find the perfect place for Formal so that everyone is happy with it."

"That's why I stopped by," Lora-Leigh said. "Besides the scones, of course," she added, taking a second one.

"Yeah, big help you are," Roni teased. "Every place I find, you shoot down."

"To be fair, let's review the options so far, shall we?" Lora-Leigh said. "The Leopard Lounge. Leopard-print wallpaper and red velvet booths, need I say more? The Palm Ballroom, a fine banquet facility if you want a Copacabana feel with neon palm trees and a dance floor bordered with plastic pink flamingos. And Club Underground, perfect for cage and pole dancing; not so perfect for black tie."

Roni looked dismayed, until Jenna bent over laughing. It was contagious, and soon Roni was giggling, too.

"It's not my fault I don't know Latimer very well," Roni said, gasping to catch her breath. "How was I supposed to know Club Underground was a strip club?"

That made Jenna laugh even harder, until finally she lay on the floor, out of breath and exhausted. "I think you need a break," she said to Roni. "Turn off your laptop for ten minutes, have another scone, and focus on something else."

"Like what?" Roni asked.

"How about Lance?" Jenna singsonged. "You've sure been happy this week, so things must be going *really* well."

"I hope they are," Roni said with a smile. "I mean, I *think* they are. We had another date which was great, and we're supposed to go see a movie together tomorrow night, too."

"Sounds like you're passing crush status and moving straight toward true like," Lora-Leigh said.

"Maybe," Roni said with a smile. "But I don't know; sometimes he's a little hard to read. Like, the other day, he left me a message on my BlackBerry, but when I called him back, he told me he was in the middle of studying for his first big Anatomy quiz, and then asked if we could talk later." She shrugged. "He's premed, so I guess it makes sense that he takes his classes really seriously."

"Of course it does," Jenna said.

"I'm paired up with him to do a debate on genetic engineering for our Poli Sci midterm in a few weeks, but I'm a little nervous about it," Roni said. "We've gotten together a couple of times already to work on our argument, and he keeps mentioning how important a good grade is to him. So I really don't want to screw anything up on the debate. I mean, I study, but not like he does. And I want him to think I did a good job with my end of the project."

"Roni, you're great at everything you do," Jenna said. "And you will be at the debate, too. Besides, I think Lance is just as into you as you are into him, especially if calling you a dozen times in the last two weeks is any indication."

"Oh, that reminds me!" Roni said. "Tiger called for you twice while you were in class. That boy is so head over heels."

"I know. I think maybe things are starting to get serious," Jenna said, feeling her cheeks catch fire.

"Tell us, Miss Driscoll," Lora-Leigh said, adopting a German accent and scrutinizing Jenna melodramatically, "vat kind of 'serious' are ve talking about, exactly?"

"You *know*," Jenna said with a nervous giggle. "I think I might be ready to . . . to . . ." She couldn't say the words out loud. Her face was blazing now, and her heart was in free fall.

"Hmm, I see," Lora-Leigh said, still in Freud mode. "And have you taken this step with others before?"

"No," Jenna finally managed to stammer. "It always seemed like such a huge deal, and I wanted it to be with the right guy. Have y'all?"

"Not me," Roni said. "The idea of sleeping with someone

my parents set me up with was *way* too disturbing. And I didn't want my first time to be with some snobbish Ivy Leaguer named something like Thurston the Third." She laughed. "I'm holding out for someone who really means something to me."

"What about you, Lora-Leigh?" Jenna asked.

"Frighteningly enough, it seems that I'm the residing expert on the subject," Lora-Leigh said. "Prom night last year with Cory Donahue in the back of his Chevy suburban in Research Park."

Jenna gaped. "Research Park? *Here,* on the Latimer campus?"

Lora-Leigh smirked. "Don't look so shocked. There's a reason why it's called 'Research' Park, and it has nothing to do with the science studies the Bio students do there." She laughed as Roni and Jenna both blushed this time. "Anyway, everything was moving along just fine until the campus police pulled up behind us and shined their spotlight into the back of the truck. After that, we were not so politely asked to leave. Cory and I laughed about it the whole way back to my house."

"That's one way to remember your first time forever," Roni said with a laugh.

"I'd prefer candles and mood music to a bullhorn," Jenna added.

"I didn't think you'd want a repeat of *my* experience, but—hey—it worked for me." Lora-Leigh laughed. "See, that's the thing about it. It's got to be your way, on your terms, when you're ready."

Jenna nodded. "That's how I want it to be if I decide to go ahead with it. But at this point, I'm just not sure what do to.

Part of me really wants to share this with Tiger, but . . ." She sighed, not quite believing she was actually about to fess up to her friends. "We talked about it and he told me he's had experience already."

"Maybe that's a good thing," Lora-Leigh said. "Then he can sort of show you the ropes."

Jenna bit her lip. "I wish I could see a positive side to it, but right now I'm having a hard time with it. I can't stop thinking about the girl he was with before." She stared at the carpet. "What if she was really great at . . . well, *it*? How can I live up to that when I don't know what I'm doing? What if he compares me to her afterward? Or . . ." Her heart shuddered as she said out loud what she was really afraid of. "What if he was in love with her?"

Lora-Leigh whistled under her breath. "You're going to drown in all those what-ifs if you're not careful. Maybe just focus on the fact that Tiger only has eyes for you right now."

"I wish I could," Jenna said quietly. "But ever since Tiger and I talked, I can't stop thinking about it."

Roni gave Jenna's hand a squeeze. "What about talking to Tiger about this? It's obvious he cares about you, and he'd probably want to know what you're worrying about."

"I second that," Lora-Leigh said. "If you guys are thinking about baring all, so to speak, you've got to be up front with him, just like he was with you."

"But there's no way I could talk to Tiger about all of this," Jenna protested. "It's way too embarrassing."

"Well, losing the big V is an up-close and personal experience, and if you're not comfortable from the get-go, then you won't be able to relax and enjoy the moment," Lora-Leigh said.

"I know," Jenna said. "And I don't want to have any regrets. Part of me feels ready, and part of me freaks every time I think about it, especially when I think about Tiger's past."

"Give yourself some more time to process everything," Roni said. "And then decide what's right for you."

"And in the meantime, if you do decide you're ready to take the leap and you need any pointers," Lora-Leigh said, "we could always head for Club Underground. I hear the girls there have some jaw-dropping moves."

"Lora-Leigh!" Jenna squealed, launching a pillow at her head. As she laughed with her friends, she knew that whatever happened between her and Tiger, she'd have their support 100 percent.

Roni tried (again) to focus on the announcements Beverly was giving about Greek Week on Sunday night, wanting so much to show support for her Big Sis by listening intently to her orchestrate her first meeting as Chapter President. Beverly and the other new officers had been sworn in three weeks ago, and Roni'd looked on proudly as Beverly vowed, "I swear to uphold the values set forth by the sisters of Zeta Zeta Tau and represent them always, doing honor and justice to my sisters both by my leadership and by my example." But tonight was Beverly's first night conducting a meeting solo, with Marissa only sitting near her in case she needed help. She was doing an amazing job so far, and Roni felt horrible that she wasn't paying better attention. But all she could think about was that in just a few minutes, when the house meeting was over, she was going to have to tell

Melody that she still hadn't found a venue for Formal. She'd been dreading it all day, but now she had no choice.

"So the Greek Week teams will be posted in the foyer for everyone's reference as the planning gets under way," Beverly was saying. "I just found out from our Social Chair, Louise Campbell, that our team will be Poseidon, the Blue Team, made up of Zeta Zeta Tau, Phi Omicron Chi fraternity, and Beta Xi sorority."

"Did you hear that?" Jenna shriek-whispered to Roni and Lora-Leigh, bouncing a little up off the floor. "We're on Tiger's team!"

"That's great, Jenna," Roni said, trying her hardest to look happy for her friend, even though she was still panicking inside.

"Our team should be Aphrodite instead of Poseidon," Lora-Leigh said, laughing a little at Jenna's enthusiasm. "Let's just hope that love does conquer all, and kick some major ass in the competitions, okay?"

"It's possible," Jenna said. "Tiger came to watch me march in the Palm Beach Orange Harvest parade yesterday, and we won first place for our performance. Maybe he's my good-luck charm."

"Maybe he'll be ZZT's good-luck charm and win the Greek Week championship for us," Lora-Leigh said.

"We'll be competing by ourselves in the talent show," Beverly continued, "but we'll be teamed with the Foxes and the Beta Xis for the softball tournament, tug-of-war, and other sports events. As for the cheer competition, I know that Greek Week is still a month away, but you should all start brainstorming some ing some ideas for cheers. ZZT's always had brilliant cheers, and we want to make sure this year is no exception." Beverly smiled. "Aside from Formal, Greek Week was my absolute fave ZZT event last year, and I know y'all are going to enjoy it just as much as I did."

Roni phased out for the last of the announcements (all she heard was something about upping the recycling efforts in the house), and then jumped up as Beverly adjourned the meeting, rushing into the foyer to catch Melody on her way out.

"Melody!" she cried, finally spotting her walking out of the living room. "Do you have a sec?"

"Um, I've literally got only one sec," Melody said, checking her watch. "I'm already late meeting up with my LSAT study group." She sighed. "But I guess five more minutes won't matter. What's up? How are the formal plans coming along?" Roni took a deep breath and cleared her throat. Here went nothing. "Actually, that's what I wanted to talk to you about," she said. "I'm having a lot of trouble finding a venue."

"Oh, really?" Melody said, frowning. "Did you try the Fairview Country Club? Or Regency Hall?"

Roni nodded, thinking it was a little strange that Melody could just tick off those places like she was already so familiar with them. It had taken her hours of Web surfing with Lora-Leigh and several trips to meet with banquet planners and event coordinators to come up with those two locales. Then again, Melody had lived in Latimer longer than Roni, so it made sense that she would know more places. But if that was the case, why hadn't she looked into the venue herself? "I tried both," Roni explained, "but they said their liability insurance wouldn't cover an event of that nature. To be honest, I think they're worried that we're going to trash their facilities because we're a sorority. The Latimer Grand Hotel and Emerald Resort said the same thing. It's the whole Greek-partying stereotype." She sighed. "I really want to get this right, but I'm sort of running out of ideas. I thought maybe you might have some?"

"I wish I did, but it sounds like you're covering all the same ground I would," Melody said, patting her on the shoulder. "Did you look through the formal planning binder? I think there are some notes in there from prior years about venues. And you should've called the DJ and florist by now, too. You need to book them way in advance. . . ."

Roni stared at Melody, her mind reeling in confusion. "Um . . . what binder?"

Melody's brow furrowed. "The one I gave you when we met last week? I'm surprised you haven't read it yet. It's got all of the contact numbers you need and the details on the formal budget. You should really take the time to look at it."

"But . . . but I never got a binder from you," Roni said. "All you gave me was this to-do list." She pulled the crumpled, coffee-stained list Melody had given her out of her pocket.

Melody frowned. "Of course I gave it to you. I'm positive I . . ." Her voice died away, and she gasped, her eyes widening. "Omigod, I am such a complete space cadet! You're right. . . . I totally forgot to give you the binder. I think it's still upstairs in my room. . . ." She hesitated a second, deep in thought, then said, "You know, I hate to do this, but I've really got to run. The binder's on my desk upstairs. You can just let yourself into my room and get it, okay?"

"Oh, okay," Roni said hesitantly. "But . . . then, when will we go over the binder? Do you want to get together sometime tomorrow?"

"I'd love to, but I can't," Melody said. "I've got an interview for an internship, and I'll be gone most of the day. But the binder's pretty self-explanatory." She smiled. "As for finding a venue, I'm sure it's just a matter of hitting on the right location. I know you can do it."

But how? Roni thought. This was not exactly the type of help she thought she'd get from Melody. In fact, it wasn't any help at all.

"Listen," Melody continued, "I've really got to go before my study group kicks my butt. Just keep me posted, okay? It's going to work out fine."

And with one final wave, she was out the door, leaving Roni staring after her with a sinking spirit. Now what? Back to the drawing board, she supposed. She almost found herself wishing that she'd chosen to be on the Greek Week Committee instead of doing formal planning. Jenna and Lora-Leigh seemed to have it so much easier with their committee responsibilities. But then again, who was Roni to complain? She was the one who'd wanted to be an assistant in the first place. And she'd gotten what she asked for; it just wasn't exactly turning out the way she'd hoped.

She sighed, then walked over to take a look at the Greek Week team listings, hoping that it would take her mind off Formal for a few minutes. Each team was named after one of the Greek gods or goddesses, and the frats and sororities seemed to be pretty equally distributed among the teams. Aphrodite: Pi Theta Epsilon, Alpha Mu, Omicron Chi Omega; Apollo:

Sigma Sigma, Zeta Theta Mu, Eta Lambda Nu; Zeus: Delta Kappa, Tau Delta Iota, Omega Phi . . . The list went on, until each sorority and fraternity at LU was accounted for, and Roni's heart quickened with excitement just looking at it. Aside from mixers and swaps, she hadn't interacted much with the other chapters yet.

She was looking forward to it, but she just hoped that by the time Greek Week came, she'd be done with most of the formal planning so she could really relax and make the most out of Greek Week. Of course that meant she'd have to work even harder now to get everything for the formal done. And at the rate she was going, it didn't look good.

She quickly got the binder from Melody's room and then headed back to Tuthill to log onto her laptop. She better do another Internet search and make some more phone calls. Maybe she'd have better luck with banquet halls outside of Latimer. But after an hour of dead ends, she was even more disheartened. She stared at the list of "no"s in her notebook, so lost in her thoughts that she didn't even hear her BlackBerry until the third ring.

"Hey," Lance said, making Roni smile. "Are you okay?"

"Not really," Roni mumbled with a sigh. "I'm just contemplating how screwed up the ZZT Formal is going to be, and how it's going to be all my fault."

"Oh." There was a second of silence. "I was starting to get a little worried."

Roni blinked in confusion. "Why?"

"Well, I must have gotten my nights mixed up, but I thought

we were supposed to meet at my dorm after your meeting tonight to work on the debate."

Roni cringed, not believing what she'd done. "Omigod, I'm so, so sorry. I had this frustrating talk with Melody after the meeting tonight, and I completely forgot about coming over. I'm so horrible—"

"Hey," Lance interrupted, "it's okay."

But Roni heard a hesitation in his voice, like he wasn't totally sure she hadn't ditched him on purpose. And that only made her feel worse. "I can be there in fifteen minutes," she stammered, already throwing her debate materials into her bag. "You must think I'm such a flake, but this isn't me. Really. It's just that I haven't found a venue for our formal yet, and Melody's not helping as much as I thought she would, and . . ." She caught herself midramble, and sighed. "You know what? You don't want to hear this, especially after I screwed up tonight."

"It's all right," Lance said. "We can work on the debate stuff another night, just as long as we get it done." He paused, then added, "So, I think I'm supposed to ask if you want to talk about what happened with Melody. Does that sound right to you?"

Roni laughed in relief, glad that Lance was being such a good sport about her no-show. "That sounds right, but I don't want to talk about it. I don't even want to think about it. In fact, I just decided I'm done thinking completely for the day."

"So . . . what about a Plan B? If you're up for it, I could pick you up and take you to the Marble Slab Creamery for Cookie Lover's Delight," Lance said. "Complete and total brain freeze will be accomplished within the first three bites, guaranteed."

Roni smiled, feeling herself giving in. "Okay," she said, "brain freeze sounds perfect."

"Great," Lance said. "I'll pick you up in ten."

Roni clicked off her BlackBerry and headed downstairs to wait for Lance. She couldn't believe she'd forgotten about meeting with him tonight. It was so unlike her, and he was being so great about it. But even as she promised herself not to obsess over her chat with Melody, she found it consuming her thoughts. Formal was the one thing that even ice cream and a few sweet kisses from Lance couldn't erase.

CHAPTER 4

Lora-Leigh stared at the formulas on the dry-erase board in Dr. Hinkle's Calculus class, knowing she should be trying to decipher them for the sake of her grade. She studied them until the *x*'s and *y*'s blurred, then she shrugged. It might as well be hieroglyphics, for all she could figure. She sighed, giving up, then pulled out her sketchbook and turned to the page she'd been working on, subtly tucking it under her textbook. Inverted pleats, halters, empire waists—now this was a language she could understand. She looked at what she'd sketched so far for the Greek Week Talent Show costumes.

Minnie had come up with the brilliant idea of spoofing a dramality show of Paris Hilton, Britney Spears, and Lindsay Lohan doing "hard time" in a primadonna version of prison, complete with diamond-studded ankle cuffs. Bonni Ruiz, Louise Campbell, and Naomi Yates had the best voices in ZZT, so they were going to play the parts. Stacy Fagen was giving up the hot-pink scrubs she had from her vet-clinic internship last year to use for the girls' prison clothes. But Lora-Leigh was busy designing outfits for their performance of "They Tried to Make Me Go to Rehab" at the end of the skit. It promised to be hilarious if they could pull it off.

She was just putting the finishing touches on the sketch for Paris's jailbait outfit—a black-and-white-striped mini with a white sequined blazer and a crushed-velvet beret—when her cell vibrated with a text message from DeShawn. She smiled. It was about time. They'd been on several dates since the semester started, but they hadn't seen each other the last few days.

Pritchard#33: Hey, Curly, what r u up to?

DesignsOnU: Snoring my way thru class. What else?

Pritchard#33: I thought that was my job. =) U want to meet me and the guys for lunch at the Lucky Strike? We're going to shoot some pool afterward.

DesignsOnU: Gr8t! I'll see u there aftr class.

Twenty minutes later, Lora-Leigh slid into the booth at the Lucky Strike with DeShawn and his buds Mike and Garrett. She'd hung around with DeShawn's football friends more than a few times, and they all treated her with big-brotherly affection and razzing mixed with harmless flirting. Lora-Leigh loved every second of it.

"I ordered you buffalo wings and onion rings," DeShawn said, tugging on one of her curls and slipping an arm around her waist to give her a quick squeeze. He slid the basket of food over to her.

"Oh, baby, you know what I like," Lora-Leigh teased, digging into the wings.

Across the table, Mike snickered and rolled his eyes. "Why don't you two just kiss already and get it over with?"

"Ease up, Mike," Lora-Leigh quipped back, teasing. "I don't do well under pressure."

"Thank God we only have to put up with these two a few more months before DeShawn goes MIA," Garrett said to Mike.

"No doubt," Mike seconded. Then Mike took a bite of his burger and turned to DeShawn. "You'll get drafted in the first five rounds in April, way before Marshall and Grady."

Lora-Leigh looked from Mike to Garrett and back again. What were they talking about? Marshall Dobbs and Grady Jenkins were the Red Raiders' linebacker and quarterback, and Lora-Leigh knew they were two of the strongest guys on the team, next to DeShawn. So she wasn't surprised they were going out for the NFL draft, but why were Mike and Garrett acting like DeShawn was, too? As far as she knew, he was still debating what to do.

Before she had a chance to ask for an explanation, Garrett jumped in again. "I don't even know what Grady's thinking. He won't get picked. Not with the trash he was throwing last season. Of course, if he got picked, we'd have a new quarterback next year, so at least that'd be something." He slugged DeShawn on the shoulder. "But the NFL will never pass you up. Once the draft is over, you'll be outta here."

"That's *if* I get picked up by a team," DeShawn said, launching a french fry at Garrett. "And that's a mighty big if. Just because I'm on the draft roster doesn't mean I'm a shoo-in."

Lora-Leigh shot DeShawn a quizzical look. "Wait a sec," she said. "You're on the roster already? As in, definitely going to the draft?"

DeShawn grinned, his green eyes twinkling. "Well, yeah, Curly. I got the assessment results back from the NFL College Advisory Committee, and my chances of getting drafted look really good. I had to declare myself eligible by the end of January, so I signed on the dotted line two weeks ago. What did you think we were talking about the last five minutes?" He elbowed her. "That Calc class really did a number on you today, huh?"

"I told you Math is a drain on my artistic psyche," she joked, trying to come off as blasé, even though she was fighting off the shiver of sadness creeping into her. She wished that DeShawn had told her the news himself. After all, they were dating now. Sure, it was just casual dating, but still. She'd told him about FIT, and he'd be one of the first she'd call when she found out whether or not she got in. But she couldn't hold this against him. She knew now, and that was all that mattered.

She wrapped her arms around him, barely able to reach even halfway around his burly chest. "That's amazing, DeShawn," she said. "Congrats!" She quickly pulled away, then turned to Mike and Garrett. "So, which one of you goons is taking the draft bets?"

"I am," Mike said.

Lora-Leigh pulled a bill out of her purse. "Twenty says DeShawn is the second pick in the first round."

"That's my girl," DeShawn said with a delighted grin.

"I'd date her once you leave LU if I didn't think you'd kick my ass," Mike joked to DeShawn.

"And you actually think I'd say yes to that?" Lora-Leigh snorted.

DeShawn's laugh rumbled out of him, low and gruff. "Sorry," he said to Mike, who was theatrically clutching at his heart like it was breaking. "But you know, after me, nobody else will be good enough for her. I'll spoil her for other guys forever."

"You're both delusional," Lora-Leigh said, laughing and slugging DeShawn on the arm.

"So," DeShawn said to her, "since I know you weren't working out Calc formulas in class today, what *were* you doing?"

"Besides texting you?" Lora-Leigh pulled out her sketchbook and thumbed through her sketches for the talent-show costumes. "I'm not finished yet, but this is the general idea for the costumes for our Greek Week Talent Show number."

"Very kewl," DeShawn said appreciatively. "That shirt with 'Jailbait' on it for your Lindsay Lohan look-alike is hilarious."

Mike clucked his tongue and did a dead-on impression of style maven Cojo. "She may never make it on the red carpet, but she can pull off incarceration fabulously."

Lora-Leigh laughed. "I had no idea you were so in tune with your inner fashionista. Any time you need something to do, say the word. I'll have you sewing for me in no time."

"And that's our cue," Mike said, standing and pulling Garrett up alongside him. "The eight ball is calling."

Lora-Leigh watched as they walked to the pool table in the far corner of the restaurant. Then she turned back to DeShawn, glad to have a little time with him to herself.

"So, now that you know the draft news," DeShawn said quietly, "let's hear an update about FIT. I know you haven't heard from them yet, but do you know what you'll say if they accept you?"

Lora-Leigh stared at the remnants of her chicken wings, stalling. "I don't have a clue." She sighed. "All I used to think about was FIT and getting out of here. But lately, Latimer's actually been growing on me. Or maybe not Latimer as much as the life I have here at school."

DeShawn nodded. "I can see that. Sometimes I hate the idea of leaving LU early. Especially with the friends I've made."

"And one irresistible girl in particular, right?" Lora-Leigh teased.

"Of course." DeShawn laughed, rolling his eyes. "You'll figure everything out. And wherever you end up, you'll be happy. But just promise me one thing." He took her hand. "That you'll follow your gut, regardless of what other people think you should or shouldn't do."

Lora-Leigh smiled. "I couldn't do anything else. You know that."

As DeShawn caught her up on his latest Architecture projects and she filled him in on her Art class, it struck Lora-Leigh full force how much she'd miss him if he did get drafted. Dating had brought them closer over the last few weeks, and she'd hate to see it come to an end. But then again, she was thinking about leaving Latimer, too, so she couldn't be too hard on him for wanting to follow his dream. Besides, April was still a couple of months away. So she'd enjoy the time she had with him now and think about what lay down the road, for both of them, later.

"Aren't you going to give me any hints about where we're going?" Roni asked Lance as she watched the lights of the Latimer campus fading into the distance.

"For the third time, no," Lance said as he laughed. "It's way too much fun keeping you in suspense."

Roni elbowed him playfully, then grinned into the darkness, still excited to know that Lance had wanted to take her out tonight of all nights—Valentine's Day. They'd been dating steadily for the last month. Of course they were working on their Poli Sci debate materials a lot, too, which could have been Lance's excuse for wanting to see her so much. But she didn't think that entirely explained why he called her so often, or why he almost always waited at the natatorium after swim practice for her to get off lifeguard duty so they could hang out. Their dates were always full of surprises, which was what she liked the most about him. Not only was he a diligent student, but he had a spontaneous side that completely contradicted Roni's live-by-her-calendar rules. Last night they'd climbed the bell tower for a bird's-eye view of the campus under the twinkling night sky. For Roni, it was a total departure from the stiff etiquette she'd grown up with—fresh, challenging, and fun.

Still, though, she hadn't been certain of how he'd deal with this Hallmark holiday. Because going out for Valentine's Day . . . well, that meant more than just casual dating, didn't it? It was more of a couple thing.

Now Roni leaned toward the window, trying to pick out any familiar landmarks as they drove, but all she could see on the quiet lane were acres and acres of orange groves, the oranges a peachy pale under the clear, moonlit sky. It still seemed almost surreal to her that while her friend Kiersten was battling five-foot snowdrifts and subzero windchills in Boston, there was actually citrus food flourishing in sunny, seventy-degree temps in Florida. Roni hadn't even had to wear her Burberry coat once, and she felt a little ridiculous every time she saw it hanging dormant in her closet.

Lance opened the windows a few inches and let the sweet scent of the oranges waft into the car, and Roni breathed in deeply as they turned off the road and onto a winding gravel path through the trees.

"We're almost there," he said.

Roni gasped as a sprawling villa suddenly came into view, lighting up the darkness with an impressive array of chandeliers that could be seen through nearly every one of the dozen grand windows arching across the front. A glowing fountain graced the entrance, and terraces scattered with candlelit tables and bougainvillea stretched around the sides of the villa like welcoming arms.

"What is this place?" she whispered.

"Do you like it?" he asked, with a touch of uncertainty that Roni found completely adorable.

"It's magnificent."

"Well, that's a relief, because we have a reservation for dinner outside in just a few minutes." Lance blew out a breath, then grinned. “You’ve probably eaten at so many five-star restaurants in Boston, I wasn’t sure how this would compare. It’s called the Villa Orangerie. It’s been here since the early 1900s, run by the same family, the Leonidas, since it was built.”

Roni beamed. She’d been hoping for a little romance tonight, but *this* was total extravagance. She couldn’t believe that Lance had ever doubted she’d like it.

He parked the car and stepped out to open the door for her. “Come on, I thought we could look around for a few minutes before we sit down.” He led her into the foyer, which had a beautiful mosaic-tiled floor and gorgeous paintings of orange groves and the Florida coast. In front of her was a large, wrought-iron staircase spiraling up to an elegant bar, and to her left was a ballroom with a marble floor, three walls of windows, and a huge domed glass ceiling letting in the moonlight.

“Omigod,” Roni gasped. Why hadn’t she found this place before? “Lance, you know what this would be perfect for?”

Lance grinned. “Um . . . Valentine’s Day with a guy who’s trying really hard to impress you?”

Roni smiled. “You don’t even *need* to try,” she said. “What I meant was, this villa would be amazing for the ZZT Formal!”

“Oh, right,” Lance said, seeming to look around the villa with a fresh eye. “I guess I can see that.”

But Roni’s mind was already whirling with possibilities, and she could virtually see the perfect places for flowers, balloons, the DJ. This place was made for the formal. . . . She just knew it.

Just then, the host walked over to Lance and gave him a polite head nod. "Sir, will you be dining with us this evening?"

"Yes," Lance said. "We have a reservation under McManus. Two for seven P.M.?"

The host checked his reservation book and nodded. "Ah, yes. I'd be happy to show you to your table, if you'd like."

Lance started to nod, but Roni jumped in, not wanting to miss her chance. "Actually, before we sit down, I'm wondering if I might speak with a manager about holding a formal event here at the villa. Would that be possible?"

A fleeting look of slight annoyance crossed over the host's face, but he nodded. "We are booked solid tonight, but I'll see if Mrs. Leonida can spare a few minutes. Just a moment." And with that, he disappeared up the staircase to the second floor. Roni gazed anxiously after him while several other couples walked in, heading for the dining room.

"Roni," Lance said, "maybe we can do this after we eat? The dining room looks completely packed, and I'm afraid if we don't get to our table, we'll lose our reservation. . . ."

Roni waved her hand, intent on her mission. "I'm sure they'll hold our table. Why don't you sit down and I'll join you when I'm done? I'll be fast, I promise."

Lance hesitated, but then Roni glanced up again and gasped. "Oh! That must be Mrs. Leonida now." She watched as the host led an elderly woman down the stairs. She was wearing a sleek silk blazer with an elegant black skirt and held herself with the austere, graceful air of Meryl Streep.

"Okay," Lance said in her ear, "I'm going to head inside. I'll see you in a few?"

"Sure, sure," Roni said, but she barely glanced after him as he made his way into the dining room. She had to stay focused on Mrs. Leonida. She had to make sure she used every ounce of her Van Gelderen poise to win her over.

"Mrs. Leonida," she said, extending her hand. "I'm Roni Van Gelderen, a freshman at Latimer University and a member of Zeta Zeta Tau sorority."

"A pleasure, Miss Van Gelderen," Mrs. Leonida said, shaking Roni's hand. "Is there something I can help you with this evening?"

"Actually, there is," Roni said, and she carefully explained the details about the ZZT Formal, striving for the perfect balance of enthusiasm, deference, and professionalism, just like her parents had taught her.

Mrs. Leonida nodded politely as she listened, but she seemed thoughtfully hesitant when Roni finally finished with the request to use the villa for the formal. "Well, our ballroom hasn't been open to the public for events for the last five years," she said. "Mr. Leonida and I run our villa restaurant with a relatively small staff, and the event orchestration got a little too overwhelming. And Greek functions are especially filled with . . . uncertainties these days."

Oh no. Roni knew this had been coming. The same stigma about partying Greeks was rearing its nasty head again. But this was her last chance, and there was no way she was letting it slip through her fingers. "Mrs. Leonida, please," she started. "I can assure you that all of the guests attending our formal would be on their best behavior at all times. My ZZT sisters and I would never stand for anything less. We would show the utmost respect for your villa."

Mrs. Leonida nodded, considering. "Well," she said finally, "there are always exceptions to be made. And I myself was a member of a sorority years ago, a Tri-Delt." She smiled. "I remember my first formal. It was magical." She glanced around the room. "It would be nice to have our villa filled with music and dancing again."

"So does that mean we can have our formal here?" Roni held her breath as she waited for an answer, and broke into a wide, relieved smile when Mrs. Leonida nodded.

"Yes, Miss Van Gelderen, you may have your event here." She smiled kindly.

"That would be wonderful," Roni said, not quite believing what she was hearing. It all seemed to good to be true, but just like that, she had the perfect venue for Formal.

Mrs. Leonida glanced at her watch. "I'd be happy to give you a tour of the rest of the villa, and, of course, we'll have to discuss the details of the banquet contract. But I'm afraid my schedule this evening is a bit hectic."

"Oh, I understand," Roni said, "and I don't want to keep you from your guests. Could I schedule a meeting with you for later this week?"

"Of course," Mrs. Leonida said.

Roni quickly checked her calendar and agreed to meet with Mrs. Leonida again on Monday. Then, after thanking her for at least the twentieth time, she headed for the dining terrace, unable to stop smiling as she felt the pressure she'd been under the last few weeks fade away. She couldn't wait to tell Lance the great news. But when she found him, he was staring out beyond the balcony at the orange groves, a semifrown playing at the corners of his mouth.

"Guess what?" she cried. "I've got my venue!"

"That's great," Lance said, but his voice fell a little flat, and his earlier smile had faded.

"Are you okay?" Roni sat down, attempting to calm her hammering heart as she tried to decipher the mix of confusion and frustration on Lance's face. She'd never seen him upset like this before, and she couldn't think what had gone wrong in the few minutes she'd been with Mrs. Leonida.

Lance shrugged. "I was starting to feel a little strange sitting all alone in here on Valentine's Day." He nodded to a couple at a table nearby. "Those people kept shooting me sympathy looks, like they thought I'd been stood up. And the waiter came by three times to ask if I'd like to order. I didn't, but I have to admit, even the tablecloth is starting to look appetizing."

Roni's brow knitted with confusion for a second, but then she took in the breadbasket on the table, emptied of everything but a few meager crumbs. "I'm sorry," she said. "I didn't realize you were that hungry."

"I wasn't when we got here, but . . ." Lance hesitated, like he was debating whether or not to say what came next. Finally, he took a deep breath and added, "Well, I don't want to make a big deal out of it, but that was over twenty minutes ago."

"What!" Roni gasped, then checked her watch. It was almost seven-thirty! "Omigod, I'm so, so sorry. I had no idea my meeting with Mrs. Leonida went on that long. We just got to talking, and we had to settle on a time to meet to sign the contract. . . ." She sighed, guilt settling over her. "I completely lost track of the time." She stared at the tablecloth. She couldn't believe she'd blown it like this, especially after Lance had planned such a romantic night. He'd probably never consider her girlfriend material now, even if she wanted him to. "You must think I'm a total witch."

"Of course I don't," he said. "Type A, maybe. But a witch? Not in a million years." A faint smile crossed his face. "It's just that I have a big Biochem test Monday, and I spent all day studying so I could see you tonight. I guess this isn't the way I pictured our Valentine's dinner starting."

Roni smiled apologetically. "I promise that you have my absolute, undivided attention from this second forward. For the rest of the night, okay?"

"Okay, but only if we order food within the next thirty seconds before I'm forced to raid the bowl of after-dinner mints at the host's desk."

Roni laughed, relieved that Lance was cracking jokes again. That must mean she was at least partially off the hook. She quickly skimmed the menu as Lance flagged a waiter over, and soon the food was ordered and on its way.

"Well, I have to say I'm glad you finally found a venue, too," Lance said.

"Why?"

"Oh, purely selfish reasons, of course." He grinned shyly. "If you're not so busy with Formal, then maybe I can convince you to go out with me more often?"

Roni blushed with delight. If he wanted to see her more often, that meant that maybe he *was* as into her as she was into him.

"I'd love to see you more often," Roni said, beaming at him. "I don't need any convincing."

"And maybe, since I've starved myself for the sake of ZZT tonight," Lance teased, "you might allow me to be your date to the formal, too?"

"Of course!" Roni said, relief sweeping over her. "I wanted to ask you before; I just wasn't sure. . . ."

"What?" Lance said.

Roni took a deep breath, deciding she might as well lay it all out on the line to test the waters. "I just wasn't sure if that was too couple-y for us."

"Not for me," Lance said softly.

Roni's smile couldn't get any wider. "You know what? This is the best Valentine's Day I've ever had."

"Wow, and we haven't even had dinner yet. I can't wait to see what you say after dessert." He smiled. "Happy Valentine's Day, Roni."

"Happy Valentine's Day," Roni said quietly as he bent his head to hers in a kiss that sent an electric shock through her.

The rest of the night was perfect, from the moment their dinner arrived until the moment Lance kissed her good night outside Tuthill, promising to call her first thing tomorrow. Roni's feet didn't even touch the ground as she headed upstairs. She knew that sleep would be impossible until she came down from her high, but Jenna wasn't home yet to gush to (meaning she'd probably had a fab night out with Tiger). So Roni logged onto her laptop and e-mailed Kiersten:

To: K_douglas@bostonemail.com

From: veronica.van.gelderen@latimer.edu

Date: Saturday, February 14, 1:20 A.M.

Subject: Cupid calling

Hey K,

I'm guessing you and Phillip are out celebrating your first Valentine's as a married couple! How exciting! I want to hear all the details when you have a chance (well, maybe not *all* the details . . . hee-hee). I feel like we've barely talked since the wedding. I miss you. How is the whole newlywed thing treating you? I'm sure it's all amazing.

I just had the most incredible V-day with Lance. We ate dinner at this villa in the middle of an orange grove where everything on the menu has oranges in it (duck à l'orange, orange crumb cake, even whipped orange butter!). It was all delish, and the restaurant was so beautiful. In fact, we're going to have the ZZT Formal there! I talked to the villa's owner about it tonight. Lance was so patient while I talked with her, and it's all settled now. What a relief! Anyway, can't wait to catch up with you and tell you everything. Say hi to your new hubby for me. (Don't you just love being able to introduce him as your husband now? Fun!) Talk to you soon . . .

Love,

Roni

Roni signed off and flopped back on her bed, still smiling. It had been an amazing night. She'd found a venue; she had her date for Formal; and she'd actually mentioned the word *couple* to Lance without scaring him away. And maybe she was actually on her way to having Lance as her—dare she think it?—boyfriend! She hoped so, because just the thought of him now made her heart flip-flop, confirming what she'd already suspected—that she was a complete and total goner.

Jenna peeled another crawfish and sucked the goodness into her mouth, relishing the full flavor of the Cajun spices. What a perfect way to spend a Tuesday night—under the stars at a picnic table with her ZZT sisters, surrounded by cute Sigma Sigma guys (Not that she was looking. Okay, maybe she was looking just a little . . .) and mounds of boiled crawfish, corn on the cob, red potatoes, and corn bread. When the ΣΣ guys had offered to cook dinner for the entire ZZT house for a mixer, Jenna'd guessed they were in for a night of hot dogs and burgers. She had no idea the guys could actually cook. But then again, the Sigma Sigmas seemed to be the epitome of the laid-back, crawfish-boiling, Florida beachboy types.

They'd all put on Hawaiian-print T-shirts for tonight's mixer, and strung mini-margarita-shaped lights around their massive backyard deck. At the bottom of their yard was a sand-filled volleyball court, half a dozen hammocks strung up between palm trees, and some pink flamingo yard ornaments next to a makeshift bungalow bar. Darcy'd explained to Jenna earlier that most of the Sigma Sigmas were actually closet science and engineering majors, which made the whole Jimmy Buffett motif that much more hilarious. Of course, right now, the guys were all down at the other end of the picnic table using the empty crawfish shells as finger puppets, but Jenna decided she wouldn't hold that little regression in maturity against them. Not with food this good. As she picked up another crawfish from her hefty pile, she felt someone's eyes on her and turned to see Roni, staring in horror.

"How can you eat those things?" Roni said, grimacing. "You've put away twenty already and you're still going strong. They're mud-sucking bottom dwellers."

Jenna laughed as she finished peeling another crawfish and popped it into her mouth. "They're delish. You should really try them," she said between bites. She'd made sure she ate extra healthy all day long to compensate for the gorging she knew she'd be doing at the Sigma Sigma's Crawfish Boil. And since her glucose levels were all checking out great, she was going to savor every last bite of these crawfish, and maybe even go back for thirds . . . or fourths.

"They're pure heaven," Sandy said from across the picnic table, and Danika nodded in agreement, her mouth too full to say anything. "'Course, it's making me a little homesick for Alabama. My daddy can boil some mean crawfish."

"It's time to get in touch with your southern side," Jenna said, making another attempt at convincing Roni, who still hadn't touched her plate. "You might not be born a southerner, but you can be an adopted one instead."

"Come on, Boston," Lora-Leigh said, diving into her own pile enthusiastically. "I know you think lobsters are the garbagemen of the sea and all that. But down here, crawfish are a true delicacy. It's all about keeping an open mind."

Roni tentatively picked up one crawfish, and seemed to actually be contemplating peeling and tasting it. But then she dropped it, sighing and shaking her head. "I can't do it. Its little beady eyes keep staring at me."

"Here, then," Jenna said, "have my corn bread. You have to eat something. Otherwise, you might offend the Sigma Sigmas."

"Oh, I'll be fine," Roni said, nibbling on the corn bread. "I had a late lunch with Lance after Poli Sci today anyway."

"Isn't that the fourth time you've seen him since Saturday?" Lora-Leigh said. "And today's only Tuesday."

Roni laughed. "It's not all couple stuff, believe me. When Lance and I get together to work on our debate, he's all business. When he shifts into study mode, it's like I'm not even in the room anymore. But anyway, Valentine's Day shouldn't count against me. Besides, how many times has Jenna seen Tiger this week?"

"Not *that* many." Jenna giggled and shrugged. "Okay, so maybe I've seen him every day."

"That explains the permagrin you've been wearing all night," Sandy said.

"It's not just Tiger," Jenna said. "I found out from Papa Skank today after our parade practice that I might be moving up a chair in marching band at the end of this year. He might love ripping into me during practice, but I guess he thinks I have some talent, too."

"That's great!" Roni said, hugging her.

"Congrats, girl friend!" Lora-Leigh said. "That means, next year, you can harass the lowly freshmen with the best of them."

"Oh no. Not me," Jenna said. "Us poor frosh deserve just as much respect as anybody." After getting raked across the coals by Papa Skank last semester, she could never do it to anyone else. No way.

"So enough with the band talk. I'm dying to know what *you* did Saturday night for Valentine's Day?" Lora-Leigh asked her teasingly. "Any big *firsts*?" she added with a wink.

"No," Jenna said, blushing furiously. "I'm in a holding pattern right now."

"Still haunted by the ghost of the girlfriend past?" Lora-Leigh asked.

Jenna nodded. "Every time I think about being with Tiger, suddenly all I see is the gorge face of his mystery girl. I don't even know her name or anything about her, but I can't get past it." When Lora-Leigh gave her a half-scolding look, Jenna threw up her hands. "I know, I know! Before you say it, I know I should've talked to him about it already, but I keep chickening out. What if he thinks I'm some sort of jealous psycho?"

"I think I can safely say that the thought wouldn't even cross his mind," Roni assured her. "But if you're not ready to have the chat yet, then take your time."

"I second that. And even if there weren't any earthmoving breakthroughs on V-day," Lora-Leigh said, "I'm sure y'all did something sickeningly romantic."

Jenna smiled, relieved to have a change of subject. "He actually did the sweetest thing. We had a picnic dinner in his room. And for dessert, he gave me sugar-free heart-shaped cookies that he'd baked himself in the Phi Omicron kitchen. He'd written a different message on each one of them, like 'I'm Sweet on You' and 'Will You Be Mine.' "

"That's adorable," Danika said. "Y'all are such a perfect couple."

"What about you, Lora-Leigh?" Jenna asked. "DeShawn called on Saturday, didn't he?"

Lora-Leigh nodded. "Sure. But we're not into the whole chocolate-and-roses thing." She grinned. "No offense to those of you in the throes of full-blown couplehood, but it's way too sappy for our taste. So he invited me to the Valentine Schmalentine barbecue at the athletic dorm instead. We made a bonfire of cheesy heart-shaped cards and hung a banner from the patio that said 'Kill Cupid.' For those of us adamantly opposed to Hallmark holidays, it was very therapeutic."

"Speaking of therapeutic," Jenna said to Roni, "I just spotted Melody over by the food tables. Now's your chance to tell her about the Villa Orangerie." She called to Melody and waved her over to their table, knowing Roni'd been looking for her ever since they got here, dying to tell her the news. And Jenna knew how much it meant to Roni to get Melody's approval. She'd been looking for the venue for weeks without luck, and this was her moment to revel in her success.

"Hey, girls," Melody said, walking over. "Y'all having fun?"

"Definitely," Roni said with a smile. "And I have some great news, too. I finally found a venue for Formal!"

"That's brilliant," Melody said, after Roni'd described the

villa to her. "I went there for dinner once with an ex, and it's gorgeous." She hugged Roni. "I knew you'd find the perfect place. You're a natural at event planning!"

"Thanks," Roni said, her cheeks virtually glowing from the praise. "I'm so glad you're happy with my choice. I met with Mrs. Leonida last night to take a tour of the entire villa and negotiate the details of the banquet contract. The only catch was that Mrs. Leonida wanted us to have Formal on Sunday night because she wanted to keep the restaurant open Friday and Saturday, since those are their biggest moneymaking nights. I know a Sunday-night formal is a little unusual, but I thought the villa was well worth it."

"Absolutely." Melody nodded enthusiastically. "You handled everything perfectly. And now that we've gotten that big hurdle out of the way, you can focus on planning the song list with the DJ and picking out the decorations and favors. Now that you have the binder, I'm assuming you've been in touch with the florist?"

"I've left her a couple of messages," Roni said, "but I'm still waiting for her to get back to me."

Melody frowned slightly. "That's not like her. I've worked with her before and never had a problem." She sighed. "Am I going to have to get involved? Because I really don't have time this week . . ."

"No, no," Roni said quickly. "Everything's under control."

Jenna gave Roni a "hang in there" glance, seeing the strain in her face even as she tried to pretend everything was okay. She knew all this was getting a little overwhelming for Roni. In fact, just this morning, Roni'd told her that she hoped Melody would take over a little bit more now that the venue'd been chosen. And understandably so. Jenna'd already seen the hours Roni'd put into finding a venue, and she hated to think of her friend stressing out like that from now until Formal. But Roni was too polite, and too type A, to make a fuss over this. She'd do what she was asked without so much as a sigh (at least, she'd hold off on the sighing until she and Jenna were alone back in their room).

"I couldn't have asked for a better assistant," Melody said now, giving Roni another half hug. Then she turned to all the girls. "Come on, have y'all met my Sigma Sigma friends Holden and Jay yet?"

Jenna shook her head alongside the other girls.

"Well, you have to meet them," Melody said, leading the girls over to another picnic table filled with Sigma Sigmas. "This is Holden." She nodded to one of the lankiest guys Jenna'd ever seen. He had to be almost seven feet tall, and he looked like he'd only ever grown up and never out. And he was sitting in front of three massive piles of empty crawfish shells.

"Last year, Holden won the crawfish-eating contest hands down," Melody said. "What was your final count, Holden? Two hundred and fifty?"

"Two fifty-nine," Holden said proudly. "But I'm going to break my own record this year. I'm already at two forty-eight and counting."

Jenna giggled as Holden belched and everyone instinctively took a precautionary step back. But Holden just smiled and dug into a fresh pile of crawfish.

"Jay's over by the Jacuzzi," Melody said. "Let's go say hi."

The Jacuzzi, Jenna learned a few seconds later, was actually a huge metal tub the guys had filled by siphoning steaming-hot water from the kitchen sink, through the kitchen window, and down the side of the house into the tub. It was only big enough for two people, at most, but somehow three Sigma Sigmas (including Jay) had managed to squeeze into it along with Hallie, Heather, and Keesha, who were all laughing hysterically as they sang "No Shoes, No Shirt, No Problem."

"Move over, y'all, I'm coming in," Lora-Leigh said, impulsively climbing into the Jacuzzi in her jeans and handmade crinkle tunic tank.

"The more the merrier," Jay said, flinging a friendly arm around Lora-Liegh's shoulder and passing her a beer. "Anyone else like to join us?"

"Thanks, but I'll pass," Jenna said, laughing as Lora-Leigh tried unsuccessfully to dunk Heather.

Just then, Darcy came over, grabbing Jenna by the arm.

"Come on, girl," Darcy said. "Matt, Rob, and Heath are kicking off a water-balloon volleyball tournament down in the yard. You've got to come play."

"They're using water balloons instead of a volleyball?" Jenna asked with a giggle.

"That's the idea," Melody said. "It's a blast. I'll go down with y'all, too."

Jenna shrugged, laughing. "Okay, I'm in. Just give me one sec."

She glanced in Roni's direction to see if she wanted to come along, too, but she'd already been surrounded by three devoted Sigma Sigmas, all offering to get her drinks, or food, or anything else her heart desired. With her classic beauty, slender physique, and thick, sleek raven hair, Roni was a veritable guy magnet, even when she didn't send out any flirt signals.

Jenna walked over and eased in next to Roni, whispering, "Just wanted to check to see if you needed any help escaping your adoring fans."

Roni laughed. "No, I'm fine," she said. "A little friendly flirting never hurt anyone. I'll come find you if it looks like any of them are in danger of asking me out."

"Does that mean you're OTM?" Jenna asked teasingly.

Roni grinned and blushed. "Yeah, I guess so. The only guy I can really see myself with right now is Lance."

Jenna nodded, completely understanding that. "I feel the same way about Tiger," she said. "Okay, come play some volleyball with us when you're done breaking hearts."

Roni laughed. "I will."

Jenna caught up with Darcy and Melody as they walked down the patio steps toward the volleyball court, now lit up with tiki torches. She could already see a dozen guys tossing water balloons back and forth, "warming up" for the tournament, and she knew one thing for certain. It was going to be one crazy night, and she was going to enjoy every second of it.

CHAPTER 5

Roni took a swig of her latte on Friday morning and gave Lance yet another apologetic glance as she nodded into her BlackBerry. "I understand that Maddy's not there right now, but this is the fourth time I've called your shop in the last week. And she hasn't returned any of my messages."

"Well," snipped the assistant on the other end of the line, "that's probably because Maddy's vacationing in Cancún right now."

"Cancún!" Roni put her head in her hands. Out of all the times she'd called Maddy's Florist Shop, why hadn't the assistant ever mentioned this before? Now how was Roni supposed to put in the order for the formal floral centerpieces? "Can you tell me when she'll be back?"

Roni could practically hear the assistant frowning into the phone. "You know, that's personal information. . . ."

"I understand that," Roni said, switching into her most

polite, smooth-talking Van Gelderen voice. "But I'm planning on placing a very large order with Maddy which I'm sure she'll be thrilled with. I'm working on a tight schedule, and if I don't know when she'll be back from her trip, I might just have to look into another florist—"

"No, no," the assistant quipped. "That won't be necessary. She'll be back in two weeks, and I'll have her call you as soon as she can."

Roni smiled triumphantly. "Thank you. I appreciate your help." She jotted down the date of Maddy's return in her notebook, said a polite good-bye, and hung up. Then she glanced up at Lance just in time to see a look of irritation pass fleetingly over his face.

"I'm sorry." She sighed. "That took longer than I thought. I've just been waiting for that phone call, and I had to take it." She twisted her hair nervously around her finger. "I can't believe the ZZT florist is on vacation. I just hope we won't have to pay extra for a rush job now."

"Well, they're just flowers, right? Who notices flowers during a dance, anyway?" he said half jokingly. "I'm sure all the sisters will forgive you if they're not completely perfect."

Roni stared at him. "But they have to be perfect! The whole formal has to be, otherwise everyone at ZZT will think I didn't do my job. . . ."

"But it's not all your job." Lance shook his head, frowning slightly. "It's Melody's, too, remember? You're supposed to be *helping* her, not doing everything for her."

"I'm sure she's doing her fair share of planning, too," Roni said. At least, that's what she kept trying to tell herself, even though she couldn't imagine what might be left for Melody to plan, with all the work she'd already done herself.

"It doesn't sound like she's doing anything, Roni," Lance said. "It seems like she's all delegation and no work. And she just assumes that you can pick up the slack for her, like you don't have anything else important to spend your time on." He shook his head doubtfully. "You thought you'd be done with the big formal planning once you found a venue. But last night you spent the whole night biting your nails at the comedy improv we went to, practically in tears because the decorations you ordered are on back order. And then there's the florist, and the list of songs you have to put together for the DJ. For the last few weeks whenever I've seen you, you're glued to your BlackBerry." He sighed.

"I get it, I get it," Roni said, making an attempt at lighthearted laughter. "You know what?" She held up her BlackBerry. "I'm turning this thing off, okay? No more interruptions, no matter what."

She pulled up the cheeriest smile she could muster, and finally Lance gave her a genuine smile in return, then flipped open his Poli Sci notebook. "Okay, not to sound like a complete nerd, but if we're formal-free for a few minutes, we better start working on the debate. I've got class in less than an hour now. I thought we'd have more time. . . ."

"I know," Roni whispered, guilt shooting through her. But she'd already apologized, so she knew the only thing left to do was get down to business so Lance would feel better about the progress they were making on their project. She pulled out her debate notes and mustered up an enthusiastic smile. "Okay, so what do we have left to do?"

"Well, do you have those articles from *Scientific American*?" Lance asked. "We can go over those first."

Roni blanched as her stomach hit the floor. "What articles?"

Lance stared at her, all traces of his fleeting good mood disappearing from his face. "The ones you said you were going to look up on microfiche and copy for our arguments?"

Roni sucked in her breath, her head in her hands. She couldn't believe this was happening. "Oh no . . . Lance, I . . ."

"Forgot?" Lance said quietly. "You forgot."

"I can go to Helman's right after my eleven o' clock class. I'll copy the articles by this afternoon, and then we can go over everything tonight. . . ."

"I have swim practice tonight," Lance said. He sighed, then met her eyes soberly. "The debate's on Monday, Roni. It makes up half our midterm grade, and I'm not even sure we're going to be ready."

"We'll be ready," Roni said. "I'll fix this. I can't believe I forgot in the first place. I never forget things like this. I've just been so stressed about Formal, I don't think I've gotten a decent night's sleep the last three nights running." Her voice died away under an uncontrollable sigh. She was sure Lance didn't want to hear another word about Formal today, especially not after this. "I'm sorry."

"I know you are. But, Roni"—he held her gaze steadily—"aren't you worried about what else you might be sacrificing for ZZT? It seems to take up all of your spare time. You know, swim team tryouts aren't that far away. Are you still thinking about going out for the team?"

Roni shook her head reluctantly. "I'd love to, but right now I don't see how I'd have the time. I'm swamped with ZZT activities and responsibilities already, and I only just became a member. After seeing how much work is involved in planning the formal, I can't imagine what type of time commitment ZZT is going to take up next year." She sighed. "I'm thinking that maybe I should just hold off on the swim team for now."

Lance frowned. "That's a real shame. You have a lot of talent, you know. Is sorority life really as rewarding as swimming for you?" He shook his head. "It just seems like it's all socializing and not much else."

Roni stared at him. Could he actually be serious? Was that all he really thought ZZT was? All his sorority jokes aside, this was the first time she'd ever really heard him seriously belittle the Greek system, and it made her stomach turn over uneasily. "It's way more than that," she said quietly. "It's very important to me, maybe even more important than the swim team at this point."

Lance nodded, then shrugged. "Well, it's your choice. But the LU swimmers will be missing out on one fast—not to mention gorgeous—addition to the team."

Roni smiled. "Thanks." Then she looked down at their debate notes, feeling renewed guilt that she'd forgotten to do her part of the research. She never forgot things like that, and now she wanted to make it right. "You know what? I'm going to head over to Helman's right now and copy those articles. I still have an hour before my class, and that should give me enough time."

"Are you sure?" Lance said. "I can do it."

"Not a chance. You've already done more than your fair share of prepping for this." She leaned over to give him a hug. "Let me pick up some of the slack, okay? I deserve it, especially after letting you down already."

He slipped his arm around her and kissed her lightly. "Thanks."

"So . . . am I forgiven?" She leaned into him and let his familiar scent—spicy soap mixed with a hint of chlorine from the pool—wash over her.

"As long as we ace the debate . . . of course you are," he joked. Then his eyes lit up. "Hey, I've got an idea. Next week, we'll both be swamped with midterms. But the week after, let's get out of town for the day. We can drive down to Palm Beach and go out for lunch. You know, just get some R and R and be brain-dead for a while. No stress about Formal, or debates, or anything. How does that sound?"

Roni smiled. It sounded heavenly, except for one thing . . . "You're talking about the weekend of March sixth, right?" she asked, and her heart dove to her toes when he nodded. "That's Greek Week. It starts that Wednesday and goes through Saturday."

"Oh, right," Lance said, disappointment masking his face. "So much for that, then."

"We can still go!" Roni tried. "Maybe another weekend . . ."

"What, when you're not booked up with ZZT functions?" He shrugged, frowning. "Man, as involved as I am with all the sorority drama going on with your house, I feel like I should be made an honorary member."

She glanced at him, all her confidence fading away. "Is this just about the formal and Greek Week, or is something else bugging you?" she finally got up the courage to ask, not sure she wanted to know the answer. Maybe this wasn't about Formal at all; maybe Lance was just getting annoyed with her. Or tired, or bored. He had seemed pretty busy lately with his course work, but what if that was just a cover-up? Maybe he didn't want to see her anymore. She waited while Lance stared at the table, bracing herself for the worst-case scenario.

"Roni, I hate to bring this up, but I'm starting to think that this is more about us than about the formal," he finally said.

"What do you mean?" she asked, struggling to keep her hands from visibly shaking. Here it came. . . . He was going to give her the "let's just be friends" spiel.

Lance's face turned red as he said quietly, "I don't even know why I'm saying this, because I'm probably just setting myself up. But . . . if you're not into dating me anymore . . . just be straight with me, okay? You don't have to use Formal as an excuse."

"What?" She stared at him, her heart jackhammering in the back of her throat. She couldn't believe this. Here she'd been thinking that he was getting tired of her, and he'd been worried about the same exact thing! "Why would you even think that?"

Lance shrugged. "I know you've told me you like me, but you're so tuned out when we're together lately, I thought maybe you'd changed your mind."

"No way," Roni said firmly, not wanting to leave him any room for doubt. "I love hanging out with you."

Lance nodded, then smiled faintly. "Then maybe you can hang out with just me, and not the florist and the DJ and Melody and—"

"Of course," she said. "I'll try harder not to let Formal stress me out, and I promise that if we drive down to Palm Beach, I won't even mention it at all. We can go the weekend after Greek Week. I'll put it into my BlackBerry right now so it's set in stone. Okay?"

Lance hesitated, still frowning, until Roni took a chance, jumping out of her chair to playfully hug him. "Please please please please please please please," she crooned, clinging to his neck with exaggerated affection.

Finally, much to her relief, he laughed, and his icy mood was broken. "All right, all right." He smiled, then gave her a quick kiss. "Now cut it out before the barista giving us the evil eye over there yells at us for PDA overkill."

Roni giggled, relieved that the tension between them was gone. Before she hurried to Helman's, she made plans to meet Lance at the natatorium before his practice so he could look over the articles. He seemed happy with that compromise, and as he kissed her good-bye, she felt like they'd recovered from their nerve-racking morning. But as she got ready for bed later that night, her mind unwillingly replayed the earlier tension with him, and an uneasiness settled in her stomach. She told herself that everything was back to normal. Of course it was. He'd kissed her and smiled at her when he'd said good-bye, just like he always did. The only thing was, every time she thought about Lance's comments about ZZT, a small spark of fury lit inside her. And that wasn't normal at all.

Saturday morning, Lora-Leigh snipped the last piece of extra thread from Naomi Yates's Britney Spears outfit for the Greek

Week Talent Show and held it up to give it a final once- over. Now she just had to have Louise, Naomi, and Bonni try on their outfits. She'd make any last adjustments, and she'd be finished.

"So?" Lora-Leigh asked her roommate, Virginia, who was busy painting her lips a ghoulish purple. "What do you think? Does it say 'Britney in the Big House'?" She had created some ultra-low-rise vinyl flare pants with a ball and chain hanging from the hip, a black-and-white tuxedo bib halter, and black-and-white-striped opera gloves to complete the look.

Virginia scanned the outfit with her "Corpse Bride" thickly lined eyes. "God, I hope so," she said. "I can't stand pop stars. They're so . . . bubbly." She grimaced, like that was a fate worse than death. She was about to turn back to her makeup, but then she hesitated. "Hey, do you think I could have those pants when the talent show's over? My skull-and-crossbones corset top would look too cruel with them."

"Anything for you, my little vampress," Lora-Leigh joked just as her cell rang.

"Hi, Mom," she said, after checking the caller ID. "What's up?"

"Hello, sweetheart," her mom said. "I just wanted to let you know that you have some mail here at the house. I can have your dad drop it by ZZT later this week sometime, or—"

"What kind of mail?" Lora-Leigh interjected, her heart catapulting through her chest. Maybe today was the day. Maybe she'd finally hear something back from FIT.

"Oh, let me see," her mom said absently, and Lora-Leigh

could hear paper shuffling in the background. "There's a letter from your friend Brian from his new training post in San Diego . . ." More paper shuffling ensued. ". . . and a letter from the Fashion Institute."

Lora-Leigh was practically throttling the phone with the grip she had on it. "What kind of letter?" she blurted, the blood pounding in her ears. "What does it look like? Is it small or big? 'Cause if it's small, then it's probably a rejection. But if it's big, then maybe . . ." She couldn't even finish the sentence for fear of jinxing her chances right then and there.

Her mom laughed. "Oh, it looks big to me, and heavy, too. So, when can we drop it—"

"I'm coming over right now," Lora-Leigh said, cutting her off. "I'll be there in ten." She grabbed her keys and was out the door before she even remembered to click her cell shut.

"What did you do, fly here?" her mom cried, laughing, as Lora-Leigh burst through the kitchen door of her house less than ten minutes later.

"It's not that far, Mom," Lora-Leigh said, playing it off as coolly as she could. She wasn't about to tell her about the three *very* yellow lights (okay, so they were technically pink) she'd barreled through, or the several other traffic rules she'd bent to the max on the way over.

"Your mail's right here," her mom said with a smile, sliding two envelopes across the counter.

Lora-Leigh grabbed the hefty envelope from FIT, feeling the weight of it in her hands. With her heart racing, she ripped it open and pulled out a letter and—yes!—an admissions packet. A grin was already breaking across her face, but she skimmed the letter that was included, just to be sure:

> *Dear Ms. Sorenstein,*
> *We are pleased to inform you that you've been accepted to the Fashion Institute of Technology for the fall semester—*

"Well, are you going to keep me in suspense?" her mom said with a mischievous smile, no doubt having already guessed the news.

"I got in!" Lora-Leigh sang out, catwalking across the kitchen like it was a runway at New York's Fashion Week.

Her mom pulled her into a hug and gave her a warm kiss on the cheek. "Congratulations, honey," she said. "I know you've wanted this for a long time." She stood back to look at Lora-Leigh and brushed a curl off her forehead. "Now you can finally escape Latimer and your old-fogy parents."

"Not that old, Mom," Lora-Leigh said with a smile. She could barely believe that FIT was finally within reach, not just a dream anymore, but a concrete reality. And her mom was right. She had wanted this for what seemed like forever. And now here it was, right at her fingertips.

"So, do you want to stay for dinner?" her mom asked. "I'll make your favorite—knishes—and we can celebrate."

Lora-Leigh's mouth watered at the thought, but she held back. "Thanks, Mom," she said, giving her a quick peck on the cheek, "but I've got to run. Save me some knishes. Maybe I'll swing by for brunch tomorrow." She grabbed the FIT envelope and headed for the door. Right now she could only think of getting back to Tuthill, because there were two people there she was dying to share her news with.

Lora-Leigh heard their laughter echoing in the hallway long before she reached Jenna and Roni's room. The door was propped open for her, like it usually was; and when she stuck her head in, she saw both girls practically rolling on the floor in fits of giggles. Lora-Leigh'd been all prepared to bust in with the FIT news, but now, as she watched her friends laughing, the high she'd been on took a nosedive. If she went to FIT, she wouldn't be saying good-bye just to her humdrum hometown; she'd be saying good-bye to all of this—Jenna, Roni, and the rest of her sisters at ZZT. She'd miss her two best friends so much. Even though she'd started this semester with her heart set on FIT, now she had one foot out the door and one cemented here. And suddenly a part of her just wanted to forget about the FIT packet in her hands and get in on the fun with them without dampening the mood by spilling the news.

"Omigod, Lora-Leigh," Jenna gasped, wiping the tears of laughter from her eyes. "You have to hear Roni's idea for the Greek Week cheer. She wants to set it to 'Please Come to Boston.' "

"I couldn't help it," Roni said through hiccuping laughs. "It was the first song that came into my head. 'At Zeta Zeta Tau, we never wear a frown. Boston isn't our kind of town. We aren't Red Sox fans, and we only drink *iced* tea. We're the blooming white rose of the South, the girls from ZZT.' "

Jenna started giggling before Roni was even finished, and it spread to Lora-Leigh and Roni.

"You can take the girl out of Boston, but you can't take the Boston out of the girl," Lora-Leigh said, shaking her head. "Sounds like I came just in time. Of course the cheers I learned at frat parties in high school involve a lot of lurid references to drinking and sorority girls in 'compromising positions.' "

"Those are definitely out," Roni said.

"Oh, come on," Lora-Leigh said. "Some of them are fun." She put her hands on her hips and pasted a Vaseline-on-the-teeth cheerleading grin onto her face. Then, clapping in time, she chanted:

"You take the legs of Mischa Barton
The vamp of A. Jolie's the best,
You take the grace of Nicole Kidman
And off of Carmen take the chest
We need the chest!

"And then you put them all together
Far hotter than the rest
We keep the guys drooling forever
ZZT girls are the best!"

Lora-Leigh gave a quick jumping jack and ended with a right punch into the air, leaving Jenna and Roni in hysterics.

"I could definitely use Carmen Electra's chest," Jenna said between laughs.

"You and me both, girl friend," Lora-Leigh said. "Of course maybe we'll just take Roni's instead."

"I don't think so," Roni said. "I grew these at age ten and hated them until I turned fifteen. But now I've come to appreciate them, and there's no way I'm parting with them."

That got them all started again, until finally, Jenna came up for air and said, "Face it, y'all. Coming up with cheers is just not our forte. Maybe we should leave it to the other sisters."

"What, and admit defeat?" Lora-Leigh said. "Never. Come on, we can come up with something."

The three of them bent their heads over pieces of paper, brainstorming, until Roni suddenly jumped up. "Wait a sec, guys," she said, flipping on the Bose iPod dock her parents had given her for Christmas. "I've got an idea." She clicked through her song list, and then hit "play," a smile spreading across her face as the music to the Beatles' version of "You Really Got a Hold on Me" came on.

Lora-Leigh immediately saw where Roni was going with this as she listened to the lyrics. "You won't just like her," she started, thinking out loud as she went. "You'll really love her. See, you'll be always thinking of her. Oh oh oh. A ZZT girl will help you out gladly. She'll make you love her madly. 'Cause ZZT's got a hold on you. ZZT's really got a hold on you."

"I like it." Jenna nodded. "Keep going."

They listened to the song three more times, jotting down ideas for their cheer along the way. Finally, they sang through their version together with the music in the background.

"That's it!" Roni said. "It's perfect."

"So now we just have to see what the rest of the sisters think about it," Jenna said. "Darcy told me we'll vote on a cheer at the meeting after next."

"Everyone will love it," Lora-Leigh said confidently. "And no offense, but it beats 'Please Come to Boston,' hands down."

"What can I say?" Roni said with a shrug. "I tried."

"So now that we've got a brill cheer"—Lora-Leigh took a deep breath—"can I talk to y'all about something else?" She slowly retrieved the FIT packet that she'd tossed on Jenna's bed earlier, and held it up for them to see.

"Omigod!" Jenna gasped. "You got in, didn't you?" She didn't even wait for Lora-Leigh to answer; she just threw her arms around her in an enthusiastic hug.

"Yeah, I got in." Lora-Leigh grinned as Roni got in on the hugging act. "Okay, okay, let's not overemote."

"But this is amazing," Jenna gushed. "You're going to move to Manhattan."

"And we're going to come shop—er, visit, whenever we can," Roni added.

"Hang on a sec," Lora-Leigh said. "I didn't say whether or not I was going, did I?"

Jenna and Roni froze, exchanging questioning glances.

"What do you mean?" Roni said. "We thought . . ."

"I know, I know," Lora-Leigh said. "That I couldn't wait to get the *H-E*-double *L* out of Latimer." She shrugged. "The great irony is, after all this, I'm not sure what I want to do anymore. I'd hate to leave ZZT, and hate to leave you guys even more."

"We'd hate that, too," Jenna said quietly, her brow creasing just at the thought. "But you have to do what's right for you."

Roni nodded. "And not worry about us."

"You mean you're not going to grovel and throw yourselves at my feet to get me to stay?" Lora-Leigh asked. "Well, that sucks. I was at least hoping to get some good mopeage out of you two."

"Oh, they'll be plenty of that if you leave, believe me," Roni said. "We're just putting on the happy faces for your benefit right now."

"Yeah, actually, if we talk about this too much longer," Jenna said, "my eyes are going to fog up." She bit her lip, and then smiled at Lora-Leigh. "We just want you to be happy, no matter what you choose."

"Thanks," Lora-Leigh said. "I have until March twelfth to send back the official acceptance letter. That's right after Greek Week . . . only three weeks away. So I guess I better get busy with some serious soul-searching, right?"

"Three weeks," Jenna repeated. "I guess that means Roni and I have three weeks to convince you to stay here." She looked like she was making a visible effort to keep that optimistic smile pasted on her face. "Well, whatever happens, just the fact that you got in is incredible! We should go out and celebrate."

"My thought exactly," Lora-Leigh said. "DeShawn called me on my way here and said he's meeting up with some of his buds at Morgan's later tonight. So what do y'all say to a little dancing?"

"What are we waiting for?" Roni answered.

"Maybe we can call Tiger and Lance and get them to meet us there, too," Jenna suggested.

"Great," Lora-Leigh said. "I'll go glam myself up and be back down in fifteen."

As she left the girls to go get ready, she smiled. Sure, she didn't know what she'd decide to do in the end, but she didn't want to focus on that right now. She just wanted to relish the fact that she'd actually gotten accepted! Now FIT was at her fingertips, there for the taking. They wanted her, and she felt like that was an accomplishment in itself. Tonight, she was going to celebrate and have the time of her life right here in Latimer. And tomorrow, she'd start trying to figure out her future.

CHAPTER 6

Lora-Leigh took another bite of Miss Merry's creole catfish casserole and cringed. She was trying to get through the ZZT dinner on Sunday night without gagging, but it was an uphill battle.

"Hey, Chez Jen," she whispered to Jenna, "did you bring the goods like we talked about?"

"Yes, I brought the leftover lasagna from my cooking class," Jenna whispered with a nervous giggle. "It's upstairs in Darcy's room. But keep your voice down. I don't think Mrs. Walsh would be too happy if she found out I was smuggling in food from the outside."

"Please," Darcy said in a low tone, "Mrs. Walsh would probably be the first one to raid my minifridge to get at it."

"So the plan is to meet in your room after the house meeting, right?" Camille asked Darcy, and she nodded. "I don't know if I can wait that long. I'm starving."

"What are you guys plotting over there?" Roni piped up,

eyeing them suspiciously. "Jenna, you look completely guilty."

"I do?" Jenna said. "I'm innocent, I swear!"

"Hmm," Roni said. "I'm not buying it."

"Seriously," Lora-Leigh said. "We were just having a little Greek Week chat, that's all." She knew Roni was much too loyal a ZZT to ever contemplate noshing smuggled food. In fact, even though she suspected that Roni was more grossed out by Miss Merry's cooking than anyone else, Roni still got through every meal (with grits being the exception. Oh, and the Sigma Sigmas' crawfish, of course). Her taste buds had a higher pain tolerance than Lora-Leigh's, that was for sure.

"It's true, Roni," Jenna said, trying (and failing) to look innocent. "I was just asking Lora-Leigh for advice on the Greek Week T-shirts. Betsy put me in charge of recruiting our players for the softball team and choosing the T-shirts for the entire Poseidon team. It has to be something that the Phi Omicrons and the Beta Xis will wear, too."

"And the Beta Xis are some high-maintenance chicks, so we really need to give some thought to the tees," Lora-Leigh said. "I heard their house rules state they have to get regular manis and pedis to look their best at all times. I bet most of them have never played a sport in their life. To them, primping is a sport."

"Be nice!" Camille said, smacking the back of her head. "You're making them sound like a bunch of prima donnas."

"Well, I've never seen one of them without flawless makeup and hair."

Darcy snorted. "It's true."

"And they're on our softball team?" Jenna said with dismay. "We're so going to lose. . . ."

"Eh, your Prince Charming and the other Phi Omicrons might save the day," Lora-Leigh said. "And we'll make sure the team shirts are something that even the Beta Xi divas are willing to wear. Since we're the Poseidon team, maybe something with a trident spearing the other houses."

"So does that mean you'll help me with the design?" Jenna asked sincerely.

"And maybe you could help me with the formal tees, too?" Roni jumped in. "I need a concept to go with the annual Romance and Roses theme."

"Wow," Lora-Leigh said. "It's great to be in such high demand. Such is the life of any great visionary, I guess." She grinned as Roni and Jenna rolled their eyes. "Of course I'll help y'all. I'm all finished with the talent-show costumes anyway, except for the girls' final fittings, so I need another project."

"How did the costumes turn out?" Camille asked.

"Fabtastic, if I do say so myself," Lora-Leigh said. "It's Hollywood marries Alcatraz." She'd loved every minute she was working on the costumes. Of course designing T-shirts for Greek Week and Formal wasn't exactly designing gowns for the Oscars, but she had to start somewhere, right? It suddenly occurred to her that if she decided to go to FIT, she'd get to design outfits all day, every day. *And* she could spend all her free time shopping in Manhattan's garment district for one-of-a-kind fabrics. What could be better than that? Just the thought made her fingers itch for some fabric and her sewing machine. But as soon as she found herself smiling at the prospect of roaming the streets of the Big Apple as a budding fashionista, the reality of leaving Latimer behind hit her head-on. Half of her was riding a high over FIT, and the other half was feeling sick at the idea of having to choose between it and her life here. But she forced herself to refocus on her friends as they laughed and chatted enthusiastically about the talent show, wanting to enjoy this time with them and wait until she had some alone time to weigh all the pros and cons of her decision.

"I can't wait to see Naomi do her Britney Spears imitation," Darcy was saying now. "She was practicing the other night, and it was dead-on." She glanced over to where Beverly was escorting Mrs. Walsh out of the dining room. "Hey, we better finish up, y'all; the meeting's about to start."

It was then that Roni noticed the untouched casserole on everyone's plate but her own. "I can't believe you guys aren't eating that," she said. "It's amazing."

Resisting the urge to point out that catfish were right alongside crawfish in the bottom-dweller category, Lora-Leigh slid her plate toward Roni with a smile. "Here, have mine."

"Really?" Roni asked, already digging in enthusiastically. "Great."

Lora-Leigh was still laughing five minutes later as Beverly started the house meeting with her announcements.

"With Greek Week only two weeks away," she said, "we've got a lot of planning to do. Betsy will give us a quick update on the Greek Week Committee activities as well as areas where y'all can get involved in the fun."

With that, Betsy took the floor. "The Greek Week Committee needs everyone's help to paint a house banner that we'll hang over the porch for the duration of Greek Week," she started. "I know y'all are going to be swamped with midterms this week, but the committee will be painting the banner on Wednesday night after dinner, if you want to help. Lora-Leigh came up with an incredible idea for the design. We'll be painting a huge trident, Poseidon's symbol of strength. To show our unity with the rest of our team, the prongs on the trident will spell out Zeta Zeta Tau, Phi Omicron Chi, and Beta Xi in each of our house colors." Betsy held up the sketch Lora-Leigh had given to her earlier in the night, and everyone clapped while Lora-Leigh beamed proudly. "Jenna and Lora-Leigh are also designing T-shirts for everyone to wear, and they should be available early next week.

"Jenna's just posted the sign-up sheets for each of the events," Betsy continued. "We'll need at least five sisters to sign up to help build the chariot for the chariot race; and five for the tug-of-war, Twister contests, relay race, obstacle course, and softball tournaments. We'll need everyone involved in the cheer competition. Anyone who has a cheer idea can present it at next Sunday's meeting, and we'll decide on our official cheer then."

Lora-Leigh exchanged glances with Roni and Jenna, silently acknowledging that next week they would unveil the "ZZT's Got a Hold on Me" cheer they'd been practicing in private. Lora-Leigh hoped the other girls would love it as much as they did.

"We'll have a practice cheer session on Tuesday night before the official kickoff on Wednesday," Betsy said. "And for those of you who sign up for the chariot building, that will take place at the Phi Omicron house next Monday night."

"Tiger's helping out with that," Jenna whispered proudly. "He and Mike and some of the other guys already made a Home Depot run for PVC pipe and plywood."

Lora-Leigh rolled her eyes. "The call of the tool belt. No guy can ignore it."

Beverly rejoined Betsy at the front of the room with an enthusiastic smile. "I know we're going to kick some major butt in Greek Week this year. I can feel it. And maybe we'll even beat the Tri-Os, too. Last year, they knocked us for a loop with their talent-show history-of-dance montage. But this year, they're not going to know what hit 'em."

"Damn straight!" Lora-Leigh shouted, making everyone cheer louder.

"Okay, moving on," Beverly said, "we'll have an update from Melody now on Formal."

Lora-Leigh felt Roni straighten and tense next to her as Melody stepped to the front of the room.

"Hey, y'all," Melody said with a smile. "I have some great news. After a long search, I found the perfect venue for Formal—the Villa Orangerie." She held up some color printouts and then gave them to Keesha, who was sitting toward the front, to pass around to everyone. "Here're some pics I printed out from the villa's Web site that'll give you the idea. But it's an amazing place—beautiful inside and out. I'm so glad it was available for our special day."

As oohs and ahhs and applause sounded from around the room and the girls all hovered over the pics of the villa, Melody gave a brief rundown of the progress she'd made so far with the DJ and decorations. But Lora-Leigh was too furious to pay any attention, especially when she saw Roni's crestfallen face and sunken shoulders.

"That's it," Lora-Leigh whispered, starting to stand up. "I'm outing Miss Melody ASAP. There's no way she's getting away with this. So uncool."

"You can't," Roni hissed, grabbing her arm and pulling her back down onto the floor. "Just . . . just forget about it. It's no big deal."

"Are you kidding me?" Lora-Leigh said, feeling heat rising from her cheeks. "She's taking all the credit for finding the venue that you busted your ass looking for. And you're just going to sit there and take it?"

"Lora-Leigh's right," Jenna said, concern written all over her face. "Melody's totally out of line. We should say something."

"I don't want to stir things up," Roni said. "Not here, in front of everybody. It wouldn't be right, or sisterly." She looked at Lora-Leigh with pleading eyes. "Please, Lora-Leigh, keep quiet, just this once. For me."

The last thing Lora-Leigh wanted to do was back down, but she didn't want to cause her friend any more pain. "All right," she relented, "I won't say anything. But for the record, it's dirty pool, and you should call her on it."

Lora-Leigh hoped that, just this once, Roni might put aside her sense of propriety to stand up for herself. But since she stayed quiet, lost in her own thoughts for the rest of the meeting, Lora-Leigh didn't think the odds of that happening were too likely at all.

• • •

"I just don't understand why she did it," Roni said twenty minutes later as she finished telling the entire story to Beverly in the privacy of Beverly's room upstairs. She was still reeling from what Melody had done at the meeting. After all the hours of work she'd put in during the past few weeks, this was a stab in the back, any way she looked at it. "I mean, I know I'm just her assistant, but still . . ."

"She shouldn't have done it," Beverly said, frowning. "It's not something one sister should ever do to another."

"It's not just that she took the credit," Roni said, "but she made it sound like I hadn't done a thing to help. That's what bothers me more than anything. Everyone's going to think I'm a total slacker."

Beverly laughed and launched one of her pillows at Roni's head. "Don't be ridiculous," she said. "No one could think that for even a second. You've gone above and beyond from day one, and everyone knows it. What about confronting her about it? I could be with you. . . ."

But Roni just shook her head. "That would be completely awkward, and it's just not worth it. I can't deal right now, not with midterms. I have my Poli Sci midterm debate tomorrow and—" She gasped, feeling a wave of nausea wash over her.

"What's wrong?" Beverly asked, leaning over her.

"Omigod, omigod!" Roni grabbed her purse off Beverly's bed, then scrambled for the door. "I was supposed to meet Lance at his dorm right after the meeting. We were going to go over the argument for our Poli Sci debate. He's probably been waiting for me for over an hour."

"Go, go, go," Beverly said, waving her out of the room, "You go prep for your debate and then enjoy some downtime with your boy."

By the time Roni got to Stewart Hall, it was already close to nine. She'd tried calling Lance's cell a few times on her way through campus, but it went straight to voice mail. She found Lance bent over his textbooks in the lobby, looking tired and stressed.

"I'm so, so sorry," Roni said, leaning over to kiss him on the cheek. God, why did it feel like she was constantly apologizing to him for one screwup after another? "My ZZT meeting ran late and it went horribly. I stayed a few minutes to talk to my Big Sister about it all, and I guess I lost track of time."

Lance sighed and gave her a small smile, but he didn't look happy. "That's all right," he said, rubbing his temples. "I had to study for my Anatomy midterm anyway. I have that tomorrow, too."

"I know," Roni said. "Are you ready for it?"

"I'll find out tomorrow morning at eight A.M.," he said. "So, what happened with your meeting tonight?"

Roni sighed. "Melody happened," she started, and then, in one long tirade, she vented the whole story.

"I hate to say it, but I tried to warn you about this before," Lance said matter-of-factly when she was finished. "She's been using you for weeks. She doesn't strike me as the sensitive, caring type."

"But she's always been nice to me," Roni said, not wanting to believe that Melody was as catty as Lance was making her out to be. "And we're sisters. Sisters don't do things like this to each other. It goes against everything we stand for."

"You make it sound like she's violated something as serious as the Hippocratic oath," Lance said. "But you can't let it get to you. It's just a little Greek drama, that's all, and we have bigger things to worry about anyway. Like our debate tomorrow."

"I know," she said, trying not to let his remark about the "little Greek drama" get under her skin. "It just feels like a stab in the back, that's all."

"That seems a bit extreme, though, don't you think?" He frowned. "Honestly, I'm not even sure why you want to be a part of ZZT if you spend all your time stressing over things like this."

"What?" She stared at him.

"Well, being in a sorority is supposed to be fun, but it doesn't seem like you're having much of it. With everything that's happened with Melody, your experience has been sort of negative so far."

"That's not true," Roni started, shifting uncomfortably in her seat. "I love ZZT, and I'm having the time of my life."

"Okay, then," Lance said, "shrug this off, and get back to enjoying your sister-bonding stuff. In the overall scheme of things, this isn't a big deal."

He gave her a hug, but it wasn't the long, comforting hug Roni'd hoped for. And she had the unsettling feeling that he was just humoring her instead of sincerely sympathizing. All too quickly, he released her and pulled out his Poli Sci notes.

But she couldn't just let this go. This was something he needed to understand about her. "It *is* a big deal," she said, her back bristling with tension. "You make sororities sound ridiculous, like we're a bunch of brainless social butterflies giggling all day long."

"I didn't say that," Lance said. He continued to flip through his notes without glancing at her, like he was dismissing everything she'd said.

"But you're thinking it," Roni said. "I can see it in your face." She sighed. "You don't get it. The girls at ZZT are like my family. You know my mom and dad aren't exactly involved in my life, and I've only heard from my friend Kiersten a few times since she got married. She's focused on her new life now. My best friends are my ZZT sisters."

Lance stared down at his textbook, but Roni could tell that he wasn't focused on the words on the page.

"So," she said, taking a deep breath. "Don't knock ZZT, because when you do, you're treating me like I'm ridiculous, too. I'm not. And neither is ZZT."

Lance stayed quiet for a minute, and then finally shrugged. "Okay," he said. "I'm sorry. It's been a long day, and I'm completely spent from all this studying. It must be giving me a short fuse. But the thing is . . . ZZT's just not something I can relate to, you know? I'm sorry about Melody. I'm sure it's upsetting. But maybe you're letting it get to you more than you should. You've been so frustrated about it lately, it seems like it's all you've talked about and thought about."

Roni twirled her hair around her finger nervously. It was true that she'd vented to Lance almost every day for the last month about her ZZT duties. And maybe, after he'd heard all of that, ZZT wouldn't sound like much fun to him, or to anyone outside the Greek system. But she shouldn't have to feel like she was constantly defending ZZT to her own boyfriend. If he really cared for her, then he'd care about her life in ZZT, too. Still, though, with midterms looming, this wasn't the time for her to confront him about it.

"I'm sorry I've complained so much lately," she said quietly, reaching for his hand to keep the peace. "I'll try to be better about that."

"Don't worry about it," Lance said. "I have stuff I'm stressing about right now, too . . . like my swim meets and my grades. I have to do well in my courses, or there's no point in me going the premed track. If I'm not at the top of my class, I'll never get into a good med school." He sighed. "So, do you think we could maybe stop talking about ZZT for the rest of the night and just focus on finalizing our debate? It's late already, and if I don't get some sleep, I'll be worthless tomorrow when it counts."

"Sure," Roni said, forcing a smile onto her face. "But . . . are you okay?"

"Of course," he said, quickly pecking her cheek. "We're good. Everything's fine."

But disappointment weighed her down as she and Lance studied. She had wanted him to handle this so differently than he had. She'd wanted understanding, and instead Lance had basically shrugged off the whole thing like it was just some silly catfight. He said they were good, but Roni didn't *feel* good . . . about any of it.

Jenna whooped as she watched her pink golf ball shoot over the drawbridge, through the doors of the miniature castle, and out the other side, finally diving into the seventeenth hole with a satisfying *thunk*.

"Another hole in one for me!" she squealed, rushing over to

grab her ball, then taking a bow. "That's my third one! First I ace my World Lit midterm, and now I'm sinking every other putt!" She beamed, feeling like this day couldn't get much better. Her last midterm had ended at three this afternoon, and she walked out of it feeling almost certain of a good grade. In fact, she'd felt that way after all her midterms, especially her Culinary Arts practicum. But then again, cooking had never been anything but fun for her, so even making a spinach soufflé in under an hour was a breeze, and the look on Dr. Pierpont's face when she'd tasted it was priceless—absolute bliss.

Last semester may have been a struggle, but this semester Jenna was back to her old self, acing exams and already at the top of two of her classes. Both the parades she'd had for the Marching Raiders were over and done with, and her Raiders Concert Band practices were cushy compared to the grueling parade routes, so she could coast through the rest of the semester, no problem. And now that the cramming for midterms was over, she could kick back and enjoy her Friday night out with Tiger, Roni, and Lance at the Putt-Putt Playland.

"I wish I had your luck," Roni mumbled to her as she fished her ball out of the minimoat surrounding the castle. "My Business Math midterm was a nightmare, and so is my swing. And I'm playing with a polka-dotted two-foot club. How can I keep missing the ball with a baby club? This game should be a gimme."

"Nothing in golf is ever a gimme, trust me," Tiger said. "But Jenna's unbelievable." He laughed, shaking his head. "This is starting to get embarrassing."

"I made peace with *my* embarrassment when I realized we

were the oldest people here by about a decade," Lance said, nodding to the scattered groups of kids playing golf around them. "And that the munchkins were leaving me in the dust."

"But *I'm* supposed to be the golf pro here," Tiger said.

"Not when it comes to miniature golf, you're not," Jenna singsonged, reveling in her victory. "Besides, the last time I played with you on a real course, I played a two-hundred-stroke game, and you played an eighty-six-stroke game. This is sweet, sweet revenge."

"Face it, man." Lance slapped Tiger amicably on the back. "Golf might be your game, but putt-putt isn't."

"I blame it all on the Jack and Coke I had before we came here," Tiger said, leaning over to concentrate on his ball. He swung, and the ball ricocheted off the castle tower and shot toward the miniature jousting knights below. "Fore!" he yelled, just before the ball crashed into the knights. "Hmm, I think there might have been a few casualties that time."

"I don't know," Lance said. "I think the alcohol might have actually improved my game."

"I beg to differ," Roni said with a laugh. "You almost took out that poor squirrel on the last hole. And he wasn't a prop."

"See, there *are* benefits to being the designated driver." Jenna smiled. "I might not be able to drink, but my reflexes are like lightning."

Tiger leaned over to Roni and stage-whispered, "You realize she's never going to let any of us live this down."

Roni nodded. "That's all right. I've still got her beat with my backstroke."

Jenna stepped up to the eighteenth hole, carefully positioned herself over her ball, and swung, driving the ball straight into the mouth of the gigantic papier-mâché clown head decorating the final hole. "Yes!" she cried. "I am the reigning putt-putt queen. Let's play another eighteen!"

"Oh no," Roni said, finally walking up to the hole to hand-drop her ball in after her fourth attempt to hit it in failed. "I'm retiring my club before I become a danger to myself and others."

Lance sank his ball, then slipped his arm around Roni. "I vote for a go-cart race next."

"Definitely," Tiger said. "Burning some rubber will help me recover what's left of my manhood."

"Unless we girls beat you at that, too," Jenna joked.

"This is so much fun," Roni said as she and Jenna headed toward the racetrack, leaving the guys trailing behind them to chat. "I'm so glad we came along with you guys tonight. Especially with the way things have been between me and Lance since last Sunday. We were so in need of an icebreaker."

"He seems all right now," Jenna said, trying to sound as positive as possible.

"I guess so," Roni said. "We found out this morning that we got an A on our Poli Sci debate, so that made him happy. And we still hung out a lot this week. But every time I mention anything having to do with ZZT, he gets this look of annoyance on his face. It's like he's thinking, 'Here she goes again . . .' And the whole topic of Melody and Formal is definitely off-limits."

"That's not good," Jenna said as they stepped into the line for the go-carts.

"I know," Roni said. "Sometimes I just feel like I'm tiptoeing around on eggshells now."

"But you should feel comfortable talking to him about anything." Jenna paused, then sighed. "I can't believe I just said that, when I have my own totally taboo topic right now with Tiger. Since I don't even have the guts to bring up the whole *S-E-X* issue again, I'm probably the last person you should ask for advice on relationships."

"But that's a lot bigger deal than Formal," Roni said. "I can understand why it's tough to talk about. Lance and I shouldn't be hitting road blocks when we talk about ZZT, you know?"

Jenna nodded, and gave Roni an encouraging smile, wanting so much to see her face worry-free again. "I'm sure y'all will work everything out. I mean, he can barely keep his eyes off you, in case you haven't noticed."

"Shhh," Roni said. "Here they come." She nodded to the guys, who were only a few feet behind them now.

"So," said Tiger, giving Jenna a playful pinch in the waist, "are you ready to meet your match?"

Jenna elbowed him. "I think you should be asking yourself that question," she teased.

Tiger looked at Lance and shrugged. "I knew we should've gone to the pool hall tonight."

"They forget I've driven through downtown Boston during rush hour," Roni whispered to Jenna with a giggle. "They're doomed."

Jenna laughed and pulled Roni toward the waiting go-carts. "Come on," she said. "I feel a battle of the sexes coming on."

Two hours later, Jenna was still laughing as she watched Tiger practicing putting in his room back at the Fox house. After losing two go-cart races, a skee-ball competition, and a round of foosball, he and Lance had finally admitted defeat, but Tiger was still a very reluctant loser.

"I just want to fix this glitch in my swing," Tiger muttered, more to himself than to Jenna, "then we can watch a movie." He swung his putter again, and watched as his ball rolled across the carpet and missed the empty plastic cup he was aiming for by about three inches. "I can't believe I missed again!" he cried, letting his club fall to the ground as he plopped down onto the bed next to Jenna. "I'm losing my touch."

"No, you're not." Jenna tried her best to hide her smile (he was so adorably boyish when he was frustrated!), then tucked herself under his arm so she could rest her head on his shoulder. "We'll go to the driving range tomorrow morning and you'll be whacking them two hundred yards, I'm sure."

She gave him a quick peck on the lips, and a smile flickered across his face. "What was that for?"

"To cheer you up," she said. "Did it work?"

A mischievous glint sparked in his eyes, and he said, "I don't know. You caught me off guard that time. Maybe try again and I'll pay closer attention."

Jenna blushed, then gave him a second kiss. "Well?"

"Yup, I'm starting to feel better." Tiger wrapped his arms around her and bent his head to kiss her neck. "*Much* better," he said, just before his lips found hers in a long, deep kiss.

Jenna relished in the kiss, but just as she was relaxing and giving in to it, an ugly thought burst into her brain, killing the moment. How many other girls had Tiger kissed this way? And how many of those kisses had led to . . . She cringed and instinctively pulled back from him before she could stop herself.

"I'm sorry," she mumbled in answer to Tiger's worried gaze. "I'm okay." But as she started to kiss him again, there were those thoughts again.

"Jenna?" he whispered. "What's going on?"

She met his eyes and suddenly she knew that she couldn't put off talking to him about this anymore. If she did, she'd always feel that she was living in the shadow of his old girlfriend, and she'd never be able to move past it.

"This is terrible," she cried, flopping down on the futon in exasperation.

"What?" Tiger said, sitting down beside her. "The kissing, or my breath? Wow, maybe it's the pizza I had for lunch. I have some Altoids in my desk. . . ."

Jenna found herself smiling in spite of her pounding heart. "No, the kissing is fantastic." She sighed. "It's me. *I'm* the problem." She took a deep breath to steady herself as her nerves roiled, then she met Tiger's gaze. "The thing is that lately I've been thinking a lot more about us, and whether or not I want to, um, well, *be* with you."

"Okay," Tiger said, giving her hand a squeeze. "And what have you been thinking?"

Jenna shook her head as a fiery blush crept across her cheeks. "The truth is, I've sort of been panicking more than thinking." She swallowed thickly and bit her lip. "I mean, you already know what you're doing, and I—I don't have a clue!" She sucked in her breath and let the deluge of questions pour out. "What if I'm not good at it? And what if the other girl you've been with was better than me? And what if . . ." She froze, not being able to get the rest of the words out. "What if afterward, you still wish you were with her instead of me?"

She closed her eyes and dropped her head, not daring to look at Tiger. She wasn't sure she'd ever be able to look him in the eyes again, not after that completely mortifying confession. But then she felt his lips gently press against her forehead, and his arms slip around her.

"Jenna," he whispered. "First of all, there is no comparing you to *any* other girl, because you're one of a kind, and no other girl holds a candle to you."

"But . . . did you love her?" she whispered.

Tiger hesitated, staring at the floor, then finally answered, "Yes, I did, but it feels like forever ago." He took her hand and met her gaze. "And, Jenna, you're the only girl my heart belongs to now."

Jenna opened her eyes and glanced at him doubtfully, but all she saw was complete and total honesty shining out of his eyes. A wave of happiness and relief washed over her as she realized that he meant every single word of what he'd just said. "Thank you," she said quietly. "You saying that means a lot to me."

"Well, you mean a lot to me," Tiger said. "And as for the rest of what you said . . ." He paused to kiss her lightly. "It would be a learning experience for both of us. We'd take one small step at a time. No good or bad, just the two of us sharing something special."

Jenna nodded and exhaled, only then realizing that she'd been holding her breath. All of the nervousness she'd felt leading up to this washed away with Tiger's sweetness.

"That's what I want," she said quietly. "Something special."

"Then it will be," he said. "So . . . are you feeling better about everything now?"

Jenna smiled and nodded. "Much better. And, I think I'm getting closer to being ready." She kissed him, then paused. "But—don't take this the wrong way—your room isn't exactly the type of romantic place I had in mind when I picture my first time. It's not very private and . . ." She took a deep breath. Here went nothing. ". . . it kind of smells."

Tiger stared at her for a second, and then burst out laughing. "Well, if my room reeks, no *wonder* I'm not scoring."

"No offense," Jenna said through her own giggles, relieved that they'd somehow made it through some of the awkwardness of the last few minutes. "But it's true."

"Remind me to pick up some Febreze the next time we're out," he joked, then pulled her to him in a warm, soft cuddle. "I'm so glad you talked to me about all of this."

"Me, too," Jenna said, and she meant it with all her heart.

"And I want to make sure it's as perfect for you as it can be," Tiger said. "We can wait until the timing is right. And in the meantime, I just want to spend time with you. That's all."

Jenna snuggled into the corner of his neck, smiling. "That means everything to me," she said. "Thank you." He'd said just what she'd needed to hear. She'd never felt more comfortable with him than she did right now, resting in his arms.

CHAPTER 7

As Roni waited for the ZZT house meeting to start on Sunday, she did a mental check of the things she needed to go over with Melody tonight. The florist had finally returned from her vacation, and now the centerpieces had been ordered for the tables. Roni'd booked the buses to take everyone to and from Formal, and she'd also made several trips to Party World to scope out possibilities for decorations, but she hadn't completely made up her mind. At least she had some ideas, though.

Melody—surprise, surprise—had done absolutely nothing since the last meeting, and she hadn't bothered to call Roni to check on the status of her progress either. Of course Roni'd come to expect that and, since last week's meeting, had actually been hoping to avoid run-ins with Melody altogether. She didn't think it would be appropriate to butt heads with an older active so soon after she'd been initiated into ZZT, so she hadn't confronted Melody about taking all the credit for the formal planning. Instead, she'd decided to keep moving forward with her own planning and swallow her pride. A small voice inside of her had nagged her to quit being so diligent and let Melody pick up the slack, but her conscience wouldn't let her do that. This was her first ZZT Formal, the first for all of the new actives, and she didn't want anything to jeopardize it.

Now she took a seat with Jenna and Lora-Leigh on the couch in the ZZT living room and scanned through the "Formal To-Do" list on her BlackBerry one last time. At least if Melody did approach her for an update, she'd be ready to prove just how much she'd done, and to prove that she was above holding a grudge. Well, maybe she wasn't completely above holding a grudge, but at least she could put on a good show. Just as she was about to slip her BlackBerry back into her pocket, it buzzed with a new e-mail. She checked the screen, and her heart skipped into double time, a smile spreading on her face.

"A message from your paramour?" Lora-Leigh teased, seeing Roni's smile.

"It's from my dad," Roni said. "I've gotten a couple of pay-checks from my lifeguard job now, so I finally sent him a check for the infamous Amex bill from Morgan's last fall. Look at this."

She held up the screen so Jenna and Lora-Leigh could read it:

To: veronica.van.gelderen@latimer.edu

From: harrison.van.gelderen@vsfpartners.com

Date: Sunday, March 1

Subject: Your check

Veronica,

I must say I'm surprised (and impressed) that you kept your word about paying for your questionable "outing." I appreciate the maturity with which you handled the situation.

With thanks,

Your Father

"With thanks?" Lora-Leigh snorted. "He's about as warm as an ice age, isn't he?"

"But he said thank you," Roni said. "In a convoluted way, I think he's saying he's proud of me."

"He totally is." Jenna smiled, and squeezed Roni's hand. "You just have to look past the legalese tone."

"It feels so great to be earning some of my own money," Roni said. "And I even have some left over from the paychecks for spending money this month. I was thinking maybe I'd splurge on a new dress for Formal. It'd be nice to buy an outfit with *my* money, for a change. Of course I still have a tight budget. . . ."

"Guess we'll have to hit Loehmann's then," Lora-Leigh said. "Discount designer wear for the fashion savvy but financially impaired. I'll go with you whenever you want. Just say the word."

"Okay," Roni said. "Maybe after Greek Week is over and I get most of the formal done. It'll be my reward."

"And you deserve one after dealing with the whole Melody

nightmare," Lora-Leigh muttered. "That girl put the 'meow' in catty."

"Shhh," Roni whispered, mortified by the thought that one of the sisters might overhear them bad-mouthing Melody. "I don't want to be unsisterly."

"And we don't know her side of the story either," Jenna said, as always, ready to jump to anyone's defense.

"I'm over it now, anyway," Roni said, trying to sound convincing.

Lora-Leigh gave her a "yeah, right" look, and opened her mouth to argue, but just then Beverly called the meeting to order, and thankfully, Lora-Leigh had no choice but to be quiet. The meeting flew by in a flurry of announcements about Greek Week. Beverly and Betsy quickly went over the breakdown of the Poseidon teams for each event while Jenna passed out the Greek Week T-shirts. Sandy, Danika, Minnie, and Stacy had all signed up for the tug-of-war; Lora-Leigh, Camille, and Amy Tubbs had signed up for the Twister competition; and Roni, Lora-Leigh, and Jenna were all on the Poseidon softball team and were helping to build the chariot for the chariot race.

"We're playing against the Zeus team in the softball tournament on Thursday afternoon," Lora-Leigh said with a frown, looking at the schedule of events that Betsy had passed around.

"I take it that's not a good thing," Roni said.

"Zeus is made up of Tau Delta Iota, Delta Kappa, and Omega Phi," Lora-Leigh said. "The Tau Delts are the stars of LU's lacrosse and basketball teams."

"But that doesn't mean they can play softball, does it?" Jenna said worriedly.

"They can play *anything*," Lora-Leigh said. "They're born athletes. And the Delta Kappa girls are the biggest tomboys on Sorority Row. I mean, I do throw a mean curveball, but I'm no match for a ΔK girl."

"I don't know how to throw any kind of ball," Jenna said forlornly. "The last time I tried to play baseball was in fourth grade in a mandatory Phys Ed field day. After two strikeouts, I finally hit a grounder, but then I tripped running to first base and broke my wrist." She blushed at the mere memory of it. "And that's when I swore off sports forever, and learned to play the trumpet."

Roni laughed. "But, Jenna, if you don't like playing softball, then why did you sign up for the Poseidon softball team?"

Jenna smiled sheepishly. "Tiger told me he was signing up to play, and I wanted to do an event with him. But now I'm worried I'm just going to humiliate myself."

"So play up the naive, 'I don't know the first thing about sports' card," Roni said. "Ask Tiger to teach you how to catch and throw, and he'll think you're adorable."

Lora-Leigh grinned slyly. "I bet that's not all he'd like to teach you about either."

"Lora-Leigh!" Jenna shrieked, looking by turns embarrassed and horrified.

"Okay, Lora-Leigh, leave poor Jenna alone," Roni whispered as Jenna sent her a pleading look. Lora-Leigh shrugged and quieted, and Roni saw Jenna heave a sigh of relief. Jenna'd already filled in Roni and Lora-Leigh on her chat with Tiger about his past, and even though Jenna was feeling much better about it all, Roni knew that she was still testing out her comfort level with giving up the big V. For now, it was better if Jenna had some time to process without Lora-Leigh's lighthearted teasing.

And luckily, there wasn't a chance for any more discussion about Tiger because just then Beverly announced that it was time to hear the ideas for the ZZT Greek Week cheer. "Okay, y'all," Jenna whispered to Roni and Lora-Leigh, "time to unveil our cheer."

Ashley Nardozzi, Amy Tubbs, and Hollis Hendricks had come up with a cheer set to the tune of "Girls Just Wanna Have Fun," but it was gently rejected when Darcy reminded everyone that the Eta Lambda girls had done something too similar last year for their cheer. Margo and Sue-Marie had created a semi-rap chant based loosely on the lyrics to Beyoncé's "Irreplaceable."

"That works," Roni said, clapping as Margo and Sue-Marie finished.

"Yeah, but it doesn't have the fabulosity that ours does," Lora-Leigh said.

When Beverly gave them the go-ahead, Roni popped the CD she'd burned from her iPod into the living-room sound system, and she, Lora-Leigh, and Jenna stood up and did their "ZZT's Got a Hold on You" cheer. Roni could see the smiles breaking out across the room before they'd even finished, and when the song ended, it was to the unanimous cheering of everyone in the room.

"I think we found our cheer," Beverly said, grinning as Roni sat down again with Lora-Leigh and Jenna. "Great idea, y'all. If your enthusiasm is contagious, then we'll be kicking some serious butt in the cheer competition on Friday night." Then her face grew more serious. "Now, since I think we're well prepared for Greek Week, I have one final announcement to make that's not Greek Week related."

Beverly glanced at Marissa, who was sitting closest to her, ready to step in if she needed any assistance. Marissa gave a subtle nod of approval, and Beverly continued. "Melody has decided to step down as Formal Planner."

Roni could barely keep her mouth from falling open in surprise. What? Had she heard Beverly right? As her stomach lurched nervously, she scanned the room for Melody and caught sight of her in one of the ladies' chairs in the corner, blushing and staring uncomfortably at the carpet.

"What's going on?" Lora-Leigh hissed, nudging Roni.

All Roni could do was shake her head. "I have no idea," she whispered.

"So in light of this news," Beverly went on, "all of the officers have collectively agreed that we'd like to ask Roni, who is currently acting as Melody's assistant, to take over as the Formal Planner for the remainder of the semester." She gave Roni an encouraging smile. "Roni, are you willing to take on this new role?"

Roni tried to clear the questions fogging up her head long enough to answer. "Of course," she finally managed to stammer. "I'd love to do the job." *Especially since I'm already doing it*, she thought.

"Great," Beverly said.

Roni sat in a daze for the few minutes left of the meeting, wondering how this had all happened. But she didn't have to wait too long to get an answer, because as soon as the meeting was over, Beverly motioned to her to follow her into the empty dining room.

"So are you in shock?" she said when they were safely out of earshot of the other girls.

"Completely," Roni said. "Can you clue me in?"

"Well, after you and I talked last week, I decided that I had to do something about the problem with Melody," Beverly said. "I mean, now that I'm President, I have to make sure that things stay fair, you know? But I wasn't sure what to do, so I talked to Marissa, and then she and I talked to Melody."

"Oh no," Roni groaned. "She must hate me."

Beverly put a hand on her shoulder. "Now don't go freaking," she said. "As soon as we asked Melody about it, she fessed up to everything. She wanted to be able to list the ZZT officer position on her résumé for law school. I'm sure she's already told you about her LSAT prep course and how she's up to her eyeballs in prelaw courses right now. She just wasn't prepared for the Formal Planner job. And you were so enthusiastic about the planning from the beginning, she didn't think it would be a big deal if she gave you some extra stuff to do."

"*Some* extra stuff?" Roni repeated. "I guess that got a little out of control."

Beverly nodded. "But she felt terrible about the whole thing, and she volunteered to step down right away. So, are you okay with the workload?"

Roni laughed and shrugged. "Sure," she said. "I've done so much planning already, I'm actually in really good shape for the formal."

"That's what I figured. Such a perfectionist." Beverly gave her a hug. "I'm so glad it all worked out."

Roni smiled. "Me, too." Just then, she caught sight of Melody peeking sheepishly around the door.

"I was wondering if I could talk to Roni for a sec?" she asked Beverly.

"Sure," Beverly said, then waved to Roni and left the two of them alone.

"I just want to apologize for everything," Melody said. "I should never have taken advantage of you the way I did." She sighed. "I didn't mean to, but I was getting so stressed with my classes and internship apps, and you were so willing to help out. I just got carried away."

Roni smiled at her. "It's all right," she said. "I'm just sorry you're so stressed."

"Me, too, but it's self-inflicted," Melody said with a short laugh. "I chose prelaw, and now I've got to suck it up and deal with the insanity of it all. My LSAT practice test is in two weeks. I'm not going to survive."

"Yes, you will. I'm sure you'll ace it, and you'll be completely ready for the real thing when it's time," Roni said sincerely. "And please don't worry about Formal anymore. Let's just forget about the whole thing, okay?"

Melody grinned, looking very relieved. "That sounds good to me."

As Roni made her way out of the dining room, she smiled. It was going to be a great week, and an even greater month. Greek Week would be a blast, and then, before she knew it, the formal would be here. Now that she and Melody had cleared the air, she could move forward with her formal planning without the frustration she'd felt before.

She immediately thought of calling Lance to tell him the good news, and she'd already pulled up his number on her BlackBerry screen when her fingers froze, hovering over the "send" button. She wanted to share this moment with him, but she wasn't at all sure how he'd respond to hearing about another formal minidram. She'd been tiptoeing around the topic with him lately, and maybe now wasn't the best time to bring it up. She hated holding anything back from him, but she didn't want to risk sparking more tension between them again. Making her final decision, she slid her BlackBerry into her pocket and hurried to meet up with Jenna and Lora-Leigh. At least if she couldn't celebrate her victory with Lance, she could do it with her two best friends.

There was no doubt about it. It was going to be the best formal ZZT had ever seen. As the official Formal Planner (got to love that!), she would make sure of it.

Jenna didn't know how long she and Tiger had been out on the dance floor, and she didn't care. Lora-Leigh'd had the great idea to take Roni to Morgan's for a girls' night out to celebrate her "promotion" to Formal Planner, but Jenna'd already had a date planned with Tiger, so Roni and Lora-Leigh told her to bring him along.

Jenna hadn't wanted to mess with the girls'-night vibe, though, until Roni had assured her it was totally fine for her to invite Tiger. "You shouldn't ditch him if you had a date," Roni'd said, and that was all Jenna'd needed to hear before calling Tiger to ask him to join them.

Now she was vaguely aware that somewhere in the background, Roni and Lora-Leigh were dancing, too. But the rest of the room was basically just a blur, and it had nothing to do with alcohol, since neither she nor Tiger had had anything to drink tonight except water. No, her light-headedness was all because of Tiger, pure and simple. All she could think about was the closeness of his body and the electricity she felt bouncing between them. Ever since their talk on Friday, she'd been finding it harder and harder to stop thinking about him, or about *it*. She felt way more comfortable about Tiger's past now, and she knew she was getting closer to being ready. She just wanted to make sure everything would be perfect when she took the leap. But somehow, the fact that the whole *S-E-X* question was on the table made Tiger even more irresistible to her, especially on a night like tonight, when he was looking especially cute and being especially sweet.

"You know I'm crazy about you, don't you?" he whispered into her ear, pulling her closer and pressing his lips lightly to her neck.

"I don't know why, but that's okay. I'm not picky." Jenna giggled. "By the way, if I haven't already said it, thanks for meeting me here tonight. I know we were supposed to have a one-on-one date, but I really wanted to share this night with Roni, especially since things are tense between her and Lance. It means a lot to her."

"You've already said thank you about ten times," Tiger teased. "So I'm going to say for the tenth time that it was no problem.

I don't mind sharing you with your friends. As long as I get to keep these"—he kissed her lips lightly—"to myself."

"Deal." She laid her head on his shoulder and closed her eyes, hating that the slow song they were dancing to was about to come to an end.

As it did, Lora-Leigh and Roni came over.

"Okay, you two lovebirds," Lora-Leigh said. "Time to break it up. Word on the street is there's a party back at DeShawn's dorm, and he just called me to say we're invited. So how about we call it quits here and head out?"

Jenna hesitated. She wasn't in the mood for a loud, crowded party, especially when all she really wanted was to spend a little alone time with Tiger. She glanced at him, trying to read his thoughts. But she didn't have to, because after a second, he said, "You know, I think I'm done for the night . . . all partied out."

He looked at Jenna, and she jumped in with "I'm pretty tired, too." She turned to Lora-Leigh. "Would you mind if we called it quits?"

Lora-Leigh looked from Jenna to Tiger and back again, then smiled slyly. "I see how it is . . . in the mood for a little moonlight mugging, huh? Well, don't let me stand in your way." She waved to them and backed off the dance floor.

"Have fun!" Roni called after them, following Lora-Leigh toward the door.

Jenna blushed at Lora-Leigh's singsongy teasing, wondering what Tiger thought of it all. But he just laughed good-naturedly and waved, then turned back to Jenna with a smile.

"So," Jenna said, "do you want to hang out at the Fox house for a while?"

"Actually, I have somewhere else in mind," Tiger said mysteriously. "I was going to surprise you with it on our date tonight. So, do you want to take a little drive?"

"Sure." Jenna's heart skittered as she wondered at his sudden secretiveness.

But she didn't have to wonder long, because it was only a short fifteen minutes later that Tiger parked his car in front of the Latimer Hilton under a sky full of brilliant stars.

"Here we are," he said, grinning. "We have a suite on the tenth floor with a hot tub and balcony. Ours for the whole night."

Jenna sucked in her breath as her stomach bottomed out. Of all the places she'd imagined Tiger surprising her with tonight, a hotel had never even crossed her mind. "Wh-what are we doing here?" she finally managed to eek out.

A flicker of confusion crossed Tiger's face, and his smile dimmed slightly. "I thought . . . I mean . . ." He ran his hand through his hair nervously. "You said you wanted your first time to be special, and that you didn't want it to be at the Fox house, so . . ."

"So you booked a room at a hotel?" Jenna sighed, biting her lip. "Without talking to me about it first? Why would you do something like that?"

Tiger stared at the steering wheel, his brow furrowing in the moonlight. "I thought you'd be happy." He blew a puff of air out of his mouth in one long, exasperated stream. "I guess I got it all wrong, huh?"

"I said I wanted it to be special," she said quietly, "but I didn't say I was ready yet. I don't know when I'll be ready."

"Oh."

There was a long silence as they sat there, lost in their own thoughts.

"I'm sorry," Tiger finally whispered. "I'd never want you to think I expected it of you. I can wait forever, if that's what you want. I just misunderstood everything."

"It's okay," she said, but it didn't feel okay. Not even close. A mixture of doubt and embarrassment coursed through her as she tried to make sense of where, and how, they'd gotten their signals so crossed. How could she make him understand that because she'd waited so long for this step, when she did take it she wanted it to be on her own terms? Even if she tried to explain it, she didn't know how that would sound to him. "I'm sorry, too" was all she could say now. "Maybe I gave you the wrong impression when we talked before. Maybe I've been leading you on—"

"No," Tiger said firmly, cutting her off. "You haven't done anything wrong. Tonight was all my fault." He leaned over to give her a hug, but his arms around her felt somewhat tentative and awkward.

"No, it wasn't your fault," Jenna said quietly. "I should have been clearer. I just need to think about this . . . to make sure I'm ready for the next step. To make sure it's what I want at all."

Tiger nodded. "Okay. Take all the time you need." He kissed her lightly on the cheek, then turned the car back on. "How about I take you home, and we start over again in the morning, and pretend that none of this ever happened?"

"Sounds good," Jenna said. She let out a sigh of relief as they pulled out of the parking lot, but even as the hotel disappeared from view, she knew she wouldn't be able to pretend that this night had never happened. And neither would Tiger. Now that the whole idea was out there, it was hovering over their relationship like a three-ton elephant, way too big and too awkward to ignore. And it wasn't about to go away any time soon.

Jenna dipped her paintbrush into the can of gold glitter paint, then ran it smoothly across the plywood. She was just about finished painting the carriage of the Poseidon Chariot, and Lora-Leigh was busy adding some decorative flourishes to the sides that had already dried. She and Lora-Leigh had met up with Camille and Darcy at the Fox house on Monday night to help build the chariot for the Greek Week kickoff chariot race on Wednesday afternoon. Stephanie and Jill, two Beta Xi girls, had come over to help out, and they were busy spray-painting chariot helmets and a trident off to the side.

"This is going to look awesome," Jenna said, standing up to walk around the carriage, which, after three hours of work, was really starting to look like something straight out of *Gladiator.*

"Yeah," Darcy said, "with Lora-Leigh as the art director, how could it not?"

Lora-Leigh glanced up from the silver sharks she was painting with intricate detail on the side of the chariot. "I'm feeling especially inspired today. I'm channeling all my nervous energy into my paintbrush. It's amazing what a few sleepless nights can do to the creative mind. I feel like Picasso after twelve espressos."

"So you're still worrying over what to do about FIT?" Jenna asked tentatively, half afraid to know the answer. She knew how much her friend was stressing over her decision. She'd been a little short-tempered and more sarcastic than usual over the last few days, and every morning at breakfast there were circles under her eyes. Now, if Lora-Leigh told her she'd made up her mind to leave LU, Jenna was in serious danger of waterworks in front of everyone. Her nerves were already shot after her über-awkward moment with Tiger last night, and this could potentially send her hurtling over the edge into a Niagara Falls–worthy crying jag.

But much to her relief, Lora-Leigh groaned and said, "I don't think Einstein could've put any more thought into this than I have so far, and I still don't have my decision. All I know is that when I start thinking that this might be my one and only Greek Week ever, I go clammy. But then I think about never getting my chance at FIT, and I have the same reaction . . . a brutal cold sweat." She threw up her hands. "I have one week left to make up my mind, and I'm at a complete standstill." Then she shrugged, like she was shaking away the rest of her thoughts on the subject, and refocused her attention on her painting. "No matter what happens next week, I'm going to treat this Greek Week like it could be one of my last chances to leave my mark at ZZT. Which means this chariot is going to be a masterpiece."

"I'm sure it will be," Jenna said, taking Lora-Leigh's cue and changing the subject.

"It might fall to pieces halfway through the race," Lora-Leigh said, "but I'm going to do everything in my power to make sure it looks amazing before it crashes and burns."

"Be nice, Lora-Leigh," Jenna half scolded. "The guys are trying." She glanced over to the tarp in the driveway where Tiger,

Mark Dickson, and Chris Stevens were arguing over how to mount the racing-bike wheels to the chariot's metal axle.

"Look," Mark was saying. "It's not my fault that the axle is too wide for the wheels. The rule book said we could only spend a max of two hundred on materials. This was the only axle I could find on sale."

"Yeah well, you screw up my Vortex bike wheels, and y'all are toast," Chris grumbled. "I need them back after the race."

Jenna tried her best not to laugh, but it *was* funny. She hid a giggle in the sleeve of her hoodie so that Tiger wouldn't hear. After ending last night with him on a supremely uncomfortable note, it felt good to be doing something with him where they could just relax and have fun. And being surrounded by a dozen other Greeks focused on this project was helping to ease the tension, too. But still, whenever Jenna's eyes met Tiger's, she felt her face flush crimson all over again at the memory of the Hilton. Neither one of them had fully recovered yet, and who knew when they would?

Now, as Tiger clumsily dropped a box of nails on the sidewalk, Jenna caught Lora-Leigh rolling her eyes. "Face it, Jenna, your man might be a cutie, but an engineer he is not." She nodded toward the Sigma Sigma house across the street, where the Apollo Team was welding together a veritable tank of a chariot out of aluminum siding. "Check out the ΣΣ guys. They even have blueprints of their model, for crying out loud."

"Who cares?" Camille said, elbowing Lora-Leigh. "They've won the chariot race for the last two years running, but they bomb in all of the sporting events. I think we're better off with the brawn than the brains, anyway."

"Hey, my guy has brawns *and* brains, and don't you forget it," Jenna said, smiling.

"Aw, Persephone defending her Cupid," Lora-Leigh said. "How sweet."

Stephanie and Jill came over to join them just then, holding the empty can of spray paint in their hands.

"We're done with the helmets," Stephanie said. "Thank God. I'm well on my way to a migraine from the fumes." She sighed, looking down at her hands. "And I got paint all over my hands, too. Do y'all know how I get that off?"

"Paint thinner," Lora-Leigh said, holding up the small bottle of turpentine that was out for the cleanup after they were done.

"I am *not* putting that on my hands," Jill said, eyeing the bottle with disgust. "I just got a manicure yesterday."

Jenna stifled a giggle, remembering what Lora-Leigh had said about the Beta Xi girls. Stephanie and Jill were nice enough, but they did seem a little bit prima donna-ish. Oh well, Jenna was sure they'd still be great teammates in the end.

"Stand back, ladies," a voice said behind them, "and make way for the men with the tools."

"God help us," Lora-Leigh muttered as they turned to see Tiger, Chris, and Mark carrying the wheel and frame toward them. But she shut her mouth after Jenna sent a warning look her way.

The guys were all business, talking about wrenches, screws, and alignment as they worked to secure the axle and wheels to the bottom of the chariot cart. Jenna and the other girls exchanged amused looks as they watched Tiger pinch his finger between the cart and the axle, Mark strip two screws, and Chris try to put the axle on backward. Finally, the guys got the last nut and bolt in place and stood back to admire their work.

"Well," Tiger said, grinning proudly, "how does it look?"

"Great!" Jenna gushed, hoping a little positive reinforcement would let him know that everything was okay between them (or, that everything *would* be okay . . . eventually).

Lora-Leigh snorted into her sleeve, and Jenna guessed she was honing in on the wheels, which were a tiny bit crooked.

"Who wants to take it for a test drive?" Chris said.

Darcy and Jill exchanged a glance and hesitantly stepped forward.

"I guess we will," Darcy said, "since we're the ones who are going to be riding in it on Wednesday."

"Go slow, though, okay?" Jill said as she tentatively climbed into the chariot with Darcy. "The helmets are still drying, so we can't wear them."

Together, the three guys lifted the front of the chariot with the PVC handlebars they'd attached to the frame, and then took off running down the driveway. The chariot wheels wobbled unsteadily, but amazingly, held on. And Jill and Darcy managed to keep their balance in the cart, too, mostly because they were holding on to each other for dear life, half laughing, half screaming. Then the chariot disappeared around the corner of the street.

"I hope they have a last will and testament," Lora-Leigh said, shaking her head.

Jenna was still laughing when she saw Roni coming up the driveway.

"Did you happen to see if my boyfriend was still alive somewhere out there?" she joked, but Roni didn't seem to hear her. She was biting her lip and frowning, lost in her own thoughts.

"Hey," Jenna said, meeting her halfway down the driveway. "Are you okay?"

Roni blinked like she was coming out of a daze. "Oh yeah," she mumbled. "Fine. Sorry I couldn't get here sooner. I worked a double shift at the natatorium since I'm taking off on Thursday and Friday for Greek Week."

"No prob," Jenna said. "We just finished up the chariot and were getting ready to head back to ZZT for dinner."

Roni sighed, plopping down on the front lawn. "After all that, I didn't even get here in time."

"After all what?" Jenna asked, sitting down next to her.

"I saw Lance at the natatorium while I was working," Roni said. "Normally he waits for me after his swim practice, but today I wasn't getting off until later. So he told me he was going to head to the library and study, and then asked me to have dinner with him after I got off work." Her hair was still wet from the pool, and she was twisting a strand of it around her finger absentmindedly. "But I told him I couldn't have dinner because I had to help you guys with the chariot tonight. And that did it. He got this irritated look on his face and told me to forget about dinner—that it didn't matter anyway."

Jenna slipped her arm around Roni. "Are you sure he was mad?"

But Roni just shook her head. "He was. He left without even saying good-bye."

"You know what? He's probably just having a bad day," Jenna said. "He must have been happy when you told him about getting the Formal Planner position, right?"

Roni shrugged. "He didn't say much about it. Actually, he hasn't said much of anything about ZZT stuff lately. But I'll see him in Poli Sci later this week, and he's supposed to come to the Greek Week Talent Show on Saturday night."

"See?" Jenna said. "Everything will be fine. I bet you on Saturday night, he'll be ZZT's biggest fan."

"I hope so," she said quietly, then looked up at Jenna with watery eyes. "I really care about him."

"I know," Jenna whispered. "And he feels the same way."

"Thanks," Roni said. "I needed to hear that." She gave Jenna a small smile. "So, how are things with you and Tiger today? Back to normal?"

Jenna's face dimmed just a bit. "Not really," she said quietly. "I mean, we're fine as long as we pretend like last night never happened. We're just basically avoiding the whole issue right now. I think we're both afraid to bring it up again. And that's okay by me, because I'm not even sure I can go down that road with him now."

"Really?"

Jenna bit her lip. "I was feeling good about everything, until yesterday. Now I'm just totally confused. I feel like he completely jumped the gun, just assuming I'd be okay with anywhere and any time. It made me worry that he doesn't take it as seriously as I do."

"If he cares about you, which I know he does," Roni said, "then he'll take it seriously."

She sighed. "I don't know. After what happened, I feel like he doesn't get it at all." She bit her lip. "How could he think taking me to a hotel would make me happy?"

"Guys aren't always thinking." Roni half laughed. "He was probably as mortified as you were."

"Oh, he was, but it just made me more nervous about everything." She shook her head. "I just wish I could know for sure how things will be afterward."

"Nobody can know that. It's the risk you take going into it." Roni squeezed her hand. "But you'll figure it out. And in the meantime, he's willing to wait, which gives you all the time you need. No pressure."

Jenna nodded, then smiled. "Thanks. *I* needed to hear *that*."

She hugged Roni, then pulled away, gasping as she saw Tiger coming up the driveway with a bent bike wheel under one arm and some broken PVC pipe in the other. Mark and Chris were following behind, carrying the cart, which had miraculously escaped unharmed. Jill and Darcy came last, laughing hysterically, arm in arm.

"What happened?" Jenna asked.

"Apparently, it helps to use more than one screw when attaching an axle to a cart," Tiger mumbled, giving Mark the evil eye.

"Slight oversight on my part," Mark said with a short laugh. "So back to the drawing board."

Jenna looked at Roni, and the two of them burst out laughing. The frown that had etched Roni's face was gone, and Jenna was relieved to be distracted from her thoughts. She only hoped that everything would work out in the end for Roni and Lance, *and* for her and Tiger.

CHAPTER 8

Jenna took a deep breath, adjusted her batting helmet one more time, gave Tiger a weak smile from the dugout, and walked to home plate with an undeniable sense of impending doom. How many times had she warned everyone about her batting skills? And how many times had Lora-Leigh, Roni, Darcy, Tiger, and the rest of the Poseidon softball team assured her that it didn't matter how poorly she played? They'd told her that Greek Week was all about Greek camaraderie and fun. And so far, it had been.

The kickoff chariot race last night had been amazing. More than three hundred Latimer residents and university staff and students had turned out, and the LU Panhellenic Association had announced this morning that already the Greek community had earned more than $3,000 for the Special Olympics from ticket and T-shirt sales. The race had been a blast to watch, and Jenna had never seen anything quite like the insane enthusiasm that each Greek chapter was showing for its team. The cheers, chants, and screams from the sidelines were deafening as each team tried to outshout and outspirit its rivals. War paint, crazy team hats (like the foam sharks the Foxes were wearing for the Poseidon Team), and posters were just some of the things the chapters were using to root for their teams.

Poseidon had come in third place (without losing any wheels or the axle, this time). They'd earned fifty points for the team. They'd also gotten a hundred points for participation, since every member of their chariot team had shown up for the race. But most of the other teams had gotten a hundred points for participation, too, so that was a gimme. The Apollo Team had taken first, thanks to the Sigma Sigmas (for the *third* year running), and Hera had placed second.

Afterward, there'd been a massive tailgate barbecue in the Daniel Stadium parking lot, and Jenna'd had a chance to get to know at least a dozen Greeks she'd never met before. For the first time, it made her feel like she was part of something much bigger than ZZT, and that the whole Greek community shared a sense of kinship.

But now, as she took a few practice swings with the bat, she was worried that that feeling of kinship was about to meet a tragic end. Because no one was going to feel warm and fuzzy toward her when she embarrassed the entire Poseidon Team. They had two batters on base—Abby from Beta Xi was on second and Tiger was on third, trying to get to home plate. It was the top of the fifth, and the Zeus Team was already ahead, 12–2.

"Go, Jenna!" Lora-Leigh screeched from the dugout, and then she and rest of the ZZTs, Beta Xis, and Phi Omicrons on her team crouched down in the dugout to do their Poseidon cheer. Of course, as soon as her team finished, Zeus started up with their cheer, something about being the alpha god and smiting all of the lesser gods in their wake. Jenna's heart was in her throat as she nodded to the Zeus's pitcher, Fiona, to show she was ready.

Fiona launched the ball, and Jenna saw a mass of white shooting straight for her head, first the size of a pea, then an orange, then a watermelon. She squeezed her eyes shut, swung, and—*crack!* She opened one eye, and saw the ball bouncing along the ground, and shooting right between Fiona's legs. Oh. My. God. She'd actually made contact with the ball. She, Jenna Driscoll, the athletic misfit, the band geek, the—

"Jenna!" Lora-Leigh howled, rattling the fence in front of the dugout. "What are you doing? Run!"

Jenna dropped the bat and took off for first base, not stopping until her feet touched the plate, just as first baseman Ben Stevens tagged her with the ball.

"Safe!" the ump cried, and the stands behind the Poseidon dugout went wild. Jenna could just make out Beverly, Sandy, Danika, and Darcy jumping up and down, screaming her name. And there was Tiger jogging to the dugout from home plate, giving her a thumbs-up. Jenna checked the scoreboard and gaped: 12–4. That meant she'd brought home Tiger *and* Abby, scoring two runs for Poseidon. It was nothing short of miraculous, especially for her.

The rest of the inning went by in a blur. Jenna made it to second base, but then Mia, one of the Beta Xis, came up to bat and struck out, making the third out for Poseidon. Jenna jogged over to the dugout, where Lora-Leigh immediately attacked her, rumpling her hair and clapping her on the back, and the rest of the team offered up high fives.

"From Marching Raiders Band Geek to Softball All-Star," Lora-Leigh said. "You should be proud."

"That was great!" Roni said, hugging her. "And you were so freaked before!"

Tiger grabbed her by the waist, kissing her. "Hey, slugger," he said. "Way to play ball." Jenna grinned, relieved that they were still able to share some spontaneous moments without hesitation.

But then Tiger leaned in to whisper, "You keep hitting like that, and I can't be held responsible for my actions."

"Um, thanks," Jenna stammered awkwardly, and just like that, the enjoyment she'd gotten from their kiss was gone. She blushed, a flurry of confused emotions racing through her. Of course she wanted Tiger to be attracted to her, but now she found herself reading much more into every joke he made. Was he getting frustrated that she hadn't made the decision to be with him yet? Were his jokes a subtle way of letting her know that he was more than ready?

Tiger quickly gave her one more peck on the cheek before heading to the outfield for the start of the next inning. Jenna stared after him until Lora-Leigh yelled at her to cover right field, forcing her to focus again. She brushed off the rest of her thoughts about Tiger, grabbed her glove, and hurried to join their team.

She kept her mind on the game after that, but as the innings flew by, Jenna soon realized that her two runs batted in hadn't upped Poseidon's chances of winning. By the eighth inning, the score was 24–4, and Zeus was pretty much already doing a victory dance. But strangely, it didn't seem to matter. Because the worse Jenna and everyone else on the Poseidon Team started playing, the funnier the whole thing seemed. Soon every head-on collision, every missed ball, and every strikeout was only making them all laugh harder. It had to be the worst ball ever played at LU, but their team seemed to be having the best time out of anyone. And when the game was finally over, Lora-Leigh led everyone in a hysterical rendition of "We Are the *Losers*, My Friends."

While the Zeus Team went on to play two more games against Athena and Hermes to determine the tournament champion, the Poseidons met up with the other losing teams at Morgan's. And as soon as they crossed the threshold, it didn't even seem to matter anymore what the Greek letters were on everyone's T-shirts. They were all talking, laughing, dancing, and having a blast. Before Jenna knew it, she had her arms linked with an Alpha Mu and a Psi Kappa Upsilon, singing "Margaritaville" at the top of her lungs. As she sang, she smiled at Tiger, Lora-Leigh, and Roni, who were singing along, too. Jenna knew one thing for certain. If this was only the second day of Greek Week and she was already having this much fun, she couldn't wait to see what the rest of the week would bring.

Lora-Leigh bent into a stretch, touching her toes, and then stood up to inspect the dozen Twister mats stretched out before her on the turf at Daniel Stadium. They'd been liberally doused with several cans of whipped cream just minutes before. She could still make out the colored circles on the mat, but barely.

"Remember, you have to play nice, Lora-Leigh," Camille said. "No shoving the Tri-Os into the whipped cream or anything. We break the rules in the Twister competition, and we automatically forfeit."

"Who said anything about breaking the rules?" Lora-Leigh asked innocently. "I'm just fantasizing about seeing one of them bite it. What's the harm in that?"

She turned toward the sidelines to see Roni, Jenna, Sandy, Danika, and at least a dozen other ZZT sisters cheering them on in the huge crowd.

"This is it, ladies," Lora-Leigh said, huddling with Keesha and Camille. "The fate of Poseidon hangs in the balance. We took first in the tug-of-war and second in the slip-'n'-slide obstacle course, but tanked in the three-legged relay. The Ares Team has the most Greek Week points so far, but we're only a hundred points behind them. If we win Twister and place first or second in the cheer competition tonight and the talent show tomorrow, we might win the whole thing."

Keesha looked doubtful. "But you're up against the Ares Team for this, and they have the Chi Pi Rubberman."

"The what?" Lora-Leigh snorted.

"Rob Jeffries, aka Rubberman," Camille said, motioning to a six-foot-five, skin-and-bones guy jogging in place with the other Ares Team members. "Rumor has it his entire body's double-jointed. He's a senior this year, and he's been the reigning king of the Twister competition three years running."

Lora-Leigh scrutinized Rob, watching his sober face masked with determination.

"He may be a Twister god, but has he ever had a girlfriend?" Lora-Leigh asked Camille.

Camille thought for a sec, then shook her head. "I don't think so. At every mixer we've had with Chi Pi, he's always been a token wallflower."

Lora-Leigh grinned, rubbing her hands together as she plotted. "Then, ladies, I think I've discovered Rob's Achilles' heel."

Camille and Keesha both looked at her with questions in their eyes, but they didn't have time to ask what she meant, because the official Twister referee stepped forward just then to start the competition.

"Everyone take your places!" he ordered. Lora-Leigh took her stand at the edge of one mat next to April, her Beta Xi partner for the game. Keesha and Camille took places at their mats, too, Keesha pairing up with Wes from the Fox house, and Camille with Britney from Beta Xi. Lora-Leigh turned to April, giving her a thumbs-up, and then eyed their opponents. Cheryl from Tri-O had her hair up in a flawless French twist, and Lora-Leigh almost had to laugh. That perfect hair was going to end up snowy white with whipped cream. Whether she knew it or not, poor Cheryl was going down. Rob was all business, even stretching his fingers out as he waited for the ref to spin the Twister wheel. That was until Lora-Leigh winked at him.

"I just love whipped cream, don't you?" she said in her sultriest Demi Moore voice. "It's so much fun to roll around in."

A muffled giggle escaped from April. But Lora-Leigh just smiled, watching as the possibilities sank into Rob's naive mind. The tips of his ears suddenly blushed crimson, and he dropped his eyes to the ground, clearing his throat nervously.

In that moment, Lora-Leigh knew she owned the Twister game, *and* poor, unsuspecting Rob. This was almost going to be too easy, but she would enjoy every second of it.

The ref spun the wheel, starting the tournament with a "Right foot, Green" command, followed by "Left hand, Yellow," "Right hand, Red," and "Left foot, Green."

It took only until the third spin for Lora-Leigh, April, Cheryl, and Rob to get completely tangled, arms and legs twisted, bent, and stretched in every direction. And by the fourth spin, Lora-Leigh found herself with one arm tucked under Rob's shoulder, the other arching over his back, and their faces only inches apart.

Lora-Leigh knew this was the time to make her first move. "Mmm," she whispered. "Do I smell Bvlgari Black?" She moved in closer to his neck. "I love a man with a masculine cologne. *Very* sexy."

A sheepish grin crossed Rob's face, and Lora-Leigh noticed his knees start to shake slightly.

For the next fifteen minutes, Lora-Leigh made sure that every move she made kept her over, under, and around Rob. At about the twentieth spin, April and Cheryl head-butted while they were both moving toward the same yellow circle, and collapsed together into a giggling heap of whipped cream. Lora-Leigh laughed triumphantly when she saw Cheryl's French twist emerge from the whipped cream looking like Andy Warhol's hair. Now it was just between her and Rob.

On the next spin, she pinned Rob just inches away from the Twister mat, her arms and legs balanced on either side of him. She moved her lips toward his, and only stopped when she could smell an Altoid mint on his breath. Sweat was beading up on his forehead, and he was trying in vain to look anywhere but directly at her.

"Well, Rob," she whispered. "I do believe I have you in a bit of a compromising position." She grinned slyly. "Now . . . whatever *am* I going to do with you?"

And that was all it took. Rob sputtered, turning almost purple with embarrassment; his feet slid out from under him, and he landed—*splat!*—flat on his back in a sea of whipped cream.

Lora-Leigh jumped up, shook the whipped cream from her curls, and took a bow toward her sisters on the sidelines, who were all doubled over laughing.

Then, she leaned down to give Rob a helping hand up.

"Good game," she said, offering him a formal handshake.

"Um . . . yeah," Rob muttered, clearly trying to piece together where it had all gone wrong. "Good game." He started to walk away, then turned back toward her. "I don't suppose . . . ?"

"Sorry, but I don't think I'm your type." Lora-Leigh smiled kindly. "But you know, you should really meet my ZZT sister Emma Cox." Emma had just the right blend of brains, sweetness, and innocence to be a great match for someone like Rob. "I think y'all would be perfect together. Look for me at the cheer competition tonight and I'll introduce you to her."

"Sure thing." Rob grinned and waved, then went to rejoin his teammates.

"And that," she said, turning to Keesha and Camille, who were waiting for her, both completely covered from head to toe in whipped cream, "is how you win a Twister game."

"Poor, unsuspecting soul," Camille said, laughing. "He had no idea who he was dealing with."

"But I bet he loved every second of it," Lora-Leigh said as the other girls rushed over to join them.

"Come on, y'all," Jenna said, tugging on Lora-Leigh's arm. "You have to get changed and then we have to practice our cheer one more time before the cheer competition at five o'clock."

"And I need to refuel, too," Lora-Leigh said, patting her grumbling stomach. "Flirting takes a lot out of a girl, let me tell you."

She turned to head back to the ZZT house with the other girls, but as she did, a sudden, sobering thought pierced her mind and went straight through to her heart. If she didn't come back to LU next year, if she went to FIT instead, this would be her first and last Greek Week . . . ever. She'd done some checking since she got her admissions packet and had found out that there was no Greek life at FIT. It was a design school with one goal—to groom students for the fashion industry. And even though Lora-Leigh was sure she'd bond with some great fellow fashionistas, it would be completely different from the social life she'd built here with ZZT.

But in a few more days, she'd have to make a final decision about FIT, one way or the other, and just the thought of that made her skin go clammy and cold. She looked around at her friends, thinking about what a blast they were having at Greek Week, and suddenly she knew beyond a doubt that her college experience would never be the same without them. It didn't matter how many new friends she made at FIT, she'd never equal the sisters she'd found here at LU. Granted, her whole universe wasn't fashion here, the way it would be at FIT, but she'd definitely made a niche for herself, carving out outfits for ZZT and honing her design skills on her own. Against everything she'd ever thought about herself, LU had actually become a part of what she wanted out of her life, a part of her dreams. And even though she didn't have to make up her mind today, she had a feeling her heart already knew the choice she wanted, and needed, to make.

Roni craned her neck in her seat to look toward the back of the Pullman Amphitheater one more time, but there was still no sign of Lance. She turned back to face the stage, where the Foxes were doing a hilarious skit called "The Worst of *American Idol*." Everyone in the audience was laughing hysterically, and Roni was trying to get into the spirit of the Greek Week Talent Show, too; she really was. She didn't want to be a downer, especially since the Greek Week Champion Team was going to be announced when all the points were tallied after the show.

The Poseidon Team was head-to-head with the Ares Team—the Tri-Omegas, Chi Pis, and Alpha Sigmas. Last night, ZZT had placed second in the cheer competition, but they'd won first place for their house banner. Now, if Phi Omicron, ZZT, and Beta Xi could accumulate enough points with each of their talent-show performances, Poseidon had a real shot at the championship. And so far, the Foxes were doing a great job of entertaining everyone.

Heath Carmen and Ty Werther did some hilarious impressions of some of the worst *American Idol* performances. Meanwhile, Jed Nielson was giving bitingly witty commentary in his role as Simon.

But even though there was a smile on Roni's face, and she laughed at all the right moments, waves of disappointment kept washing over her when she least expected it. She couldn't believe that Lance wasn't here yet. Sure, they'd been playing phone tag for the last few days because Roni'd been so busy, going straight from her classes to the Greek Week events. But during the five minutes they'd talked before their Poli Sci class on Monday, he'd told her he would be here. And now it was almost time for ZZT to give their performance, and he was nowhere to be seen.

Even DeShawn had shown up to root for ZZT, and while Roni was happy for Lora-Leigh that he was supporting her, it didn't seem right that he was here and Lance wasn't. Lora-Leigh and DeShawn weren't even a serious couple and he'd still made the effort to come. Which said a lot for DeShawn, and a lot less for Lance.

Roni pulled out her BlackBerry and checked the screen one more time, hoping there'd be a message from Lance saying something—anything—but there were no new calls or messages. She slid it back into her pocket with a sigh just as Jenna gently touched her arm.

"Lance is still MIA?" Jenna whispered, concern showing in her eyes, and Roni nodded. "Maybe he forgot? You could call him. . . ."

But Roni shook her head. "No, now's not the time for that." If he was on his way, calling him would only make her look needy and whiny. And if he wasn't coming . . . Well, she wasn't up for the lengthy conversation she was sure would happen if that was the case.

Lora-Leigh checked her watch. "There's still ten minutes before ZZT goes on. He could make it."

Roni smiled. "I know." It was possible he'd still show up, but Roni's gut told her otherwise.

"Omigod!" Jenna gasped, latching onto Roni's and Lora-Leigh's arms. "Y'all . . . check out Tiger! He's spoofing Sanjaya."

Roni looked up to see Tiger strut onto the stage wearing a wig of dark, curly locks, an acid-washed denim blazer, and torn jeans. He slid across the stage on his knees and began belting out "You Really Got Me" at the top of his lungs. Just then, twenty other Foxes ran onto the stage in drag, screaming and falling all over themselves for Tiger as Sanjaya's tween fans. Roni cracked up along with Jenna and Lora-Leigh.

Everyone in the audience was on their feet, singing and dancing along by the time the Foxes finished their show. Next up were the Tri-Os, and Lora-Leigh groaned as the girls tap-danced onto the stage in top hats, fitted tux jackets, and black stockings for their "Tribute to Broadway."

"I can't watch," she mumbled, edging her way past Roni and Jenna toward the aisle. "ZZT's up next, so I better get backstage to make sure there aren't any costume crises in the making."

"I can't wait to see Naomi, Louise, and Bonni," Jenna said,

already giggling as Lora-Leigh disappeared down the aisle while Roni and Jenna turned back to the show.

The Tri-Os were in the middle of singing "One" from *A Chorus Line,* linked arm in arm and giving perfectly synchronized eye-high kicks.

"They're good," Roni whispered to Jenna.

Jenna nodded. "*Really* good. I don't know if we can beat that."

Roni rolled her eyes as one of the Pi Theta guys tried to jokingly crawl onto the stage to follow the Tri-Os as they danced their way into the wings. "Well, even if the Tri-Os get an awesome score from the judges, I don't think the Chi Pis or the Alpha Sigs did that great. So maybe the final Ares Team score won't be high enough for them to win."

"Fingers crossed," Jenna said, then she and Roni went quiet as the announcer introduced the ZZT skit—"Celebs in Cells."

The curtain opened with Naomi, Louise, and Bonni in their pink jail bodysuits and Britney, Paris, and Lindsay wigs, sipping champagne and eating chocolate-covered strawberries in their cell, which came complete with a chandelier, wall-to-wall carpet, racks of designer shoes and clothes, a TV, stereo, and silver dining cart. They were all singing "Swing Low, Sweet Chariot," and immediately everyone in the audience started howling.

Jenna leaned forward for a closer look. "Are those your shoes, Roni?"

Roni giggled and nodded. "Louise needed some designer stuff for the props, so I offered my shoe collection."

Jenna laughed. "How very authentic."

Louise immediately started off the skit by grumbling, "When are we going to get out of here? I mean—hello!—don't these people know I'm an heiress? My jewelry is absolutely going to *tarnish* in this place, and I miss my Chihuahua."

"Tell me about it," Bonni said, flipping the locks of her red Lindsay Lohan hair over her shoulder. "This ankle band is killing me," she grumbled, flashing the fake diamond-encrusted band she was wearing.

"We're so misunderstood," Naomi said. "I keep telling my lawyer that the whole thing was a mistake. That's all." Then she stripped off her pink coveralls to reveal her ball-and-chain outfit and launched into a hilarious rendition of "Oops, I Did It Again." Louise and Bonni got in on the act, undoing their overalls to reveal the costumes Lora-Leigh had made for them and singing a trio with Naomi of "Tried to Make Me Go to Rehab." As they sang, a dozen other girls from ZZT surrounded them, wearing pink coveralls and singing backup.

Roni couldn't stop laughing at the sight of her friends nailing the celebs' mannerisms and voices and poking fun at them all at once, and she noticed that the crowd thought the whole thing was hilarious, too.

"They're eating this up," Roni whispered to Jenna, but Jenna was too consumed with fits of giggles to answer.

For the final song, Naomi, Louise, and Bonni were having a spa day in their cell while singing a joke version of Paris Hilton's "Stars Are Blind." By the time they finished, the entire crowd was in an uproar.

"I think we have a hit on our hands," Lora-Leigh said as she reappeared to reclaim her seat. "Was it as funny from out here as it was from the wings?"

"Definitely," Camille said, leaning over from where she was sitting behind them to give Lora-Leigh a shoulder squeeze. "And the costumes were amazing. You did a terrific job on them."

"All in a day's work, my friends," Lora-Leigh said, clearly enjoying the compliments. Roni looked over her shoulder and saw DeShawn giving Lora-Leigh a thumbs-up from his seat. And Lora-Leigh beamed a smile back in his direction.

"Now we just have to see what the judges say," Roni noted.

"Oh, I hope they liked it as much as everyone else did," Jenna said.

"What, a perfect performance from a bunch of glamazons like us?" Lora-Leigh said. "How could they not?"

Still, Roni felt an unspoken nervousness spread throughout the three rows of ZZT girls as they waited for the last two acts of the talent show to finish so they could hear the final results. Beta Xi gave the last performance of the night, and Roni thought their free-form dance show that mixed ballet, tap, jazz, and Irish clogging was beautiful, and the tremendous amount of time and effort they'd put into practicing and making their elegant costumes were obvious.

After they finished, there was a brief break while the points from the whole week were tallied, and then Hilary Buckman, the LU Panhellenic Association Greek Week Chair, stepped onto the stage.

Roni held her breath as Hilary took the mike, and she exchanged hopeful smiles with Lora-Leigh and Jenna. This was it. The moment they'd been waiting for. Hilary started by thanking all of the Greek chapters for their participation, enthusiasm, and good sportsmanship throughout the entire four-day event.

"Now, for the results of tonight's talent show," she continued. "Third place goes to the Phi Omicron Chi house for their '*American Idol*' skit. . . ."

Everyone in ZZT and Beta Xi jumped to their feet, clapping and cheering for their fellow Poseidon Team members, and Jenna practically climbed over Roni and Lora-Leigh to get to where Tiger was sitting up front with the Foxes to give him a congratulatory hug.

"Second place," Hilary went on, "is awarded to Tri-Omega for their 'Tribute to Broadway.' "

More deafening cheers broke out from the Ares Team, and Roni applauded politely. "Stop scowling," she said, nudging Lora-Leigh, "it's not good sportsmanship."

"All right, all right," Lora-Leigh said, finally resigning herself to a halfhearted golf clap.

"And finally . . ." Hilary smiled. "First place goes to . . . Zeta Zeta Tau for the most original and creative skit of the evening, 'Celebs in Cells'!"

Suddenly Roni couldn't hear anything except the screaming and clapping of her sisters as they all crushed together for a giant group hug.

"Omigod!" Jenna squealed. "I think that means that we might've earned enough points for Poseidon to win the whole thing."

And sure enough, just seconds later, Hilary gave the total point tallies for each of the Greek Week teams. Apollo came in third with 650 points, Ares second with 775, and Poseidon with a total of 800 points!

The cheering from the Fox, ZZT, and Beta Xi houses was so loud that Roni actually felt the amphitheater floor vibrate. Hilary waited until the celebration had died down before asking the presidents of each chapter to come forward to receive their championship trophy and award.

Beverly, Jimmy, and Cheryl (the Beta Xi President) stepped onto the stage together; they all took a trophy and lifted it proudly over their heads, and another cheer from the three houses was unleashed into the theater.

"As this year's Greek Week champions," Hilary said, "each of your chapters will be given a thousand dollars to put toward the philanthropy of your choice." She smiled and shook each of the Presidents' hands, and then thanked everyone collectively for their efforts. "I'm proud to say that our Greek Week earned over ten thousand dollars for the Latimer Special Olympics. This year's event has been the most successful to date. So please keep up the good work, and keep up the friendships and the bonds you've made with each other during this week. Remember, being Greek isn't just about being a part of your individual chapter. It's about being a part of the whole—a part of a community of service, friendship, and family. See y'all at Greek Week next year!"

The theater erupted into excited chatter and laughter as everyone congratulated one another with hugs and handshakes.

"Way to go, Curly!" DeShawn said, lifting Lora-Leigh off her feet in a massive bear hug. "I knew ZZT would kick ass with you on board."

"How could you expect anything less?" Lora-Leigh said with a coy grin.

Beverly came down the aisle holding the ZZT trophy over her head, and all three Poseidon chapters broke into their cheer, rattling the rooftop. Roni laughed, belting out the cheer at the top of her lungs as she hugged Beverly, Jenna, Sandy, and all her other sisters. It was only when Tiger swooped in, spontaneously dipping Jenna backward in a theatrical victory kiss, that Roni felt a pang of melancholy again. As she watched DeShawn and Tiger hovering over their girls, Roni's awkwardness over Lance's absence grew.

He should've been here with her to share all of this. And now it was too late. He'd missed everything.

"So, who's hosting the after-party, my peeps?" Lora-Leigh boomed so that everyone in Poseidon could hear her, loud and clear. "It's time to celebrate!"

"We should do a pub crawl on the Strip tonight," Tiger said. "Last year, Morgan's and the Lucky Strike offered half-price drinks all night to the reigning Greek Week champions, and they're supposed to do it again this year."

"Music to my ears," Lora-Leigh said. "Let's go!"

She was already halfway up the aisle with a crowd of ZZTs, Foxes, and Beta Xis following. But before Roni could join them, Jenna pulled her aside, worry creasing her face.

"Are you okay?" she asked quietly. "If you don't feel like going without Lance, I'll head back to Tuthill with you and we can just hang there."

Roni gave herself a millisecond mental talking-to to adjust

her downer attitude, and smiled. "Are you kidding? And miss out on all the fun? No way!"

"Do you want to call him real quick before we head over to the Strip?" Jenna asked. "Tiger and I will wait for you."

"Nope," Roni said decisively. "I'm sure he had a good reason for not coming, but I'll find out what it is later. I'm not about to let anything spoil my fun tonight."

Jenna threw an arm around her. "Good. Then let's go before Lora-Leigh starts dancing without us."

Roni laughed, shaking the last drop of disappointment out of her system. As she followed the rest of the Poseidon Team across campus to the Strip, she made up her mind to forget everything else except for their Greek Week victory. Tonight was all about celebrating with her sisters and her newfound Greek friends.

CHAPTER 9

As Jenna hurriedly opened the door to her room on Thursday after class, she had only one thing on her mind, and she blurted it out before she even set down her backpack.

"Have you talked to Lora-Leigh yet?" she asked Roni, who had her nose buried in her Archaeology textbook.

Roni glanced up and shook her head. "No, but it's driving me crazy, too." She sighed, tossing her book to the end of her bed. "I've been thinking about her FIT deadline all morning. Do you have any idea what she decided to do?"

"Of course not," Jenna said. "She still hadn't made up her mind when I talked to her about it before Greek Week started. But you know Lora-Leigh. She doesn't tell all until she's good and ready." She bit her lip. "What if she accepted, Roni?" she whispered, not wanting to say it too loudly for fear of jinxing everything.

"Then we'll be happy for her," Roni said. "We have to be happy for her, if it's what she wants."

Jenna flopped back onto her bed, staring at the ceiling. "I just don't know if I can handle that on top of everything with Tiger."

"Are you still trying to decide what to do?"

Jenna nodded. "And he's been great about giving me plenty of time and space to figure things out. But lately, things have gotten a little weird between us in the making-out department."

"Really? Why?"

Jenna sighed. "Well, first, I've been worried about sending the wrong signals. I don't want him to think I'm leading him on, so I've been a little cautious. But he's super careful with me now, too, very polite and always asking if I'm okay. Like last night when we were hanging out in his room, we kissed for a while, and then he was the one who stopped. That's *never* happened before." She felt her worry increase even as she talked about it with Roni. On the surface, everything between her and Tiger kept moving along just like always, wonderful and fun. But underneath, she felt this current of awkwardness, and she couldn't help feeling it was her fault. "Do you think it's normal for Tiger to pull back a little bit, or is he getting frustrated that I haven't made up my mind yet?"

"Don't even think that," Roni said. "If he did lose his patience, then he's not the type of guy you'd want to be with anyway, right?"

"Right."

"I think what Tiger's doing makes sense. It's got to take a lot of discipline to draw the line when you've been down that road before, you know?"

Jenna nodded. "I guess I never thought about it that way. But maybe he is just trying to respect my wishes."

"I know he is," Roni said, giving Jenna's hand a squeeze. "He's a great guy and he'd do anything for you."

Jenna smiled, knowing in her heart that it was true. "I'm so tired of worrying about this. I just want to forget about all the what-ifs and let my heart decide."

"Then that's the way it will happen for you," Roni said. "All of a sudden you'll forget to be scared, and everything will fall into place."

"I hope so," Jenna said, but then suddenly, all of her worries about Tiger flew out of her head as she caught sight of Lora-Leigh peeking around their door. "Omigod, Lora-Leigh, where have you been?" she cried, jumping up to drag her friend into the room. "Don't you know you're torturing us with all this suspense?"

Lora-Leigh grinned. "You know I'm all about dramatic effect." She dropped her bag and stretched out on the floor. "Besides, I had some important business to take care of this afternoon."

Jenna's heart sank, but she bolstered herself and put on her best encouraging smile for her friend. She took a deep breath and said, "So you *did* send in your official acceptance letter?"

Lora-Leigh paused. "Mmm, not exactly." She dug through her bag and pulled out several sheets of paper. "I'm going to send this instead, as soon as y'all read it for me."

Jenna and Roni exchanged a questioning look, but then Jenna took the papers from Lora-Leigh and scooted next to Roni on her bed to read them. Her heart stopped at the first few words on the page.

After much thought and careful consideration, Lora-Leigh had written, *I've decided to decline your offer for admission to FIT.*

"What?" Roni gasped, her eyes jumping to Lora-Leigh's face. "Are you sure this is what you want?"

"Just keep reading," Lora-Leigh ordered.

Jenna bent her head over the letter again, reading the next paragraph, where Lora-Leigh requested a three-year deferral of admission.

I know this is a highly unusual request [Lora-Leigh explained in the letter] *but my reasons for making it are well founded and heartfelt. In the past, attending FIT was the only dream I had for myself, but this year, that's all changed. Now my dream revolves around Latimer University as well. I'm a part of something special here, something that goes beyond my love for fashion. Here, I have a love for my school, my sorority, and my Zeta Zeta Tau sisters. My passion for fashion will never fade, and neither will my dream of attending FIT. But for the next three years, my commitment is to Zeta Zeta Tau and my undergraduate education. I don't want to give that up, and it's my hope that I won't have to. So, if there is any way I can achieve both my dream of finishing my time at LU and my dream of later attending FIT, I would consider myself very fortunate. And I know that I will bring even more to FIT as a graduate of LU and a member of ZZT than I can right now.*

"Wow," Jenna said quietly as she finished reading. "I had no idea you felt that way, Lora-Leigh."

"I didn't either," Lora-Leigh said, "until I started thinking about what I would be leaving behind if I started FIT right now.

But this way, I'm not giving up on FIT either. Who says a girl can't have it all, especially a girl with my taste in clothes?" She smiled. "So does the letter sound okay?"

Jenna looked at Roni, and they both nodded.

"It's perfect. It says everything it needs to," Roni said. "But . . . do you think they'll really let you defer?"

Lora-Leigh thought for a minute, looking more serious than Jenna had ever seen her. "I don't know," she finally said. "But this feels right, so I have to go with it. And hope for the best."

"We'll hope for you, too." Jenna wrapped her arms around Lora-Leigh in a big hug. "But in the meantime, am I allowed to say how glad I am that you're not leaving? At least, not leaving yet?"

"Me, too!" Roni said, getting in on the hug.

"Pour it on, ladies." Lora-Leigh laughed. "You know I love hearing how completely indispensable I am."

Jenna slugged Lora-Leigh playfully with a pillow, relishing the relief she felt that Lora-Leigh was staying. She had to hand it to her. Lora-Leigh was one huge risk taker, and Jenna hoped it would pay off, for her sake. She just wished that she could be more like that sometimes, throwing caution to the wind and living in the moment. But maybe she could, after all . . . with someone like Tiger.

Lora-Leigh smiled proudly as she watched Jenna get to her feet with the rest of the trumpet section to belt out the fanfare to the Mozart concerto they were playing. She'd thought the Marching Raiders Band was impressive marching onto the field at Daniel Stadium, but that was before she heard the Raiders

Concert Band play in the Pullman Amphitheater on Thursday night. The concert band was half the size of the marching band, but with the benefit of a string section that had a more sonorous, less brassy sound. The concert band focused on classical pieces, and with the impeccable acoustics in the amphitheater, every piece rang out richly and beautifully. When Jenna'd invited Lora-Leigh and Roni to the spring concert, Lora-Leigh'd expected a good performance, but nothing this notable.

The concerto ended on a unified note, and everyone in the audience was immediately on their feet giving thundering applause. Lora-Leigh whistled loudly from the front row, laughing at Roni's look of mortification when Tiger, on the other side of her, joined in.

"Come on, Boston," Lora-Leigh said. "You know that performance deserves way more than hoity-toity clapping."

Roni just shook her head, laughing, then they both turned back to the stage to see a beaming Jenna, looking beautiful in her simple black wrap concert dress, taking a graceful bow with all the other band members before she headed offstage.

"I'm going to meet her backstage," Tiger said, barely able to edge by them with the two dozen white roses he was holding in his hand. "We'll see y'all in the reception area in a few, okay?"

Lora-Leigh and Roni nodded, and they watched him hurry toward the theater wings with the roses.

"They make such an adorable couple," Roni said, smiling after him. "I can't believe he brought all of those roses for her."

"Seriously"—Lora-Leigh snorted—"between her and Tiger and you and Lance, there's a whole lot of lovin' going on around here."

Lora-Leigh laughed, but only until she saw Roni bite her lip, worry suddenly sprouting on her face. "God, I'm sorry, Boston. I forgot about the current sitch with Lance."

Roni smiled faintly. "Don't worry. It's not that things are bad between me and Lance. It's just that since the whole Greek Week no-show last weekend, he's been a little removed. It's because he's so stressed out about his classes right now, poor guy."

"I'm sure that's the prob," Lora-Leigh said, trying her best to sound completely convinced, even though her mind was flashing out a WARNING signal of the trouble she was afraid was looming on the horizon for Roni. After they'd recovered from the post–Greek Week bar crawl, Roni'd called Lance first thing Sunday morning. And of course Lance had immediately started apologizing, saying he'd been in Hades (the student-dubbed nickname for the Helman University Library) all day Saturday studying for a big Anatomy quiz on Monday. Apparently, even though midterms had just ended, Lance's Anatomy prof was so unhappy with the grades that he'd decided to quiz everyone on the parts of the test they'd done the worst on. Lance had completely lost track of time studying and had fallen asleep in one of the reading cubes, only waking up at midnight when one of the security guards told him in not-so-gentle terms that they were closing and that he needed to "depart the premises." Roni'd immediately forgiven him and spent most of the afternoon on Sunday at his dorm, quizzing him to prep for the test.

But Lora-Leigh had a sneaking suspicion that Lance hadn't forgotten a thing. He was way too conscientious for that. No, she was pretty convinced that he was pulling a passive-aggressive maneuver because he had absolutely no interest in Greek Week. Not that she would say that to Roni. No, she didn't believe in messing with other people's love lives, especially when it came to a best friend. Roni was such a complete goner for Lance, there was no way Lora-Leigh was going to tread on that paper-thin ice.

Even now, as they made their way out of the theater and into the reception area in the foyer, Roni was gushing on and on about Lance, saying, "I would never have the guts to do what he's doing on the premed track. It's insanity, and it'll only get more stressful and more time-consuming the further into his science courses he gets. Next year he'll have to take Organic Chem." Roni cringed. "Do you know that last semester two people at LU had nervous breakdowns from that class? No wonder Lance is feeling so pressured."

Lora-Leigh just nodded, but it seemed to her that Roni was trying way too hard to justify Lance's behavior. "Well, I'm sure he's going to be completely back to normal now that his quiz is out of the way," she said finally, wanting to be as supportive as possible. "Plus, spring break is next week, so he'll be able to relax and take a break from studying for at least a little while. Is he going anywhere?"

Roni shook her head. "He's staying here to study, poor guy."

"Hmm, sounds like masochism to me," Lora-Leigh joked. "I'm still bummed that we're not going with the ZZT seniors on their trip to the Bahamas. Why is it that seniors have all the fun and us lowly, financially impaired freshmen have to settle for visits with our families or anticlimactic day trips?"

Roni laughed. "We'll get our turn at an awesome trip when

we're seniors at ZZT, too. Just be glad we'll all be together at spring break. We'll still have a good time relaxing at the pool and catching up on our z's. I just wish Lance would cut himself some slack and spend some of next week relaxing, too. I mean, he already had to cancel our trip to Palm Beach this weekend."

"Well, y'all are going out tomorrow night, right? With a little TLC from you, he'll be fine, and y'all will be back to your sickeningly cute and cuddly selves by Formal."

"I think so." Roni smiled, relief spreading over her face. "But we'll try to control ourselves for your sake."

Lora-Leigh snorted. "That's nice of you, but don't you worry about me. As soon as I say congrats to Jenna, I'm meeting up with DeShawn at the Cadillac Bar to see if he wants to be my date for Formal. Who knows? Maybe we might even allow ourselves a little PDA at the dance, too. Nothing like mugging with a hot jock to get you in the mood for dancing."

Just then, Jenna and Tiger appeared in the foyer, Jenna radiating happiness as she floated over to them cradling her roses in her arms.

"What did y'all think?" she asked. "Did we sound all right?"

"You sounded like the freakin' New York Philharmonic," Lora-Leigh said, hugging her. "No, even better than that."

"Thanks," Jenna said. "But you know what's really amazing? After our fanfare, Heidi, our section leader, was chatting with me, and Papa Skank came over to us and said, and I quote, 'Not bad, Driscoll. Not bad.' I think I've finally cracked his armor."

"Good. Then he'll know to watch out for Jenna Driscoll, trumpet player extraordinaire."

Jenna blushed, and Lora-Leigh knew she'd enjoyed the compliment, even if she was still petrified of Papa Skank. The four of them moved to the refreshment table for cookies and drinks, and Jenna introduced them to a few of her band friends. But after about fifteen minutes, Lora-Leigh grabbed two cookies for the road, hugged Jenna one more time, and made her exit to meet up with DeShawn.

It took her only a few minutes to walk from the campus to the Cadillac Bar at the end of the Strip. She spotted DeShawn the second she walked through the old-fashioned swinging saloon doors. He was shooting darts in the back between swigs of Corona, waiting for her.

She grabbed a stray dart that had fallen on the floor, snuck up behind him, and shot, bull's-eyeing it right in the middle of DeShawn's board.

DeShawn swung around and grinned. "Nice aim, Curly."

Lora-Leigh gave him a quick, teasing kiss. "Can you beat it?"

"You know it," DeShawn joked. "But I've got all night to beat you at darts. And right now I'd rather watch you do that again." He handed her a set of blue darts and he took the red ones. "So, you said you had something you wanted to ask me when you called me earlier. What's up?"

Lora-Leigh shot one of her darts, bull's-eyeing a second time, and DeShawn gave a low whistle. "Dang, girl, that's a good eye."

"It spotted you, didn't it?" she joked, then went for a third, knocking the first two out of the bull's-eye with the single shot.

"You are a goddess," he said, catching her around the waist.

"And you find me irresistible."

"Always have, always will," he said, playfully kissing her neck.

"And you'd do anything for me," she said.

DeShawn smiled. "Yes, I'd do anything for my girl. You know that."

"So, you'll be my date for the ZZT formal on April twenty-sixth?" she said, her heart accelerating as she finally asked the question. Even though she and DeShawn were seeing each other pretty regularly now, she still felt a stab of nervousness as she waited for a response. This wasn't just one of their casual dates; this was heading toward a more serious, couple-y place. A place she realized she might really like to go with him.

"Oh, Curly, you're going to kill me," he said, shaking his head.

"What?" Lora-Leigh said, immediately shifting into chill mode as a defense mechanism. "Wait, don't tell me. You've already got a date with your other irresistible girl, right?"

"You'd kill me for that, too," DeShawn said, giving a small laugh. "No, the twenty-sixth of April . . . I'll be in New York for the draft. I leave earlier that week." He tugged at one of her curls and tucked his hand under her chin, briefly brushing his thumb over it. "I'm sorry. You know I would've been there in my penguin suit and everything, if I could."

Lora-Leigh smiled, immediately pushing the disappointment she felt as far down inside her as she could. She wanted to be happy for DeShawn now, for what he had going for him, and that meant forgetting all about throwing herself a pity party. "Hey, no prob," she said, giving his arm a squeeze. "The draft is way more important than keeping me company for one night. I can't believe you're going to be on television. The second you flash those pearly whites on national TV, girls all over America are going to be clamoring for tickets to your first Green Bay Packers game."

"That's only if they draft me," he said quietly. "All the NFL College Advisory Board could tell me is that I'm expected to go in the first round."

"The first round? Kudos!" She hugged him. "But you're going to miss seeing me in the to-die-for dress I'm making for Formal, so eat your heart out."

"I'll just use my imagination." DeShawn winked. "It's an incredibly dirty thing."

She laughed. "I'm proud of you, you know that? Nothing's stopping you from going after your dream, and you're going to make it."

"And what about your FIT dream?" DeShawn asked. "Why haven't I heard you mention that more lately?"

Lora-Leigh stared at the darts in her hands, not sure what he would say about the news she was about to tell him. "That dream's on temporary hold," she said quietly. "I decided to ask for a deferral of admission so I could finish out my undergrad work here. I'm waiting to hear back from them with an answer."

DeShawn let out a low whistle. "Now that's some kind of gutsy, Curly. Only you would take a risk like that."

"You don't think I should've?" she asked quietly, her stomach knotting up with second guesses.

"If that's what you want, then you *absolutely* should've," DeShawn said, looking at her with a seriousness that was rare for him. "And I hope you get everything you're asking for. You deserve it."

"Thanks," she said with a relieved smile. It was great to have him rooting for her. She'd take all the moral support she could get right now. Then, to break the serious mood settling over her at the thought of what the next few weeks held in store for both of them, she held up the darts in her hand. "So, are you going to show me what you're made of, or what?"

"I thought you'd never ask," DeShawn said. "Bring it on."

As DeShawn threw his first dart, Lora-Leigh watched him, and suddenly she realized this might be one of the last times she'd be able to hang out with him like this. The thought made her feel a strange mixture of sadness and happiness, all at once. She'd miss him, of course, probably more than she'd ever let him know. But she was so glad he was getting this chance. Now all she could hope was that she'd get her own chance—at FIT.

Jenna flopped back onto her pillows and began flipping through the *Southern Gourmet* cookbook Tiger had given her last semester, trying to decide which recipe she should try out. Since she had the highest grade in her Culinary Arts 101 class, she'd finally decided that she could cook a fab meal for Tiger without risk of setting something on fire (or giving him food poisoning). And, she'd been thinking she'd cook it for him before Formal as a surprise. She had a couple of surprises in mind for that night, and she thought a quiet dinner would be a great start to the evening.

She could cook everything beforehand in the LU Culinary kitchen, which was open outside class hours for students to drop by for hands-on study and experience, and then surprise Tiger with it. She'd been practicing some of the recipes in her cookbook already, and she'd perfected two: braised beef with bourbon-Roquefort sauce and shrimp and scallops Mornay. She was leaning toward the shrimp dish, especially because she knew Tiger was a huge seafood fan, but she wanted everything about formal night to be absolutely perfect. As she looked over the recipes again, she heard Roni mutter a barely audible curse word and toss another outfit onto her bed. Apparently, Jenna wasn't the only one having trouble making decisions today.

"Still can't find something to wear for your date with Lance tonight?" Jenna asked as Roni collapsed onto her bed next to Lora-Leigh, who was busy skimming through the address book on her cell phone.

Roni rubbed a hand over her eyes. "It's not the clothes that are the issue," she said wearily. "It's me. I'm completely freaked out. I just want everything to be okay between me and Lance." She looked at Jenna and Lora-Leigh, and Jenna could see the panic in her eyes. "What if it's not?"

"I'm sure it will be," Jenna said, sitting down next to Roni and slipping an arm around her. "He called you this morning, didn't he?"

Roni nodded. "But he didn't sound right. He sounded all businessy. He said he just wanted to 'touch base' about tonight in this real polite tone. I know that tone. It's the one my mom always uses when she's setting up a lunch with Jeanette Charlton, and she *loathes* Jeanette."

"Maybe he's just in a study delirium," Lora-Leigh offered. "You know, where your brain is so completely drained that all you can do is stare off into space and mutter incoherently."

Roni gave a short laugh. "Maybe." She eyed the pile of clothes on her bed. "I just wanted to wear something tonight that made me feel incredible, you know? For good luck."

Lora-Leigh's eyes lit up, and Jenna could practically see her mental wheels turning. "Brainstorm!" she said, jumping off Roni's bed and racing to the door. "I'll be right back."

Roni raised a questioning eyebrow at Jenna, but all Jenna could do was shrug. "Who knows what she's up to?" she said. "I've learned not to question."

Less than two minutes later, Lora-Leigh reappeared in the doorway, out of breath but grinning triumphantly. "Here it is, the latest Lora-Leigh creation." She held up a cinnamon-colored satin wrap top.

"That is glamtastic!" Jenna squealed. "Roni, you *have* to wear it."

"Even though you're taller than me, it should still fit you," Lora-Leigh said. "And the color . . . *très tois*, girl friend. You can pair it up with that black Chloé pencil skirt you have."

Relief and delight flooded Roni's face as she ran her hand over the top. "Really? I love it."

Lora-Leigh nodded. "Anything to ward off your depressimistic attitude. Put on the top. But there's a catch."

"Uh-oh," Roni said. "I'm not sure I like the sound of that."

"Oh, it's not that bad, Boston. You get to wear the top, but you have to help me conjure up a date to Formal. DeShawn's going to be MIA, and my little black book's running on empty." Lora-Leigh held up her cell phone and grimaced.

"Any chance your high school friend Brian can be your date?" Jenna asked.

"I wish, but he's stationed in San Diego now," Lora-Leigh said.

"Okay, no prob," Roni said, already slipping on the top and skirt. "Maybe one of Lance's swim-team buds. Most of them have girlfriends, but . . ."

"Story of my life," Lora-Leigh muttered. "I'm not looking for my Prince Charming. Just a guy to hang with for the night."

"There's Lance's friend Ian," Roni suggested. "He's super sweet, and he's very original."

"Original is promising," Lora-Leigh said, "but please define. I need the mental picture."

"Well . . ." Roni hesitated. "Okay, so he's obsessed with Harry Potter."

"How obsessed?"

"Um, well, he had the lightning-bolt scar henna-tattooed on his forehead."

"What . . . for Halloween?" Lora-Leigh asked.

Roni giggled, then shrugged. "For the release of Rowling's last book."

Lora-Leigh rolled her eyes. "Okay, moving on . . ."

"Hey, what about Mark Dickson from the Fox house?" Jenna asked. "Y'all are good friends."

Lora-Leigh sighed. "Sadly, Mark is dating one of the Beta Xis now, and rumor has it it's getting serious. I heard he's thinking of giving her his Fox pin at the Beta Xi Formal. And she's one of those girls who doesn't believe guys can be 'just friends' with girls, so Mark has steered clear of me ever since."

Jenna tapped her fingers against her *Southern Gourmet* cookbook, thinking. "What about one of the other Foxes, then? Tiger has a lot of single friends, and I'm sure one of them would be happy to go with you."

"No way," Lora-Leigh said, snickering. "Trying on a Fox blind date for size while you and Tiger, LU's sweethearts, stare dreamily into each other's eyes all night? No offense, but that much love in the air would suffocate me."

"Sorry," Jenna said. "I didn't even think we'd been that mushy in front of y'all the last few weeks. We've been a little cautious with physical stuff lately." She blushed. "But I think everything's going to be much better by Formal."

"Oh?" Lora-Leigh said, leaning forward with an expectant smile. "And pray tell, why is that?"

Gauging by the heat radiating from her cheeks, Jenna was sure her face was a cherry tomato by now. "I've been thinking," she started, then took a deep breath. "I've been thinking that on the night of Formal, Tiger and I would—" She broke off, not able to say the words out loud.

"Seal the deal?" Lora-Leigh said, clapping. "Kudos, girl friend! Now that'll definitely be a night you'll remember."

"I hope so," Jenna said.

"That's great," Roni said, giving Jenna a hug.

"Well, now that I know that, there's absolutely no way I'm going to interrupt your plans for romance by tagging along with another Fox. Talk about killing the mood." Lora-Leigh snorted. "Besides, I'd rather go with a friend than play the whole 'Getting to Know You' game all night."

"I know!" Roni said. "Chris Segalini or Ben Bowden!"

"The Phi Kappa Eps of drunken infamy from the Mississippi game?" Lora-Leigh laughed. "I guess either one of them would be fine, as long as I kept him to a three-drink maximum for the night. And I'd be guaranteed a fun time with a PKE guy, that's for sure. I'll give Ben a call first, and if he can't, then I'll call Chris." She nodded approvingly. "A Plan A and a Plan B. Good thinking, Boston."

"Thanks." Roni slipped on a pair of Louboutin black sling backs and twirled for the girls. "So, how do I look?"

"Eat your heart out, Rachel Bilson." Lora-Leigh gave her the thumbs-up. "You have no chiqual."

"Lance will be speechless," Jenna seconded.

"Here's to hoping," Roni said, crossing her fingers. "I just want us to have fun, that's all." Then she glanced at the clock on her dresser. "Oh, I better go! He's probably downstairs waiting for me already." She grabbed her purse and headed for the door, and Jenna and Lora-Leigh waved after her.

Once the door was safely closed, Jenna let out a sigh. "Roni's been so worried about things with him lately. She really deserves a good time tonight. I hope they have fun."

"Me, too," Lora-Leigh said. "But I have a bad feeling about it, power outfit or no."

Jenna didn't want to be negative, so she kept quiet. But as much as she tried to deny it, the fact was that she had a bad feeling, too. And she just hoped that at the end of the night, she and Lora-Leigh would both be wrong.

Roni took a bite of her chicken Parmesan and focused on chewing so she wouldn't have to think about the awkwardness that she and Lance had been sludging through for the last hour. The conversation between the two of them had consisted of Roni running at the mouth, trying desperately to make up for Lance's long stretches of silence, and the effort it was taking to keep her smile in place and pretend that everything was okay was exhausting. And Lance wasn't doing much to ease the tension. He was intently focused on his food, had barely made eye contact with her all night, and the only PDA he'd shown her so far was the polite peck on the cheek he'd given her when she'd hopped into his car. Roni had been on some uncomfortable dates before, but this was starting to get downright painful.

She'd already tried giving him the recap of Greek Week and asking him about his swim meets, but he only answered in monosyllables or nods of the head.

Making a last-ditch effort to lure him out of his cave, she gave up completely on her chicken Parm and said, "So, all the plans for Formal are finally done. I bought the last of the decorations yesterday. The T-shirts came in, too, and they look amazing, thanks to Lora-Leigh. Now all I have to do is sit back, relax, and enjoy dancing with you all night." She flashed a flirty smile and slid her hand over his. "And I should warn you, I dance even better than I swim. Think you're up to the challenge?"

She waited for a smile to flash across his face, but instead, he sighed and slipped his hand out from under hers.

"Okay," Roni said, leaning forward to meet his eyes. "I give up. I've been carrying on a one-way conversation for the last hour." She threw up her hands. "Can you *please* tell me what's going on?"

Lance stared at the tablecloth, shrugging. "I'm just sick of hearing it."

"What?"

"Greek Week, Formal, drama with Melody, mixers, chapter meetings . . . all of it." He sighed, running his hand over his forehead in frustration. "ZZT is all you talk about, all you think about. Every time I want to go on a date with you, we have to work around the ZZT schedule of social events. And when we do go out, you can't stop talking about ZZT. It's just getting a little old, that's all."

Ron stared at him, shaking her head in disbelief. "But I've tried to tell you how important ZZT is to me," she said. "It's just like the way you feel about the swim team. You love every second you're in the water or hanging out with the guys."

"It's not the same," Lance said. "The swim team *is* important. I have to practice as much as possible to stay on top of my game. When I hang out with the guys, half the time we're working out or training. Of course I take it seriously. It's not some sort of joke sport like whipped-cream Twister or a bunch of socializing—"

"Is that what you think ZZT is?" Roni frowned, bristling in defense at his words. "You really think it's all just a joke?"

"No, I'm not saying that," Lance said. "I know your friends are important to you. But you treat ZZT like it's the be-all and end-all of your existence. You don't devote this much time and energy to our relationship or to your classes, and your education should be the real reason why you're here at Latimer anyway. Working on the debate with you was totally stressful because you were so wrapped up in formal planning that half the time you forgot to do your part of the research. You won't even go out for the swim team next year because you're so afraid it might interfere with your ZZT stuff."

Roni stared at her plate, her unfinished meal swimming in front of her as she fought back tears of anger and hurt. "For the record," she said icily, rage tightening her throat, "I'm doing great in my classes. And you devote just as many hours to your swimming and your studies as I do to ZZT. I've been understanding of your priorities, so I'm not sure why you have such an issue with the way I choose to spend my free time. Plus, you don't have a clue how much I've worried about our relationship over the past few weeks. You think I didn't notice every time you got annoyed when I mentioned ZZT? You think I didn't feel you rolling your eyes behind my back when I stressed over the problem with Melody and Formal?" She latched onto his eyes with hers, almost daring him to look away, but he didn't. "I needed support from you, and all I got was irritation."

"That's not true," Lance started, the frown on his face softening a bit. "I just wanted you to relax and be happy. . . ."

"Yeah, well, if that was the case, you had a weird way of showing support." She stood up from the table. "I'm tired of always feeling like I have to censor what I say about ZZT to keep you happy. If you can't accept what ZZT means to me, then you can't accept me for who I am. And I don't want to be with someone who doesn't support me, or want me to be happy."

Lance stared at her, surprise and hurt reflected in his eyes. "So what are you saying?" he asked quietly.

Roni took a deep breath, torn between what she was about to say—what she needed to say—and what her heart wanted her to do. "I'm saying I don't think this is working anymore. ZZT will always be a big part of my life, and if you can't handle that, then we shouldn't be together."

"Roni," Lance started, "I—"

"I'll be waiting outside," she said, cutting him off for fear of falling apart right there in the restaurant, in front of everyone. She spun on her heel and wound through the sea of candlelit tables, forcing herself to hold her head up high and walk slowly and graciously. There was no way she was going to let Lance see her crumble. That was one thing she could silently thank her parents for tonight. The Van Gelderens always knew how to make a stately exit, no matter how awkward or uncomfortable the circumstances. Thankfully, a few deep breaths of the fresh night air cleared her head long enough for her to hold it all together while she waited for Lance to pay the bill and join her at the car.

"Take me to the ZZT house, please" was all she said when he opened the car door for her. He just nodded, looking slightly sheepish and down in the mouth himself.

The rest of the ride through Latimer was silent, and Roni pressed herself against the car door, staring out at the lights of campus and wishing she could will the car to go faster. The minutes ticked by painfully, and as they did, she chanted in her head, *Don't cry, don't cry, don't cry.*

And finally, at long last, Lance slowed the car, bringing it to a stop in front of ZZT. Roni glanced toward the glass door in the front porch of the house, lit up invitingly with beams of yellow light. Inside were her friends, her sisters. She needed them more now than ever before.

She turned to Lance, giving him a small, brave smile, and, with the last ounce of Van Gelderen pride and grace she could muster, said, "Thank you for the last few months. I enjoyed every moment of the time I spent with you."

And with that, she stepped out of the car and climbed the steps to ZZT. It was only when her hand was on the door handle, and she heard Lance pulling away, that she allowed the first tear to fall.

When Roni walked into the ZZT living room, she saw Lora-Leigh, Jenna, and Camille all huddled around half a dozen *Cosmos* and *Vogues*, laughing and chatting happily as they skimmed through the pictures of dresses, flagging styles they liked as possibilities for Formal. It took less than five seconds for Jenna to glance up, startle at the tears trickling down Roni's cheeks, and rush to her side.

"What happened?" she asked, pulling Roni into a hug before Roni could even open her mouth.

Roni just shook her head, afraid to speak with her tears coming fast and furious now. She let Jenna lead her to the couch, where she collapsed into the cushions next to Lora-Leigh and Camille. Camille was already busy offering her tissues, and Lora-Leigh was already wearing her battle-ax scowl.

"What did Lance do?" she said. "That jerk. I *knew* he wasn't good enough for you. . . ."

"Calm down, Lora-Leigh," Jenna said as she kept her arm tightly wrapped around Roni's shaking shoulders. "We haven't heard the story yet."

"Yeah, well, I'm going to kick his ass anyway."

"Shhh," Camille said. "Roni will tell us when she's ready."

Lora-Leigh grunted, but held her tongue. Roni gave in to the crying, forgetting all about the fact that a Van Gelderen was never supposed to appear sniffling, red-eyed, and sobbing in front of anyone. It was nice to get it all out of her system while she was surrounded by the comfort of her friends.

The girls waited patiently, and finally, Roni blew her nose one last time, took a deep breath, and told them everything. She managed to get through it with only a few modest sniffles now that she was basically all cried out, and as soon as she was finished, Lora-Leigh was the first to offer her two cents.

"Well," she huffed. "It's obvious what his problem is. Classic case of jealousy. Clearly, he doesn't feel you're focused enough on him. Guys are such babies sometimes. It almost makes me glad DeShawn and I didn't date during football season. If he'd started whining about me not paying enough attention to his football stuff, I would never have been able to deal."

"I don't know," Roni said. "Maybe this is my fault. I *have* been really preoccupied lately. And even though I wanted to help with the formal planning, maybe I complained about it too much to him. . . ."

"What?" Jenna cried. "You *cannot* second-guess yourself about this. Lance should've been more supportive when you were stressed, instead of making you worry more by getting frustrated."

Camille nodded. "Jenna's right. I mean, I've only heard the whole story tonight, but it sounds like this is much more Lance's fault than yours."

"The guy needs a serious maturity check," Lora-Leigh said. "If he wants a first-class, top-rate girlfriend like you, he needs to be a big boy and grow up. Otherwise, he's not worthy."

"You're such a tough critic," Jenna said, playfully slapping Lora-Leigh on the shoulder.

She shrugged. "Hey, nobody messes with my friends without summoning the wrath of Lora-Leigh Sorenstein."

A faint smile crossed Roni's face. "Thanks," she said quietly. "I have to admit, I could stand a little male-bashing episode right now, even if it's not completely justified." She sighed. "I know this sounds strange, but even though he was a total jerk tonight, I'm still going to miss him."

Camille squeezed her hand. "Of course you will. That's the bad thing about guys. They break your heart, but you still want them back."

Roni nodded. "Every time I think about what he said about ZZT, I get angry all over again. But maybe he didn't mean it. Maybe it was just his frustration coming out in the wrong way. He did look sad when I got out of the car tonight."

"He'll be calling you within two days, groveling," Jenna said confidently, smiling encouragingly. "He'd be an idiot not to."

"I don't think so," Roni said quietly. "He seems pretty fed up. Maybe we both need some space right now." She dabbed her eyes one last time with a tissue, then sat up straighter. "You know, I've never been to a dance without a date before."

Jenna gasped. "Omigod, that's right! The formal's only a few weeks away. Oh, Roni, I'm so, so sorry."

"That's okay," she said, and she actually believed it when she said it. "I think it might to be fun to go solo." She smiled, a renewed sense of determination settling over her. "Wait, I take that back. It *is* going to be fun. Nothing will ruin Formal for me, no matter what. Not after all the work I put into it."

"That's the way to talk the talk, girl," Lora-Leigh said. "And tomorrow, first thing, you and I are hitting Loehmann's to find you the most fantabulous dress we can."

Roni grinned. "That sounds great."

"But Lance will call before then," Jenna said. "I know he will."

"We'll see," Roni said simply.

"Okay, the night is still young, and it's time for some serious male bashing," Camille said, standing up. "As luck would have it, I just bought some Ben & Jerry's Cookie Dough Ice Cream today. It's in the freezer, calling to us. And I have all six seasons of *Sex and the City* on DVD upstairs in my room. What say we break out the comfort food and pay tribute to Carrie Bradshaw and single women everywhere?"

"Sounds perfect," Roni said, slipping off her shoes, grabbing a blanket off the back of the couch, and making herself comfy. As Camille went to get the DVDs and Jenna and Lora-Leigh went to get the ice cream and the miraculously edible chocolate-chip cookies that Miss Merry had left over from dinner, Roni sank back into the couch and closed her eyes.

She knew she'd get through this; she had to. But the more she thought about it, the more Lance's words nagged at her, and the more she worried that this was just as much her fault as it was his. Had she gotten tunnel vision so badly that she'd put Lance second to Formal? She sighed, pulling the blanket tighter around her. Her eyes were swollen from crying, her head was reeling, and her heart—her heart was physically hurting. She'd never thought a broken heart was a literal thing, but there it was, throbbing away inside her, as real as anything she'd ever felt.

CHAPTER 10

Lora-Leigh sat in her car outside the athletic dorm on Monday night, and took one more deep breath before dialing DeShawn's cell. She knew he was here. . . . He'd told her he'd be home tonight packing for his trip to New York. He was leaving first thing tomorrow morning with his parents, and since they were driving instead of flying (to save money), he was taking the rest of the week off from school. That meant that she wouldn't see him until after the draft, and then for only a few weeks at most before school ended for the year. And who knew where things would stand between them then? He could be leaving LU forever. But whatever happened, she'd made up her mind. She had to do this, she wanted to do this, before it was too late.

She punched in his number and waited while it rang once, twice . . .

"Yo, Curly," DeShawn picked up. "I'm not even gone yet and you miss me already, don't you?"

"You've got two minutes to come downstairs and kiss the best thing that ever happened to you good-bye" was all she said, and then hung up.

Lora-Leigh smiled when DeShawn knocked on her car window only a minute later.

She rolled down the window and said, "Don't ask questions, just get in."

"Oooh, I love it when you order me around." DeShawn shrugged and got into the car, his head grazing the rooftop even after he sat down. He grinned at her in the darkness. "Is this a kidnapping?" he joked. "I mean, I know you don't want me to leave, but I didn't think you were that desperate."

"I'm not," Lora-Leigh quipped, smiling, "so quit giving yourself airs." She turned off of University Drive onto Latimer Lane, a smaller, palm-tree-lined road leading to the outer edge of the campus. They drove for a few minutes in silence, until she pulled up to the entrance to Research Park and wound through the darkened streets, finally stopping in a quiet spot under the shelter of some live oaks. The park was deserted except for a few stray cars parked here and there, no doubt occupied by students getting in a good mugging session before the campus security guards made their rounds with the spotlight.

She turned off the engine and reached behind her to get the package she'd hidden in the backseat.

"What's this?" DeShawn asked when she handed it to him.

"Your going-away present," Lora-Leigh said, grinning as he ripped off the wrapping paper and lifted the lid on the box, pulling out a Green Bay Packers jersey.

"Wow, Curly," DeShawn said, holding it up so he could see it in the moonlight shining through the window. "This has to be one of the coolest gifts anyone's ever given me."

Lora-Leigh shrugged. "I thought it would bring you luck on draft day."

"It will," he said. "But you know, I've already got my number one good-luck charm right here in the car with me."

"And don't you forget it," she teased.

Suddenly, with a somberness in his eyes she almost never saw, he whispered, "You know, if I get drafted, I'm really going to miss you."

"Nah, you won't." Lora-Leigh gave a short laugh. "You'll be so busy signing autographs for all the drooling cleat chasers, you won't even remember me."

"And when you're on the front cover of *Vogue* as the newest talent in global fashion, you won't remember me either," DeShawn teased. "And speaking of fashion, have you heard from FIT about your deferral yet?"

"No," Lora-Leigh said quietly. "And I'd been trying not to think about it at all, until you brought it up." She slugged his arm. "Thanks for assuring me a sleepless night tonight."

"Oh, come on," DeShawn said. "Don't play the cool card with me. You know you've been thinking about it. What are you going to do if they deny your request?"

Lora-Leigh stared at the steering wheel. "I don't know," she finally said quietly. "It would kill me to let FIT out of my sights forever, but then again, so would leaving LU early." She sighed. "I'm not ready to deal with either possibility. Right now I'm sending all my most positive thoughts for deferral out into the universe and hoping the admissions peeps at FIT will get the signal loud and clear."

DeShawn nodded. "I'll keep my fingers crossed for you. You shouldn't have to give up anything if you don't want to, not LU, and not FIT." He slipped his hand over hers, suddenly all seriousness. "You've been a great friend this year, and you're one amazing—not to mention über-fine—girl. Thank you for the jersey, and for everything."

"You're welcome," she said quietly. She took a deep breath, knowing that if she didn't say what was in her heart now, she might lose the chance forever. "I want to thank you, too. Spending time with you meant a lot to me. You've always been more than a friend." She forced herself to meet his gaze as her heart hammered. "I care about you . . . more than I ever let on. And I know I can't expect any more to come out of this relationship right now, or maybe even ever. But if you weren't on your way to fame and fortune . . ." She shrugged. "Who knows what might've been?"

"We would've had something that lasted good and long, Curly," DeShawn whispered. "There's no doubt in my mind; it would've been something really special, for both of us."

Lora-Leigh reached for his hand. "It already has been."

He leaned over to hug her, and she slipped her hand around the back of his neck, pulling him closer until his lips met hers.

Lora-Leigh settled into his arms, knowing that as of tomorrow, there was the definite possibility that they'd be going separate ways . . . permanently. But if that was the case, they'd say good bye with no expectations, no regrets. She'd enjoyed every second of the time she'd spent with him the last few months, and if that was all their brief dating relationship could ever be, then so be it. At least now they both knew it could've turned into something unforgettable, and that would have to be enough for her.

Roni tried to focus on her Archaeology textbook as she sat in the warm sun on the bench outside the natatorium, but the one word that kept cropping up on the page, obscuring all the others, was *Lance, Lance, Lance.* His name was like a chant in her heart, pounding guilt through her veins. She'd rehashed their fight over and over again during the last few sleepless weeks, and each time the mistakes she'd made became clearer and clearer. She'd been so obsessed with Formal for so long that she'd never realized what her tunnel vision was doing to her relationship with Lance. Sure, the things he'd said about ZZT had been completely unfair and off base, but then again, she hadn't done much to improve his opinion of it by making it her sole focus the last few months. How many times had she forgotten to meet him or finish her part of their debate work because she'd been absorbed in formal planning? And how many times had he let it slide? No wonder he'd finally lost his temper. His attitude toward ZZT was misplaced, but the more she thought about it, the less she could blame him. And no matter what happened down the road between them, she at least owed him some sort of explanation.

Now she took a deep breath and checked her watch again. It was a few minutes after two. His swim practice had just ended, and any second now he'd be walking out those doors.

Sure enough, as she watched, the doors swung open and out he walked with a couple of his swim-team buddies, his wide smile gleaming as he laughed at some joke one of them had just told. But the moment he saw her, his smile dropped from his lips as fast as it'd come. There wasn't a trace of anger on his face, just a mixture of confusion and hurt.

He exchanged a few quiet words with his friends, and they quickly nodded and broke away from him, leaving him standing just a few feet away from her.

"Hi," she said, nervously pulling at a button on her cardigan. "Um . . . I was wondering if we could talk for a sec?"

"Sure," he said quietly, taking a cautious seat next to her on the bench.

Roni took a deep breath. She'd been rehearsing what she wanted to say to him for the last few days, but all at once the words she had mapped out in her head vanished, leaving her with nothing but sheer panic. "I've been doing a lot of thinking since the last time we saw each other. About what you said about my involvement with ZZT and the formal."

Lance nodded, but stayed focused on his sports duffel on the ground.

Roni clutched her hands in her lap to keep them from shaking. "The thing is . . . you were right about a lot of it. I did get a little carried away with the plans for Formal." She sighed. "It's one of the curses of being a type A. I have a one-track mind when I'm working on a project like that. But I was being selfish, too. I stuck you with more of the debate work than was fair, and I never stopped to think about how you felt about ZZT taking up so much of my time and energy." She chanced a glance at his face, but it was unreadable, a mask of seriousness. "If it seemed like ZZT was more important to me than our relationship, I'm sorry. I never meant for that to happen, and I just wanted to apologize for hurting you."

After what seemed like an eternity, Lance finally nodded. "Thank you," he said. "I appreciate that. And I'm sorry about what I said about ZZT. I know it sounded horrible, like I was buying into all the worst kinds of sorority stereotypes. But the truth is, I know ZZT's not like that. You taught me that. But that night at dinner, I was so frustrated over the whole formal thing, I just completely lost my temper. I said so many things I didn't mean. . . . It was really lousy." He swallowed nervously. "It just wasn't like me at all."

"I know." Roni nodded. "But . . . I also want to make sure you know that ZZT is very important to me, and it always will be. That's a part of who I am that will never change, and if you don't understand that, then I'm not sure what kind of future we have together."

Lance seemed deep in thought for a few minutes while Roni held her breath, wondering how this would all turn out. Finally, he looked at her with a small, sad smile. "I'm really glad we talked," he said quietly, "but I think I need some time to think about all of this. I'm not sure I can ever really relate to your life at ZZT, and I don't want it to be a constant point of tension between us either." He sighed. "I just need to figure this out before we take this any farther, you know?"

Roni's eyes welled before he even finished what he was saying, but she did her best to keep the tears from overflowing. "I understand" was all she could manage to say as she quickly stood up. "Take all the time you need. Maybe this isn't a good thing for us anymore." She started to turn away, but then risked one more look back at him. "But for the record, I think that would be a horrible shame."

"I'll talk to you . . ." Lance called after her as she hurried away with her head down to hide the tears that were falling freely now. But Roni couldn't tell whether he meant that, or whether he was just being polite. Either way, she knew she was going to dive back into her final preparations for Formal and not come up for air until it was over. It was the only thing that would keep her from thinking about Lance and the great relationship that she might have screwed up forever.

Jenna flipped through the racks of dresses at Macy's on Tuesday night, her heart skipping with excitement at nearly every gown she saw. There was a strapless teal floor-length dress with an empire waist and soft chiffon pleats cascading down; an above-the-knee cranberry pin-tucked dress; a sage halter dress with a beaded bodice; and at least a dozen other dresses in her size in a rainbow of colors, fabrics, and styles. She grabbed the sage dress and slung it over her arm, which was already aching under the weight of the six other dresses she'd pulled off the rack in the last five minutes alone (never mind the five other dresses the salesclerk had already hung in the dressing room for her). Forcing herself to head toward the dressing room, she spotted Darcy a few racks over, laughing.

"I didn't know you were planning on buying the entire dress department," Darcy teased. "And you were worried you weren't going to be able to find anything you liked for Formal."

Jenna grinned sheepishly and shrugged. "They're all so beautiful, I couldn't help myself. But when I get into the dressing room, inevitably each one of them will be too long, or too loose, or too tight in the butt. And then I'll be back to square one."

"Or, you might end up leaving here with three amazing dresses instead of just one," Darcy said with a laugh as she followed Jenna into the dressing room.

"Not with my budget," Jenna said as she slipped the teal dress over her head. "I still need shoes, and a purse, too, so I have to make my spending money stretch." She looked at herself in the mirror, and frowned. The hem of the dress was dragging under her feet, and the pleats in the skirt looked about as flattering on her figure as a teal-colored burlap sack. Most of the time, she loved being petite. But there were times when it was frustrating trying to find clothes to fit her small, curvy frame.

"Are you going to come out and show me?" Darcy called from the stall next to hers.

"Not this one," Jenna said. "I'm swimming in it. What about yours?"

"Um, I don't think so." Darcy giggled. "I can't get it to stay up long enough to show you. I think I need Jessica Simpson's bod to fill this out. So . . ." Her voice got muffled, and Jenna knew she must be shuffling out of the rejected dress. ". . . are you psyched about going to Formal with Tiger?"

Jenna smiled, hanging up the teal dress on a "No" rack and moving on to a black wrap number. "Definitely. You know I've never seen him in a tux, and he's going to look so hot." She giggled. "And it'll be so much fun to hang out with Lora-Leigh and Roni. I just wish that Roni and Lance would make up. She's being a real trouper about it, but I know she misses him."

"She hasn't heard from him?" Darcy asked.

"Not since she talked to him yesterday," Jenna said. "I guess he's still trying to figure out what he wants. But Formal's only a few days away now, so I guess that means he's definitely not coming with her. It's hard to believe, but she actually seems okay with going solo. She told me that this way, she can dance with whoever she wants to."

"I guess that's true," Darcy said. "Good for her. I think that's really brave."

"Tell me about it," Jenna said. "I don't think I would ever have the guts to do that. But Lora-Leigh's bringing Chris Segalini from the Phi Thetas, and they're just going as friends. So Roni can hang with them without being overloaded with couple PDAing all night long. I'm sure Chris will dance with her, and so will Tiger."

Jenna did a quick mirror check and decided against the black dress. It was cute, but a little blah. She reached for the cranberry dress, then changed her mind at the last minute, opting for the sage halter instead. The color was just divine. She slipped it over her head, loving the way the satiny fabric whispered silky soft across her skin, then zipped it up. As she turned to face the mirror, a smile spread across her face. The skirt of the dress was loose enough to disguise her insulin pump, but the waistline and neckline fit her perfectly.

"Okay," Darcy said, "I found one I really like."

"Me, too," Jenna said, twirling to check the dress from all angles in the mirror.

"Let's show each other," Darcy said. "On the count of three. One, two . . ."

Jenna opened her stall door and stepped out into the dressing room hallway in sync with Darcy, and they both let out gasps.

"You look gorgeous!" Jenna said, admiring the crimson dress that Darcy had chosen.

"So do you!" Darcy cried, smiling. "That dress gives you some serious curvaceousness. And the color is perfect for your skin and your eyes. I don't think I've ever seen you in anything so sexy before."

"Probably because I don't normally wear stuff so sexy," Jenna said, laughing. "But I just wanted something a little different, a little more daring. Since it's my first formal and everything. And actually"—she blushed—"there are going to be some other firsts for me that night, too."

Darcy looked at her blankly for a second, and then shrieked. "No way! You and Tiger?"

Jenna nodded. "I'm finally ready to take the next step with him, and it's going to be Sunday." The weightiness of what she was saying made her heart speed up. "I've been thinking about it for a long time. Overthinking it, actually. But I care about Tiger so much, and now I know that I want to share this with him more than anything."

"That is huge!" Darcy said.

"I know!" Jenna blushed all over again. "I haven't told Tiger about all this yet. I wanted to surprise him. I want everything to be unforgettable . . . for him and for me. So I'm cooking dinner for him Sunday before Formal, and I figured I'd tell him then. I booked a room at the Lakeview Inn, and I bought a bunch of candles and downloaded some new music on my iPod." She lowered her voice to a whisper, her cheeks reaching new heights in rosiness. "And . . . I even bought some lingerie."

Darcy smiled approvingly. "Mood music, lighting, romance . . . It sounds like you've thought of everything. I'm sure he'll love it."

"Really?" Jenna said, feeling a rush of relief when Darcy nodded. "I hope you're right. I just want it to be a night that we'll always remember."

"You both care about each other so much," Darcy said, "so it will be. But you will need something to wear to the formal that's *not* lingerie." She smiled teasingly, motioning to Jenna's dress. "So, are we going to get these dresses or what?"

Jenna nodded. "Definitely."

"Between your big surprise and your dress, Tiger won't be able to put a complete sentence together for at least a month. He'll be too busy daydreaming of you."

Jenna grinned. She hoped that would be true, especially since she had a feeling that once Sunday night was over, she'd be lost in a Tiger haze for days, too. She'd never wanted to be this close with anyone before, and she knew it would change their relationship, and change her, forever. And now that she was finally ready to take this step with him, she could hardly wait.

"It's starting, y'all!" Lora-Leigh shouted from the couch in the ZZT living room on Saturday afternoon. "Hurry up!"

"We heard you already, Sorenstein," Camille said, walking into the room balancing a massive bowl of chips in one hand and Miss Merry's famous seven-layer dip in the other (famous because it was delicious—the only dish, besides cookies, that Miss Merry could not destroy). "Calm thyself."

"Calm?" Lora-Leigh said, throwing up her hands. "There is no calm. DeShawn is about to make his first appearance on national TV as a future NFL star. This is a crucial moment in time, people. A zenith that can never be topped, except, of course, when I debut my first clothing line on the runway at New York's Fashion Week." She nervously twisted the Green Bay Packer earrings she'd donned for good luck, hoping they were doing their job right now. The other girls were all wearing green and gold, the Green Bay colors, and Jenna and Roni had even bought Green Bay hats. And then there was Camille, who was wearing a huge cheese-head hat—the most spirited of the group.

Sandy and Danika giggled as they came into the room with Jenna and Roni, carrying sodas and pints of ice cream. "We get it, Lora-Leigh," Danika said. "The very existence of Earth as we know it hangs by a delicate thread."

"Smart-ass," Lora-Leigh said, launching a pillow at her. She scooted off the couch and flopped down on her stomach in front of the plasma TV, hoping to get a better view of Radio City Music Hall as the camera panned through the audience. The theater was packed with die-hard football fans awaiting the NFL draft picks, most of them wearing the jersey of their favorite team and waving banners for the cameras. Toward the front of the theater sat the team reps, with their headphones on, ready to communicate with the coaches and managers who were making the draft decisions in the "war room" off camera. Finally, the camera settled on the stage, which was lit up with a huge arc of screens flashing montages of some of the NFL's greatest players with banners hanging above with all of the team's emblems on them.

"Is DeShawn in the audience?" Jenna asked, sitting down beside Lora-Leigh and offering her some chips.

"No, he'll be in the green room," she said, waving the chips away. How could anyone expect her to eat at a time like this? She was having enough trouble controlling the spastic butterflies in her stomach as it was. "He's waiting there with his family to hear the news about the draft. They'll probably show him on camera. They usually zoom in on the players after each draft decision, so you get to see all the good and bad emo, written all over their poor faces."

"That sounds so painful," Roni said. "How could you face that kind of disappointment on national TV? I don't know if I can watch."

"Shhh." Lora-Leigh waved her hand for silence as the draft commissioner stepped to the podium on the stage and started the clock for the first pick, setting a time limit on how long the first team had to make their choice. The Dallas Cowboys were the first team on the draft list, so they got first pick of all the potential draftees, but they only had ten minutes to make a decision. Luckily for Lora-Leigh (and her sanity) they picked quickly, drafting free agent Jarod Vaughn, the quarterback for the Buffalo Bills whose contract was up, making him eligible to be drafted by another team. The camera flashed to the green room as his name was called, and as Jarod beamed, hugging his family and agent, Lora-Leigh caught a glimpse of DeShawn in the background, sitting on the couch with his mom and dad.

"Omigod, there he is!" she shouted, leaping up to point him out to the other girls. His face looked amazingly calm, but Lora-Leigh could see him cracking his knuckles, something he always did when he was deep in thought or nervous. "Come on," she mumbled to herself. "Hang in there."

The second draft pick by the New York Giants went quickly, too, but the third, by the Arizona Cardinals, was painstaking. The ten minutes ticked by with excruciating slowness while Lora-Leigh paced the living room, getting more annoyed with each passing second.

"What are they doing?" she said, throwing up her hands. "It's not like they don't have the whole rest of the year to prep for this, and they're stalling on their decision now?"

Jenna reached for her hand. "It'll be over soon," she tried to say soothingly, but Lora-Leigh just groaned. All she could think about was that if she was this nervous here in Latimer, what a wreck DeShawn must be in Manhattan. Finally, the Cardinals made their choice, drafting wide receiver Cody Miles from Penn State University.

Lora-Leigh held her breath as the commissioner announced that the Green Bay Packers were now officially on the clock. Of course the all-knowing camera chose that moment to zoom in on DeShawn's face, given the rumor that he was in the running for the next pick. Lora-Leigh could see the sweat beading up on his forehead as his mom held onto his hand for dear life. She would've given anything to be with him right then. She'd even half seriously priced out some airplane tickets to New York, to see if she had any shot at being there. But she couldn't afford it; plus, Formal was tomorrow night, and she didn't want to miss it. But for a second, she felt physically torn, like half of her was there, sweating bullets on the couch with DeShawn, while the other half was stuck here, feeling queasy in Latimer.

The TV went into a split screen, one side staying focused on DeShawn's face and the other side panning back to the theater stage. "Green Bay has chosen," the commissioner announced. Lora-Leigh's heart went into a series of miniseizures as she waited for the draftee's name to be called. "They've chosen number fifty-two. The Green Bay Packers select DeShawn Pritchard, offensive running back, LU."

Lora-Leigh whooped, jumping up and down as her sisters crowded around the television, squealing and clapping. "Go, Pack, Go!" she shouted along with the Green Bay Packers fans chanting at the back of Radio City Music Hall.

On DeShawn's face was a Kodak-worthy mixture of relief and sheer joy as he picked up his mom and spun her around the green room laughing. And Lora-Leigh's eyes quickly welled as DeShawn stepped onto the stage in his black suit to accept a Green Bay hat from the commissioner along with a jersey with his name and number on the back. She could see him blinking fast, and she knew he was fighting tears himself. His dream was coming true.

He smiled for the cameras, and before he walked offstage, he stared right into the camera lens and winked. And in that second, Lora-Leigh knew beyond any doubt that it was meant for her.

She quickly grabbed her cell out of the back pocket of her jeans and sent a text to him with shaking fingers:

DesignsOnU: I see ur already kissing up to ur fans, you flirt you. ☺ Congrats! I can't wait to see you all decked out in the green and gold.

She sent the message, not expecting to get anything back, since she was sure DeShawn was in the middle of popping champagne with his family. But a few minutes later, a text beeped onto her screen.

Pritchard#33: Thnx, Curly! Wish u were here. But I'll put on my jersey again when I get back, just 4 u.

Lora-Leigh grinned. That was her DeShawn all right. Just imagining him in the full Green Bay uniform made a shiver run through her. He was going pro; she could barely believe it.

She snapped her cell shut and turned to her sisters. "Let's get this party started, ladies!" she said. "We have some serious celebrating to do." She popped a CD she'd burned last night into the sound system, and the Green Bay fight song boomed through the speakers. Of course she was the only one who knew the lyrics (she'd memorized them in honor of DeShawn), but Jenna, Roni, and the other girls quickly joined in the cheering.

While Lora-Leigh laughed with her sisters, munching on junk food and rehashing DeShawn's moment of glory, she realized that while he was going to start living his NFL dream soon, she was already living out one of her dreams, right here at Latimer, surrounded by the friends she loved.

• • •

Roni tied the final blue balloon onto the balloon arch that stretched over the entrance to the ballroom, then took a step into the room to survey the final product. The Villa Orangerie ballroom had been breathtaking the first time she'd seen it, but now it was embellished with ZZT panache, which made it even better.

She brushed her hair off her forehead and sighed, knowing that these were her last few hours as Formal Planner. Her job was almost done, and even though it had been a ton of work, seeing the end result now, finally, after months of preparation, gave her a pleasant feeling of satisfaction.

"There you are!" a voice called, and Roni caught sight of Beverly and Marissa heading toward her. "I was wondering where the mastermind behind all of this splendor had gone off to," Beverly said with a smile.

"Oh, I was just helping Keesha, Melody, and Amy finish the balloon arch," Roni said.

"I don't think you've taken one break in the last four hours we've been decorating," Beverly said, leading Roni to a chair. "Time to take a breather and enjoy the fruits of your labor." She glanced in Melody's direction. "I'm glad to see Melody helped out with the decorating today."

"She did a great job," Roni said honestly. Melody had thrown herself into the work, and Roni'd appreciated her willingness to help, especially after all that had happened between them with the planning. When Melody saw all the decorations, she'd said to Roni, "This almost makes me glad I was too busy to be the Formal Planner. You did a way better job than I ever would have." Roni had denied it, but *all* the girls (not just Melody) were still gushing over the decorations, making her feel like maybe she *had* done this right.

"What you've done," Marissa said to Roni now. "It's incredible. We've had some great formals since I've been a ZZT, but never anything this grand." She smiled. "I don't know how we'll top this next year."

"Thanks," Roni said, blushing. The perfectionist in her wanted to argue, but as she looked around, even she had to admit that the room looked stunning. The flower arrangements—an array of white roses mixed with blue hydrangea and irises—were beautiful, surrounded by a dozen tea-light candles and blue organza ribbon in the center of each table. There were flowers draped from each wall sconce and in an arch leading onto the dance floor, too. Balloon columns marked the four corners of the dance floor, and a satin banner hung from the back of the room that said ROMANCE AND ROSES, ZETA ZETA TAU SPRING FORMAL in glittery blue letters. She was especially proud of the favors she'd chosen—Vera Wang champagne flutes. She'd gotten them at a steep discount since she'd ordered them in bulk, and she'd even had *Romance and Roses* engraved on them. All in all, everything had come together perfectly.

"So," Beverly said, "what's left to do?"

"Not much," Roni said. "The DJ stopped by an hour ago to test his equipment and run through his song list with me, and he'll be back an hour before the dance starts. I already met with Mrs. Leonida to finalize the hors d'oeuvres and drinks." She smiled. "I guess all we do now is show up."

"And dance till we drop," Beverly said. "I can't wait to see the looks on everyone's faces when they see this place. It's like something out of a fairy tale."

"So you think the girls will all like it?" More than anything, Roni wanted all of her ZZT sisters to have a good time tonight. She hoped she'd gotten everything just right.

"Are you kidding?" Marissa said. "They're going to love it. No doubt about it."

Roni smiled, feeling a weight lift off her shoulders. She'd been so worried about how it would all come together, especially since she'd been more than a little preoccupied the last few weeks over her breakup with Lance. Even though she'd seen him a few times at the natatorium and in Poli Sci (can you say awkward?), he stuck close to his buddies at the pool, and in class he always made sure he came a little late and left a little early, sitting in the last row by the door so he could make a quick exit. There was no doubt about it. He was avoiding her like the plague. But luckily, the formal planning had kept her busy . . . and distracted. So she hadn't had the time to obsess over his silence. Now that the big day was finally here, and everything had gone off without a hitch, she could breathe a much-needed sigh of relief.

"Well," she said, checking her watch, "I've got to head over to the natatorium for lifeguard duty, so I better get going. Bev, do you think you could give me a lift?"

"Sure," Beverly said. "I'm going to get a mani and pedi at Shear Bliss, so it's on the way. And I'm taking Keesha back to ZZT anyway, so it's no prob." She glanced around the room.

"I think Keesha might be finishing hanging the last of the blue lanterns along the porch outside. I'll go get her."

Roni nodded. "I'll meet you out front, then." She said goodbye to Marissa and the other girls who were getting ready to leave as well, then shouldered her sport duffel and headed outside.

Just as she was stepping into the bright sunshine, her BlackBerry buzzed. Roni checked the screen and smiled when she recognized a text coming from Kiersten's cell number:

K_Douglas: Hi sweetie! Just wanted to send you a huge e-hug before your formal tonite! R u psyched?

LilFish: Totally. It's going to be incredible. I'll take lots of pics so u can see.

K_Douglas: Prfct! I know uv had a rough few weeks, but try to 4get about the loser ex and have a gr8t time.

LilFish: What ex? ☺

K_Douglas: That's the spirit! Ur way 2 good 4 him anyway.

LilFish: Don't I know it!

Roni grinned, even though she felt a pang in her heart each time she thought of Lance as an "ex." It seemed so . . . permanent, and she still hadn't quite wrapped her mind around it yet. But she was so glad she had great friends like Kiersten helping her through this.

K_Douglas: Watch out, Latimer, 'cause Roni Van Gelderen's going to be breaking hearts all over Florida tonight. Go get 'em, grl!

LilFish: Thnx. I'll call u 2morrow with all the details.

K_Douglas: U better! XOXOXO

Roni slid her BlackBerry into her pocket just as Beverly and Keesha joined her in the parking lot. As she slid into the backseat of Beverly's car, she took one last look at the Villa Orangerie. In just seven short hours, it would be lit up with a thousand white twinkling lights, alive with great music, and brimming with more than a hundred ZZT girls and their dates. Roni smiled, barely able to wait to see how it would all unfold.

Roni brushed her lashes one final time with Givenchy mascara, then gingerly leaned back to survey her makeup in the mirror, making sure she didn't bump elbows with Lora-Leigh or knock Sue-Marie's pressed powder from her hand. She could barely move in the ZZT bathroom, jammed as it was with nearly twenty girls all vying for hair dryers, curlers, or face time in front of the mirror. It would've been simpler to dress for Formal at Tuthill, but it wouldn't have been nearly as much fun. "Girlz Nite Out" was blaring from Beverly's iPod dock station in the bathroom, and everyone was bouncing to the beat and singing along as they got ready for Formal. The chaos of makeup kits, bobby pins, and clothing flying everywhere, along with the excited chatter and giggles of the girls, all made the cramped bathroom feel like one killer preformal party.

It seemed like the entire ZZT sisterhood had descended on the bathroom, all except Jenna, who still hadn't made an appearance. Roni had seen her this morning before she'd left to decorate for Formal, and Jenna'd been humming to herself and staring dreamily off into space. But she had been MIA since then. Roni knew she had planned to make a nice early dinner for Tiger, but then she was supposed to meet them at the ZZT house to get ready together. Now, she wasn't at ZZT, she wasn't at Tuthill, and, even stranger, her cell was off. Roni'd left her two messages, but Lora-Leigh had made her stop after that.

"Did you ever think that maybe Jenna doesn't want to be found right at this very moment in time?" Lora-Leigh had said. "Whatever she's up to, she obviously wanted to keep it on the down-low, so let's just wait until she reappears. *Then* we'll get every last detail out of her."

Roni hated to get ready with Jenna missing from their triumvirate, but with less than an hour left to the start of Formal, she didn't have a choice.

"Okay," Minnie called from the makeshift salon chair she'd set up in the far corner of the bathroom. "Who's ready for their hair next?"

"Me, me!" Lindsay cried, scooting into the chair before anyone else had a chance to sit down before her.

Minnie, who was working part-time at the Va-Va-Voom Salon this semester, had volunteered to do hair, and so far, she'd had over a dozen "customers." She'd already done Roni's in an elaborate chignon à la Grace Kelly that made her hair look like a shimmering black flower blooming at the nape of her neck. It suited Roni perfectly, making her feel decadent and beautiful.

Lora-Leigh's was made for her, too, a loose nest of curls pin-tucked haphazardly on her head, a spontaneous look that was both wild and sexy, just like Lora-Leigh herself. And it went well with the smoky eyeliner and charcoal eye shadow she was using to highlight her eyes.

"How do I look?" Lora-Leigh said, throwing her head back, pursing her Venom-glossed lips, and batting her eyelashes in a perfect cover-girl mimic.

"Runway worthy," Roni said.

"Oh, for shame," Lora-Leigh said, clucking her tongue. "I'm not even dressed yet." She motioned to her robe in disgust. "And the outfit is the alpha and omega, you know. Give me five minutes to change, and then say that."

Roni laughed, then grabbed her own wardrobe bag from the towel rack it was hanging on, unzipping it to carefully withdraw a blue sateen evening gown with a ruched waist and pleated shoulder and back straps. She quickly stepped out of her own robe and slid the dress up over her hips. As she zipped up the back and stepped into her silver Miu Miu sandals, she heard a gasp from behind her.

"Roni," Camille said, staring at her wide-eyed. "You give a whole new meaning to the word *Vogue*."

"Did you get that on Newbury Street the last time you were home?" Beverly asked, ogling the fabric. "Because if you did, I'm so coming to visit you in Boston over the summer."

"No, my budget put the kibosh on Newbury shopping sprees."

Roni smiled, her heart swelling with pride. "I got this at Loehmann's. Seventy-five percent off retail price."

"It's a Nicole Miller—the bargain of the millennium," Lora-Leigh bragged as she pulled her own garment bag off the towel rack. "And who's the red-tag huntress who found it for you after two hours of scouring the racks?"

Roni laughed, elbowing Lora-Leigh. "I know; I know. I will be forever in your debt, great fashion guru."

"I promised you designer fashions, discount prices, and I delivered, baby."

"I had no idea stores like Loehmann's even existed," Roni said. "Who would've thought you could find Versace for less than fifty bucks?"

"It's a whole new world, my friend." Lora-Leigh pulled an amethyst bubble-hem dress out of her bag. "Just wait until I take you to DSW to shoe-shop. Heaven." She slipped on her dress and jutted out her hips, striking a pose. "My first attempt at making evening attire," she said. "And what do the critics have to say?"

"*Magnifique*," Roni said, clapping, and Beverly and Camille nodded in agreement. The strapless, heart-shaped neckline brought out the graceful curve of Lora-Leigh's long neck, and the short bubble skirt was very Sarah Jessica Parker—just plain fun.

"Next year, I'm having my dress custom-made by Sorenstein Designs," Keesha said. "I could never find anything that original in a store."

"Are you sure you can afford me?" Lora-Leigh teased.

Roni smiled, playing along with Lora-Leigh's jokes, but she

felt a twinge of sadness when it hit her that for Lora-Leigh, there might not be a chance to hone her design skills at FIT anymore. She still hadn't heard from FIT regarding her request for deferral. She was keeping quiet about the whole thing, saying she didn't want to talk about it for fear of jinxing FIT's decision. But either way, this might be one of the last chances Roni had to spend with her this year. The semester was ending in just a few more weeks, and then Roni'd be headed home to Boston for the summer. She already had a summer job lined up at How Sweet It Is again. And Jenna, Roni knew, would be working as a camp counselor back in Georgia. Lora-Leigh was staying in Latimer (much to her chagrin). The summer just wouldn't be as much fun without her two best friends' company.

"Hey, space cadet," Lora-Leigh said, elbowing her and interrupting her thoughts. "Where are you mind-tripping to? It better not be to the bad, boy-angst place. Tonight, all mourning for lost loves is off-limits."

Roni laughed. "I wasn't even going there. I'm in the antimen mode right now anyway."

"I hear that," Beverly said, skimming her iPod playlist and hitting "play." "How about a little mood music to get us started?" she yelled as the opening chords to "Miss Independent" boomed through the bathroom.

As Roni threw her head back and started singing the lyrics, she smiled, flinging her arms around Lora-Leigh and Beverly. Forget about boys, forget about breakups. Tonight was all about her and her best friends.

CHAPTER 11

In high school, Lora-Leigh had been able to take or leave prom. It was a lot of buildup with very little bang. True, the outfits were always the highlight for her—sometimes fabulous and sometimes great comic relief. But with cheesy ballads, watered-down punch, and the prom queen—inevitably Latimer High's witchiest but most popular girl—posing in her crown all night long for her drooling admirers, prom was way too cliquish for her taste. But from the second she'd set foot in the Orangerie Ballroom with her friend Chris, she knew that the ZZT Formal wasn't anything even remotely like prom. If prom was a scratchy wool sweater, then the ZZT Formal was a luxurious cashmere wrap.

Since the second the music had started at 7 P.M., the dance floor had been packed with ZZT girls and their dates. It was always a sign of a happenin' party when there wasn't a single person sitting out a dance. And except for an occasional food or drink break, no one had left the dance floor yet. Lora-Leigh especially got a kick out of seeing Rob "Rubberman" Jeffries and Emma Cox staring madly into each other's eyes on the dance floor. So he *had* taken Lora-Leigh's advice and called Emma (she'd known the two of them were made for each other all along). Lora-Leigh even noticed that Roni was staying busy on the dance floor. She'd been jamming to Beyoncé's "Irreplaceable" with Beverly and Camille, and even for the slow dances, most of the other girls' dates were clamoring for a chance to dance with Roni (no surprise there). And unlike the cattiness that always pervaded high school dances when it came to dates swapping dance partners, Camille, Beverly, Keesha, and all the other girls were more than happy to let Roni take a turn on the floor with their guys. Judging from the wide smile on her face, Roni seemed to be having a great time, but Lora-Leigh wanted to make sure that it stayed that way for the rest of the night.

"Well, Boston, you outdid yourself," she said to Roni, when she and Chris danced over to the hors d'oeuvres table for a snack. She dipped a strawberry into the chocolate fountain and bit into its semisweet tartness, smiling. "I'm the least sentimental person you know, but I'm still digging my champagne flute. And the Romance and Roses T-shirts are great, too. Whoever came up with the idea of making the petals on the white rose look like a couple dancing?"

"You know who came up with it," Roni said, rolling her eyes and grinning at the same time. "You did."

"That was me, wasn't it? Sheer genius." Lora-Leigh smiled in self-satisfaction. She was pretty sure it was her best ZZT T-shirt idea to date. "This formal just keeps getting better and better. I don't think I've heard one eighties ballad so far, and the champagne punch is very tasty."

"I second that," said Chris, clinking his glass to theirs. "We had our formal last week, and when the DJ played 'The Chicken Dance,' we had to draw the line. So we threw him into the fountain outside the Wentworth Ballroom."

"You're kidding, right?" Roni said, clearly appalled by the idea.

"Not kidding," Lora-Leigh said. "You can't put anything past a Pi Theta Ep."

"He knew he had it coming," Chris said. "We were doing him a favor anyway. He's not a real DJ yet, just a friend of Ben's who wants to start his own DJ business. We agreed to let him do our formal, but I think I can safely say his days as a DJ were over before they ever started."

"So what did you do for music?" Roni asked.

Chris shrugged. "We spent the rest of the night listening to David Brent's date's dance-mix iPod playlist, which was fine, if you like three hours of Abba gold and Chaka Khan."

Roni laughed. "Well, I'm relieved that you like our DJ's song list better."

"I just wish that Jenna would get her petite self here to see the fruits of your labor," Lora-Leigh said. "We're going on a half hour now and there's still no sign of her."

"This morning she couldn't stop talking about the dress she was going to wear," Roni said. "I know she'll be here. She wouldn't miss it. I just hope she gets here soon."

"Yeah, like before Segalini drains the last of the champagne punch." Lora-Leigh elbowed Chris playfully. "Go easy on that stuff, bud. You promised that we wouldn't have a repeat of the Mississippi-game debacle."

He grinned sheepishly. "I know, and I'm on good behavior tonight, scout's honor." He set his glass down at their table just as a slow song came on. "Come on, Lora-Leigh, you want to dance?"

"Actually, why don't you and Roni go?" Lora-Leigh said, seeing an opportunity to give Roni a turn with Chris. "I've got to hit the ladies' room anyway."

Roni gave Lora-Leigh a knowing, "you don't have to" glance, but Lora-Leigh just shooed them away. "What, can't a girl go powder her nose in peace, for crying out loud?"

Chris offered Roni his arm to escort her onto the dance floor as Lora-Leigh scooted to the bathroom (where she did a brief mirror check and then waited out the rest of the song). When it was over, she emerged from the bathroom to see Roni cordially thanking Chris for the dance as he led her toward their table.

"I'm going to get us some water," Chris said. "Be back in a few."

"You know," Roni said to Lora-Leigh once Chris was safely out of earshot, "you don't have to worry about me. I've having a great time, really."

"Worry?" Lora-Leigh snorted. "Who said anything about worry? You're a girl who can hold her own, Boston; anyone can see that."

"Thanks," Roni said sincerely. "I mean, I won't lie. It does sting every now and then, but I'll live."

"Of course you will," Lora-Leigh said as Chris returned with the water. "And in the meantime, you have a plethora of adoring fans to keep you busy on the dance floor all night."

Just then, Darcy rushed over to them, dragging her date, Jim, by the arm. "Hey, y'all," she said, nodding toward the door. "Check out my little sister. Isn't she a vision?"

Lora-Leigh and Roni turned to see Jenna gliding into the room on Tiger's arm, breathtaking in a sage-green cloud of a dress. But it was the look of absolute bliss on her face that really made her radiant, and Lora-Leigh had a feeling she knew why.

"You," Lora-Leigh said, pointing a finger at Jenna and motioning her over. "Get over here. Pronto. You've got some explaining to do, missy."

Jenna giggled as Lora-Leigh ushered her over to their table with Roni and Darcy as Chris and Tiger shook hands and made small talk with Jim.

"First, where have you been all day?" Lora-Leigh asked. "And second, what's with the beauty-pageant glow?"

Lora-Leigh waited while she and Roni and Darcy watched Jenna go from beaming to blushing to beaming all over again. And suddenly she knew for sure. Now she just had to wait for Jenna to dish.

Jenna cast a sidelong glance at Tiger, making sure he and the other guys were well out of hearing range. "Well," she whispered, still feeling the rush of the events of the day bubbling through her, "if y'all really want to know, I was with Tiger this afternoon."

"I knew it!" Lora-Leigh said, whooping. "I knew you looked different."

"Well, of course you were with Tiger. We figured that," Roni said, but then she froze, her eyes widening as Jenna's words finally sank in. "Wait a minute . . . with Tiger, as in, *with* him?

"Omigod!" Roni said, hugging Jenna.

"So," Darcy said, squeezing her hand, "was it everything you hoped for?"

Jenna smiled secretively. A part of her wanted to tell her sisters everything, but another part wanted to hold everything that had happened close to her heart, treasuring the memory of it.

"It was better than I hoped," she said. "I cooked him an early dinner, and we ate it on a blanket at Research Park. Then we went to this beautiful little bed-and-breakfast in old-town Latimer, the Lakeview Inn."

"Oh, I know that place," Lora-Leigh said. "Very romantical."

Jenna nodded. "It was." She thought about the beautiful room that looked out over a pond at the back of the inn and how, from the moment they'd stepped into the room, everything had been perfect. Tiger had been so sweet, and any nervousness she had felt beforehand was washed away with his patience and understanding. Even now, with him standing ten feet away from her, she felt closer to him than she ever had before.

"Well," Darcy said, "you look completely and utterly happy."

Jenna smiled. "I am," she said. "And now I'm here with y'all, which makes me even happier." She looked around the room, taking in the soft, twinkling candlelight, the gorgeous flowers, and all of her friends' smiling faces. She glanced at Darcy and Roni, and then her eyes settled on Lora-Leigh. "I'm so glad we're all here together, right now, no matter what happens next semester."

"Oh," Lora-Leigh said, nodding in understanding, "you mean

with FIT?" She waved her hand dismissively. "That's already been taken care of."

"What?" Roni exclaimed. "You mean they didn't grant your request for deferral?"

"Lora-Leigh, you're really going?" Jenna said, trying to sound as enthusiastic as possible even though her eyes were already unwillingly filling with tears.

"And leave y'all here without your desperately underpaid but sorely needed fashion consultant? Never," Lora-Leigh scoffed. "I was just about to tell you that I'm not going. At least, not for another three years." She smiled. "I wanted to surprise y'all with the news tonight, but I heard from the director of admissions on Friday. Apparently, she was really impressed with the letter I sent her, and she said that if my commitment to ZZT was anything like the commitment I'd have for FIT, I was the type of student they'd love to have on board, no matter what. So she agreed to hold a spot for me in the program until after I graduate from Latimer, provided I take a list of preapproved fashion courses here at LU in the meantime. And she suggested I look into some fashion-related work as well, so I think I'm going to look into apprenticing at You Wear It over the summer. It's that custom clothing shop on University. And I'm going to take a Fabric and Textiles course as my elective here next year to get started on my fashion curriculum. So basically, y'all are stuck with me, for better or worse."

Jenna and Roni looked at each other, and then screamed and flung themselves at Lora-Leigh, crushing her with hugs. Darcy got in the act, too, and pretty soon Lora-Leigh was coughing and sputtering dramatically, acting like she was being strangled, even though she was laughing the whole time.

"I didn't think it was possible for this day to get any better," Jenna said, "but it just did."

"Okay, girls," Tiger said, coming over with Chris and Jim, "we're starting to feel left out in our little corner over there. If I didn't know any better, I'd swear y'all were gossiping about us behind our backs."

"Only a little," Lora-Leigh teased.

"So," Chris said, holding his hand out to Lora-Leigh, "can I have my date back now, please?"

"Since you asked so nicely," Lora-Leigh said with a grin. "Come on, let's go find Camille wherever she's off snuggling with Mike. I want to tell her the news about FIT." She winked at Jenna and Roni, waving at them as she walked away with Chris. "I'll meet y'all out on the dance floor in ten."

Jenna watched her go, then smiled as Tiger slipped his hand around her waist, pulling her closer. "And what about me?" he said. "Am I going to get a chance to dance with my sweetheart tonight?"

"Of course," Jenna said, kissing his cheek. She followed him as he led her onto the dance floor, loving the way her hand fit inside his. She wrapped her arms around his neck and tucked her head under his chin, smiling as the familiar scent of his piney soap washed over her.

"So," Tiger said, running his hand across her cheek, "would I sound like an idiot if I said thank you?"

"For what?" Jenna asked quietly.

"For today," he whispered. "For . . . everything. It meant a lot to me."

"Me, too," Jenna said.

He lifted her chin until his lips met hers, and as they kissed, Jenna felt like she was lifting off the dance floor, her whole body thrilling to the core at his touch. Then he leaned closer, whispering, "If this were one of your concerts, I'd ask you for an encore performance."

Jenna blushed and giggled. "Oh, you would, would you?"

Tiger nodded. "And would you say yes?"

Jenna grinned. "Definitely." She was still smiling at the thought when her eyes shifted to the door of the ballroom, and she gasped. "Omigod, I can't believe it."

"What?" Tiger asked, following her gaze.

Jenna stared at Lance, standing in the doorway, dressed in a tux and looking very handsome. "Well, it looks like Roni isn't going to have to go solo tonight after all."

When Roni felt the tap on her shoulder, she assumed it was Henry Leonida, Mrs. Leonida's nephew and the events coordinator for the Orangerie. He was a very nice man, but a bit of an event dictator, and he'd already approached Roni with questions half a dozen times since the dance started.

Roni glanced at Darcy and Jim, whom she'd been in the middle of a conversation with, and gave them a "just bear with me" smile. But Darcy just beamed back at her strangely, like she knew something that Roni didn't. And when Roni turned around, it wasn't Mr. Leonida she saw, but Lance, looking hesitant, humble, and drop-dead gorgeous in his tux. His hazel eyes locked on hers for a long moment, and Roni felt her knees start to tremble under his gaze. After all the hours she'd spent at the natatorium and in

Poli Sci over the last few weeks trying to silently will him to look in her direction, here he was, standing in front of her. And just like that, her heart was gone, lost to him all over again.

"For you," he said quietly, holding out a beautiful long-stemmed, white rose.

Roni took the rose with quivering fingers, a thousand questions running through her mind. *What was he doing? Why was he here?* A small hope flickered to life inside her. But the words she wanted to say seemed to fly away with every beat of her frantic heart, and all she could do was stand there, blushing in silence.

Lance glanced at Darcy and Jim uncertainly, and Roni saw Jenna and Lora-Leigh heading in their direction, Lora-Leigh marching across the dance floor with the determined, protective air of someone about to launch an assault.

"Um," he said, seeming to assess the risk to his personal safety if he didn't make a move, "can we talk for a second alone?"

"Sure," Roni said, finally finding her voice. She pulled him toward a quiet corner of the room, giving Lora-Leigh an "I'm fine" signal with her eyes to try to quell her battle stance.

When she and Lance were safely out of range, Roni turned to him, taking a deep breath. "So," she started, "this is a total surprise."

"I know," he said. "I should've called, but this was something I had to do face-to-face." He shook an unruly curl off his forehead and reached for her hand. "I don't even know where to start." He sighed. "I've been a complete and total ass."

"No, you haven't," she said. "I told you that I was the one who made the mistakes."

"It wasn't just you. I screwed things up, too. Big-time," he continued, holding her gaze. "I should've been more supportive . . . about everything you were going through this semester. About your tough time with Melody, but mostly about ZZT. It took me a while to understand it, but now I know how important the sorority, and all of your friends, are to you." He glanced around the room, taking in all the decorations and the crowded dance floor. "And if what you did with this place for Formal is any indication, I can see that ZZT can't survive without you. I've just never been a part of a group that cared about me that way, or that meant that much to me. And"—he blew a puff of air out of his mouth like it was taking an effort to say what came next—"I guess I was a little jealous, too."

"Of what?" Roni asked, staring at him in disbelief.

"Of how much fun you were having with ZZT," he said quietly, dropping his eyes. "You talked about it so much, I started to wonder whether you had more fun with ZZT than you did spending time with me."

Roni giggled, shaking her head. "How could you ever think that? That's ridiculous."

"Hey, I might be smart when it comes to Science and Math," he said, "but when it comes to figuring out girls, I'm a lost cause."

"Of course I was having fun with you, but if I told you how much, I would've scared you off. A girl has to protect herself, you know." Roni grinned. "But who do you think I talked about with my sisters?"

"See, I told you I'm a lost cause." Lance smiled sheepishly. "So . . . if I promise to grovel regularly until you're convinced that I adore you madly and without reason, do you think you might consider taking me back?"

Roni's heart shot off a series of internal fireworks. "If you keep talking like that, definitely. And I promise to keep my obsessive-compulsive overachiever work habits in check as much as I can." She didn't know who took the first step, but suddenly Lance's arms were around her, warm and reassuring, and she never wanted him to let go.

"By the way," he whispered in her ear. "That dress you're wearing could pretty much bring a guy to his knees."

"Thanks," Roni muttered, "but it would be better if you stayed standing so we could dance. And in case you need a translation, that was girl-speak for 'Would you like to dance?'" She smiled at him. "And this would be a good time for you to say yes."

"I can't," Lance said, suddenly serious, shaking his head. "Not yet."

Roni stared at him. "Why not?"

"There's something I need to do first," he said. And then, without warning, he pulled her close and gave her a kiss that nearly brought *her* to her knees. While she was still struggling to find her breath, he looked into her eyes and grinned mischievously. "*Now* I'm ready to dance."

Hand in hand, they walked onto the dance floor and found a spot near Lora-Leigh and Chris and Jenna and Tiger for the slow song that was playing.

Jenna lifted her head off Tiger's shoulder to give Roni a wide smile. But Lora-Leigh had to preface her smile with a "you better behave yourself" look at Lance.

"I'm glad to see you've come to your senses," she said to him half jokingly. "It took you long enough."

"What can I say?" He shrugged. "I'm a guy."

"So true," Lora-Leigh said.

Roni snuggled into Lance's chest as the music swirled around them. The hole she'd had in her heart for the last few weeks was closing up. . . . She could almost feel it. And she knew that no matter what happened down the road, her and Lance's relationship would be stronger and better because of what they'd been through together.

"I'm so glad you decided to come," she whispered to him.

"Hey, you think I would've missed one second of seeing you in this dress?" Lance said, bending to kiss her forehead. "Not a chance."

Roni didn't think it was possible for one person to smile as much as she did over the next few hours, but the happiness she felt just kept breaking through. And from the looks on Jenna's and Lora-Leigh's faces, they were feeling the same way. Formal passed in a blur of laughter, dancing, chatting, and soft kisses. She and Lance barely left the dance floor all night, and she relished the feel of his hand in hers. She'd missed him so much, and now he was here, and they were together again, and everything seemed to fall perfectly into place.

Roni hated the very idea that the evening would come to an end, especially when there was no sign of anyone slowing down. But when the clock struck midnight, she knew the DJ would be calling for the last song within just a few minutes. But when the microphone squeaked on at the front of the room, it wasn't the DJ who was doing the talking.

"All right, this song is for the ZZT ladies only," Beverly said into the microphone. "I want all my sisters to join me on the dance floor for this one."

As the introduction to the Beatles' "You Really Got a Hold On Me" rang out through the speakers, Roni caught Jenna's and Lora-Leigh's eyes, and they all laughed. It was the song that they'd set their ZZT cheer to! Their ZZT theme song for the semester. The three of them raced to the middle of the dance floor to join the other girls.

"Come on, slowpoke," Lora-Leigh said as she ran past Camille and grabbed her hand, pulling her along with her.

Roni crowded in with Beverly, Jenna, Darcy, Camille, and Lora-Leigh as they began singing. Roni threw her head back and belted out the words, swaying and laughing alongside her sisters:

"You won't just like her
But you'll love her
See you'll be always
Thinking of her
Oh oh oh
A ZZT *girl will help you out gladly*
You'll love her madly
Cause ZZT*'s got a hold on you,*
ZZT*'s really got a hold on you.*

"Forget the other Greek girls
Go for sophistichic girls
It's not easy to forget her

You'll remember her forever
Oh oh oh
A ZZT girl will help you gladly
You'll love her madly
Cause ZZT's got a hold on you
ZZT's really got a hold on you.

You'll love her
And all you'll want to say
Is just ZZT, ZZT, ZZT, ZZT."

The song came to an end, but the girls were still laughing, linking arms in one massive ZZT hug, and Roni could feel the love and friendship wrapping around her like a blanket of warmth and happiness.

"Y'all," Jenna said, smiling at them, "I don't know how we'll ever top this."

"Oh, we will," Lora-Leigh said. "You can count on that."

Roni laughed. "Just wait until next year." Next year, another year at Latimer, another year with ZZT—of friendship and of sisterhood forever.

GREEK ALPHABET

ENGLISH SPELLING	GREEK LETTER	PRONUNCIATION
Alpha	Α	*Al-fah*
Beta	Β	*Bay-tah*
Gamma	Γ	*Gam-ah*
Delta	Δ	*Del-tah*
Epsilon	Ε	*Ep-si-lon*
Zeta	Ζ	*Zay-tah*
Eta	Η	*A-tah*
Theta	Θ	*Thay-tah*
Iota	Ι	*Eye-o-tah*
Kappa	Κ	*Cap-ah*
Lambda	Λ	*Lamb-dah*
Mu	Μ	*Mew*
Nu	Ν	*New*
Xi	Ξ	*Zigh*
Omicron	Ο	*Ohm-i-kron*
Pi	Π	*Pie*
Rho	Ρ	*Roe*
Sigma	Σ	*Sig-mah*
Tau	Τ	*Taw*
Upsilon	Υ	*Oop-si-lon*
Phi	Φ	*Fie*
Chi	Χ	*Kie*
Psi	Ψ	*Sigh*
Omega	Ω	*O-may-gah*